MURDER IN THE CEMETERY

Book Two

The Brianna Kelly

Paranormal Mystery Series

Shirley B. Garrett

MURDER IN THE CHURCHYARD

ISBN:978-1-943065-15-8

Published by Positive Directions, LLC

Cover design by Shirley B. Garrett and Robert C. Garrett. Original cover art by Dan Pritchett.

DEDICATION

This book is dedicated to the memory of Ronald R. Moore, a man who appreciated an interesting read. He was a good friend and neighbor. Ron, you are missed.

Previous Novels by SHIRLEY B. GARRETT

THE BRIANNA KELLY PARANORMAL MYSTERY SERIES

Murder in the Churchyard

THE CHARLIE STONE CRIME THRILLER SERIES

Deadly Compulsion
Deadly Lessons
Deadly Obsessions

THE PHOENIX O'LEARY HOT FLASH SERIES

Hot Flash Divas
Hot Flash Desires
Hot Flash Decisions

Nonfiction Books by
SHIRLEY B. GARRETT, PSY.D.

Stop the Craziness: Simple Life Solutions
5 Steps to a More Confident You: Quick Tips for Life Series
5 Steps to Adapting to Change: Quick Tips for Life Series

CONTENTS

Table of Contents

ACKNOWLEDGMENTS

A special thanks to my beta readers: Gary W. Herring, James Frost, Nellie Maulsby, Jared Austin, and Kenny Emmanuel. Your time and expertise are priceless.

Many wonderful suggestions were made to improve this novel by the North Alabama Mystery Writers, the Huntsville Writer's Group, the North Alabama SciFi and Cake Appreciation Society, and the North Alabama Genre Writers.

My love and thanks to Bob, my wonderful computer-proficient husband. He not only helped with the formatting of the cover design, but also designed my website.

Dan Pritchett, thanks again for creating another beautiful original watercolor for my book cover.

My editor, Lisa Prince, has once again helped me turn my manuscript into something wonderful.

Special thanks to my family and friends for your love and support.

CHAPTER 1: BRIANNA

I stopped short, surprised to see a smiling apparition inspecting Lucille Miller's Independence Day table decorations. Her braids circled her head like a crown, lending a regal quality to her broad nose and full lips. She reminded me of an older, plumper version of Lucille.

I'm Brianna Kelly, a psychic whose life's work is to help disembodied spirits cross over. I couldn't help but wonder why this ghost was here and why she hadn't finished her journey.

Lucille had aligned two rectangular tables covered with white cloths down the sunroom's length. Like the ghost, I also smiled as I admired the three blue vases filled with white daisies, red carnations, and tiny flags that seemed to march down the middle. The abundant lush foliage of the large houseplants scattered around the room guaranteed the guests would feel like they were dining in the tropics. The bright patterns on the pillows nestled in the white wicker furniture added to the illusion. The Huntsville, Alabama heat and humidity completed the ambiance, which was why we were dining indoors.

A sudden chill passed over me, and I felt disoriented as the scene wavered before my eyes. *Oh, no! Not again.* Feeling woozy, I grabbed a chair to ground me before the bottom dropped out of my reality.

*

I stood on dew-laden grass in a cemetery, looking at a large gravestone with a three-dimensional carving of an angel draped over the top. The grave was surrounded by six ghosts looking down at someone lying there. The gravestone hid most of the person, but I could see a woman's tan arm. Her hand lay palm up on the trimmed grass, the fingers curled, exposing her long, fuchsia polished nails.

What does this mean? Will someone die? Is she already dead? Do I know the person?

*

The vision faded. I was back in the brightly lit sunroom blinking to clear my blurred vision. The whole experience left me feeling bewildered and dizzy. I don't often have visions, but this is the one psychic gift that has always frightened me the most—because they have always come true.

I endeavored to remember why I was holding the chair with a white-knuckled grip. After shaking my head to reset the circuitry, I realized that I'd come into the area to clear a space on the food-laden table for the main dish for dinner. So, I did.

It was then that the disembodied spirit floated into my peripheral vision. She appeared not to be aware of me. By using a pleasant tone, I hoped to not frighten her away before I could learn more. "Do you approve of the decor?"

The apparition looked up. She shot backward, her eyes wide with surprise. "You can see me?"

"Yes. I didn't mean to startle you. Did you live here?"

"Yes siree! I'm Lucy's mom, Gertrude Johnson. Call me Gertie."

"Lucy?" I couldn't imagine anyone calling a formidable woman like Lucille by that nickname.

She made a dismissive gesture with her hand. "That's what Leroy and I called her before she grew up and got so highfalutin'. What are you doing here?"

I introduced myself, adding, "I'm Mystery Jones's friend."

Her smile smoothed the wrinkles above her lip. "She's my granddaughter." Tilting her head to the side, she eyed me with curiosity. "How did you and Mystery become friends?"

Her tone said it all.

I've inherited my olive complexion from my mother, Olivia,

whose parents come from Sicily. My dark copper hair and green eyes come from my father, Sean, whose parents were Irish.

When Gertie was my age, racism and segregation ruled in Alabama, so a friendship between a white and a black woman would have been unlikely here in the Deep South.

I explained, "My shop, Chocolates and Delights, is next to Mystery's store in the Five Points area."

Gertie drifted closer. "You don't say. Times do change." She crossed her arms. "Then you can give that granddaughter of mine a message. She needs to visit her mama more often."

I held up both hands as a barrier. "I'm not getting in the middle of that briar patch of a situation. Keep in mind, Mystery would visit more often if Lucille weren't always on her case about pretty much everything."

I could tell from her pensive expression that Gertie was considering my words.

Shrugging, she said, "I can't disagree with you. That young'un of mine has been bossy her entire life. It started with her dolls and never stopped."

I chuckled. "I can believe it."

Lucille chose that moment to breeze in with a platter of ribs. The aroma of the grilled pork slathered in tangy barbeque sauce set my stomach to growling. My tan Chihuahua, Prissy, and Mystery's Yorkie, Phoebe, stalked Lucille, both sniffing the air. Prissy stopped and stiffened. She looked toward the ghost.

Seeing the dogs, Gertie shot through the wall.

I placed my hand on Prissy's head to calm her. "It's all right," I whispered.

Lucille placed the large dish in the spot that I'd cleared and smiled at the table full of her culinary achievements before yelling, "Y'all come on. It's time to eat." She waved her guests into the room before taking the seat at the head of the table.

I shooed the dogs into the next room. "No begging, young ladies. Go take a nap."

Prissy yipped and trotted toward the dog bed with Phoebe in her wake. My feisty fur baby always has to have the last word.

Gertie stuck her head through the wall. "Are they gone?" she floated back into the sunroom. "Dang dogs can see me and start a ruckus. I don't want Lucy to know I'm hanging around here." Her lips formed a sly grin. "At least not yet." She pointed a finger at me. "Don't you be telling her, either!"

Now I was even more curious, but I couldn't ask questions with everyone in the room.

Lucille patted the place to her right. "Adam, you come sit by me," she said with a warm smile.

Adam Craft, who owns the antique store next to Mystery's shop, shuffled to the indicated chair. He dropped into it with a grunt and hooked his cane on the table's edge. "When you are my age, the drop into your chair is the most excitement you'll get."

He'd lost his beloved wife, Agnes, many years ago, and their only child had died during infancy. Over the years, Mystery, Lucille, and I have become a kind of second family to him.

I found my place card and sat next to Mr. Craft. My beau, Detective Chris Haddington, pulled out the chair on my right. Once he'd settled his broad-shouldered physique into the seat, he flipped his thick dark hair off his forehead. His sexy wink sent a spark of excitement ricocheting through me. We met in April after Mystery and I had found a murder victim on the property of a historic church. What sealed the deal on our relationship was his acceptance of my psychic gifts.

Mystery sat across from me and her date, Ron Jeffery, sat across from Chris. Ron owns a local accounting firm. Like the number-cruncher that he is, he looked to be tallying the number of food offerings on the table. Mystery told me a few days ago that Ron's tall, lean build and sparkling brown eyes had caught her attention when he came in to purchase a security system back in April, but his kindness and quick humor had held her interest enough to accept this date.

Mystery sat ramrod straight with a tight smile. This was her first date since her husband Tyree died two years earlier. She reached up and fluffed her short curls and then didn't seem to know what to do with her hands. She's inherited her mom's voluptuous build but has her dad's lighter complexion and facial features. Lucille is attractive, but Mystery is an eight on the beauty scale of ten.

Her visible tension was mild compared to the spikes of anxiety and excitement that flew off her and stung my awareness like blowing sand.

One of my gifts is clairsentience, the ability to read the energy of people and objects. Like all my psychic gifts, this one is a blessing and a curse. At the moment, it was definitely more curse than blessing. I raised my psychic shields enough to protect my system from the overload. My mother trained me to be able to use a variety of shields at varying levels of intensity. On this occasion, I chose to tune down my sensitivity to Mystery's emotions, but I wanted to maintain my awareness of Gertie.

Tiffany Blake, a former client and Mystery's new marketing contractor, sat between Lucille and Mystery. Lucille insisted on inviting the petite blonde when she heard she was a recent widow. A widow herself, Lucille knows about the trauma of facing holidays alone.

Tiffany grinned as she sniffed the array of scents.

Patting Mr. Craft's pale, blue-veined hand, Lucille smiled and asked, "Would you say the blessing?"

I expected no less. A devout Southern Baptist, she has always insisted every meal be blessed, and heaven help the person who ever tried to sneak a morsel before the completed prayer.

Lucille cleared her throat to get our attention.

We held hands for the blessing.

Mr. Craft bowed his head of thick silver hair. "Dear Lord, please bless this wonderful food prepared by our beautiful and talented cook."

Before he could add his usual blessing for our businesses, everyone chimed, "Amen!"

He raised his head, surprise shooting his unruly brows up.

Bowls and platters heaped high with soul food delights covered the table. Their competing aromas made my mouth water with anticipation.

Gertie circled the table, sniffing with an appreciative-looking smile. Ghosts are burdened with the ability to smell the many things they can't enjoy. Perhaps it's better than nothing, but I imagine it is frustrating.

Lucille pointed her chin at Mystery. "Baby Girl, will you start the ribs?"

"Yes, Mama." She reached for the large platter piled high with succulent pork ribs. Despite having difficulty balancing it with one hand, she managed to choose a few. She then passed the unwieldy serving dish left to Ron.

"I've been so busy with all the changes happening at the store over the last few months. I can hardly believe it's already July. Where did spring go?" Mystery asked, reaching for the next dish.

Lucille chuckled while spearing a slice of her home-grown tomatoes from a plate. "Wait until you get older. Time streaks past so fast, it's hard to remember what happened yesterday."

Mr. Craft peered at her from under his brows, his blue eyes twinkling. "I'm supposed to remember yesterday?"

They laughed as if it was their private joke.

Mystery licked sauce from her fingers. "It's certainly been a life-changing three months for me." She looked over at Ron with a nervous smile.

I watched them with interest. *Two years without a living, breathing man in her life is a long time. No wonder she's a bundle of nerves.*

Tiffany grunted when she picked up a glass bowl stacked with fresh corn on the cob. She selected an ear and added it to her plate before passing the container to Mystery. "I've got you beat when it comes to life-altering events. Ron, you weren't around at the time, but I discovered my late husband was not only unfaithful, but he planned to kill me."

Ron stopped ladling slaw onto his plate and stared. "You're kidding. Right?" He finished with the slaw and passed it to Chris. "I've heard some wild rumors about your situation but I wasn't sure what to believe."

"Scary, yet true," Tiffany said, sounding as if she still had difficulty accepting the circumstances.

Lucille's mouth dropped open. She stared at Tiffany for a moment before closing it. "Oh, my."

Gertie drifted closer to Tiffany. "Now it's getting interesting."

"It's true, Lucille." Tiffany continued, unaware of the ghost's interest. "I don't know how I would've survived the whole ordeal if it hadn't been for the folks at The Mystery Shop and Brianna. To this day, I believe they saved my life. That whole incident when Jason died—"

Mystery elbowed Tiffany in the ribs before casting a glance at Ron, then Lucille.

"It, um, was bad." Tiffany stopped talking and picked up her fork.

Noticing the interaction, Lucille narrowed her eyes. Dr. Lucille Miller, Ph.D., is many things: a retired literature professor, a devout Christian, a green-thumbed gardener, and an expert soul food cook. She is *not* a fan of the paranormal and is wise enough to know Mystery will try to conceal anything that might upset her.

Gertie glided over to levitate behind her granddaughter and crossed her arms.

Mystery shivered and rubbed her bare arms while giving me an is-there-a haint-in-the-room look.

I nodded and glared at Gertie.

It took a second, but the realization hit the ghost. Gertie backed away. "Sorry, I keep forgetting that I'm a drifting icebox."

Lucille's assessing gaze shifted from Mystery to me and back to her only child.

It's obvious that food is one of Lucille's love languages. Still, I've begun to suspect that she arranges these feasts on a regular basis to find out what we're hiding. There's nothing like good food and company to loosen lips. In the past, she's always brought lunch to Mystery's shop. This was the first time she'd hosted at her home.

Mr. Craft looked up from the rib he was gnawing. Sauce smeared his mouth like a lipstick applied on a bumpy road. "My dear, it sounds like you married a true scoundrel."

"He was," Tiffany said, now focused on the bowl of fresh green beans sitting in front of her.

Chris handed the bowl of pork and beans to me. His warm smile that traveled to his blue eyes lifted my spirits.

I smiled and flipped my hair over a shoulder to keep it out of my food. "You've had it rough, Tiffany. Thank goodness things are looking up."

Mr. Craft took a bite of potato salad. His gaze rose toward heaven. "This is wonderful! What are the ingredients?"

Lucille blushed and looked pleased. "It's my special recipe." She smiled over at Mystery. "It's in my cookbook that you'll inherit someday."

"What!" Gertie shouted.

I jumped in my seat.

Chris shot a curious look my way before whispering, "Everything okay?"

I nodded.

Gertie zoomed over to her daughter and pointed an accusing finger. "That's not her cookbook. It's mine." She ghost-paced behind Lucille. "How long has this ungrateful brat been taking credit for my recipes?"

I was so fascinated by her revelation that I forgot and answered aloud. "Quite a while."

All eyes focused on me.

Mystery cocked a brow.

"Um, Mystery's been looking forward to seeing that book for quite a while. Perhaps she can copy some of the recipes?"

Lucille's pleased expression turned stern. Her gaze bore down on me like a woman intent on swatting a pesky fly. "She can have it after I'm gone."

Tiffany's head swiveled back and forth as if observing an exciting tennis match.

Gertie crossed her arms. "I told Lucy to give that cookbook to Mystery after I died. Did she do it? Nooo! That girl is stubborn as a cantankerous mule."

Mr. Craft unknowingly came to the rescue when he said, "I have good news. I sold a full mahogany dining set on Saturday that covered my expenses for the entire month."

I shot him a grateful smile. "That's great, Mr. C."

He paused the fork in front of his mouth. "That reminds me, Mystery, I need your and Brianna's help with a spirit freeloader."

Antiques sometimes come with an attached ghost, and Mr. Craft always hires Mystery's shop to help the spirit cross over. Unfortunately, in the past a few antiques with ghost hitchhikers have boomeranged back to his shop. The new owners became alarmed when the spirits started acting up. So, he has learned the hard way that it's best to clear his haunted antiques before selling them.

Mystery's fascination with anything to do with the paranormal has always driven Lucille into a hyper-protective-mom state. Mystery has a long history of poking this condition, since her business does ghost tours and sells ghost-hunting and spy equipment. The only part of the enterprise that Lucille has ever approved is the background checks Mystery does to fill in the monetary cracks and to stay in the black.

I work on a commissioned basis for Mystery. She has always called me her ghost wrangler, which I detest. It makes it sound like I saddle and ride ghosts.

I try to separate my psychic talents from my business, Chocolates and Delights, as much as possible. I prefer for my customers to not be spooked when shopping for sexy French lingerie and exotic chocolates.

Stuck to my seat curious about the possible haunting, I said, "Tell us more, Mr. C."

"I received a seventeenth-century secretary desk two weeks ago. To my surprise, the area around it is so dadgum cold, you'd think I bought a deep freezer instead of an antique."

Ignoring Lucille's glare, Mystery said, "It does sound suspicious. Tiffany will book a time for us to come inspect the desk."

Tiffany smiled across the table. "We'll talk after dinner. I can't wait to hear all about it."

Lucille shot Mystery a two-barrel glare. "Mystery Lucille Jones, when are you and Brianna going to stop chasing haints. It isn't safe. Can't you stick to selling your little cameras, recorders, and magic kits, and make background checks your main focus?"

I sat back in my chair, my Italian/Irish temper rising. *I can't believe Lucille said that to her.* I swallowed my snarky comeback and chased it down with a slug of sweet tea. Once again, my mother's advice came to mind. *Calm down. Mystery will never learn to deal with Lucille if you interfere.*

Mystery slumped in her chair, her lips tight and her eyes glistening with unshed tears.

"There she goes again." Gertie shook her head and drifted closer to Lucille. "I told her before I died that she needs to quit ridin' that child like a bronco. Did she listen to me? Nooo!"

Ron stopped eating and looked at Lucille with raised brows. "By haints, do you mean ghosts?"

"That's what she means." Mr. Craft wiped his hands and gave Mystery a playful wink. Undaunted by Lucille, he likes to poke at her dislike of anything paranormal. "I pray Mystery will ignore that advice until they get rid of my spirit stowaway."

Lucille redirected her stony glare onto Mr. Craft. "You aren't helping my cause."

He ignored her while eating his corn.

Gertie chuckled. "He don't pay her no mind. Good for him."

Ron's brow knitted as he shifted his gaze from Lucille to Mystery.

Somebody needs to change the subject fast, I thought, when I saw his expression. Ron seemed rather conservative. I didn't want him to run screaming from the table on their first date.

Mr. Craft came to the rescue again. "Brianna, I need a photo of the bronze plaque near the south entrance of Maple Hill Cemetery for research I'm doing for the Historical Society. You know, the one with the history of the cemetery. As you know, I'm not as steady on my legs as I used to be. Would you take several photos for me with that fancy new phone camera of yours, so that I can have a choice? The Society will give you credit for the photo in the book we plan to publish about Huntsville."

I perked up. "Sure, Mr. C. No problem." I picked up my glass. It was cold and wet with condensation. "Mystery, why don't we take our walk there tomorrow morning after I take Mr. C's photo?"

"Suits me, Sugar. After this feast, we'll need to neutralize some of the calories."

Mystery insists it's my duty to walk with her several times a week to help her ward off the dreaded bubble butt. She blames the dark chocolate with almonds that she purchases from my store as the sole culprit of this malady.

This seems unfair to me, since she has never asked the local Girl Scout troop to walk with her. Every January she purchases thirty boxes of Thin Mint Cookies from them, which is more than the chocolate she buys from me.

Maybe the girls in the troop could earn a physical fitness badge or something?

Ron looked up from his plate with a sad look in his eyes. "My late wife, Carol, is buried at Maple Hill. It's a peaceful place to take a stroll."

"If I'm going to work off today's calories, I need to do more than stroll," Mystery mumbled.

An idea struck me. *It might not be a bad idea to mosey past Carol Jeffery's grave while we're there to make sure she's crossed over. The last thing Mystery needs right now is supernatural complications.*

Lucille's gaze latched onto Ron like Velcro. Her expression softened. "I didn't realize you were widowed."

Ron nodded and looked down at his plate. "Carol died of breast cancer almost a year ago."

"So sorry to hear that, Darlin'. It's a terrible disease."

Ron nodded, not looking up.

"Mystery has been *so secretive* about you." Her tone made it sound like Mystery treated his past as a matter of national security.

Gertie slapped her hand to her forehead. "Good Lord! She's about to start the grand inquisition."

I rubbed the sudden twinge of pain located in the center of my forehead. *Dealing with the conversations between the living and dead is addling my brain.*

"Ron, where do you work?" Lucille asked, snagging another slice of tomato from the nearby serving platter.

Ron sat taller. "I'm an accountant. I own Huntsville Accounting Services."

Lucille leaned forward. The quality of her smile indicated she approved of his profession. "How many employees do you have?"

"Eleven."

Gertie plopped a fist on each hip. "Next, she'll want to know his Dun and Bradstreet rating."

Sweat coated Mystery's upper lip. She shot a desperate look toward me before saying, "Mama, did you make pecan pies?"

Lucille said, "Baby Girl, why are you worrying about dessert when we haven't finished eating lunch?" She shook her head. "In honor of the holiday, I made a patriotic trifle with white angel food cake, blueberries, strawberries, and whipped topping." She pointed down the table. "Would someone pass me those hush puppies?"

Hearing the word "puppies," Prissy pranced into the room and yipped.

Gertie slipped out through the wall like smoke through an open window.

Lucille smiled down at the tiny dog. "Hello, my little Darlin'."

Phoebe, wanting her fair share of goodies, trotted over and sat next to her canine friend.

Mystery pointed at our furry kids and used a commanding tone. "Your food is in your bowls. No begging at the table. Scat!"

The two dogs whined and skulked out of the room.

After a quick peek to verify the dogs had left, Gertie ghosted back through the wall and settled into the corner.

Lucille arched a disapproving brow. "Don't you be scaring my granddog!"

"Your granddog?" I said with a surprised chuckle.

Lucille's jaw tightened. Not a good sign. "It's the best I can do until Mystery provides me with grandchildren."

Red raced up Mystery's neck and flamed her cheeks. She looked ready to slide under the table to hide.

Gertie shook her head. "Mystery probably hasn't kissed the guy yet, and Lucy's already pushing for grandkids. I taught her better than that. Did she listen to me? Nooo!"

I tried to hide my laughter behind a napkin.

Chris lowered his head to hide a spreading grin. When he'd mastered his neutral cop expression, he looked back up.

Tiffany stared slack-jawed at Lucille.

Mr. Craft ignored the repartee and shoved green beans into his mouth.

Seeming undaunted by Lucille's words, Ron said, "I'm pleased as punch that this lovely lady agreed to go with me to see the fireworks after this wonderful meal." He gave Lucille a playful wink. "As for grandchildren, I'll have to give that subject some serious thought."

Gertie clapped her hands. "This man might be able to hold his own with my headstrong daughter. Tyree sure knew how to handle her when he was alive."

"I'm glad you could join us, Ron." Lucille's smile beamed with approval.

"Ms. Lucille, how did you come across Mystery's name?" Ron asked. "It's unique."

"I've been curious about that myself," Chris said reaching for his glass of tea.

"My husband Courtland, God rest his soul, had tuckered-out sperm." She looked at Tiffany and patted her hand. "They didn't have all those fancy fertility techniques like they do now. We gave up hope and focused our attention on our education. Then, one day when I was in graduate school, I woke up sick and stayed that way for weeks. I thought I had a terminal illness. The tests showed I was pregnant." She paused to sip some iced tea. "When we met with our doctor, Courtland asked how this could happen, since Doc had told us we couldn't have children. The doctor said it was a mystery, so I named my baby girl, Mystery."

Ron grinned. "That's a wonderful story."

"Thank you." Lucille leaned forward. "I understand they're having fireworks at three different locations in the Huntsville area tonight. Have you decided where to take Mystery to see them?"

"Anywhere she wants to go, Ms. Lucille. I aim to make her happy."

Lucille shot him a look guaranteed to put the fear of God into a Sasquatch. "If my baby girl is happy, I'm happy." She pointed her fork at him. "You don't *ever* want to see me unhappy."

Gertie looked heavenward. "Ain't that the truth. That girl of mine has a heart of gold, but she can sure raise a ruckus." Gertie gave me a pleading look. "I've changed my mind. I think it's best that Mystery doesn't know about me just yet. Please don't tell her or Lucy."

I turned to look at Mystery, who looked like she wanted to bang her head on the table.

I nodded. This didn't seem like a good time to tell Mystery about her grandmother's ghost.

After the table had been cleared, I managed a moment alone with Gertie.

"I can help you cross over if you'll let me," I said. "Sometimes, people die and don't realize the light is there for them and miss it."

Gertie crossed her arms. "I saw it." She raised her chin. "I ain't going nowhere until Lucy gives my cookbook to Mystery." She pointed her finger at me. "And don't you be tellin' them I'm here, either!"

I held up both hands. "I can't make that promise."

*

Chris and I held hands in the cramped back seat of Ron's black Porsche Panamera. I marveled at the number of cars snailing their way into the parking area of the Space and Rocket Center to view the fireworks. "I'm glad we left early."

Ron eased forward. The car in front of him hit its brakes, the reflection coloring his dark complexion red. "I expected this. One of my employees warned me that it might be crowded." He glanced over his shoulder at me. "We know how Mystery got her name. What about yours, Brianna?"

"I'm named after my paternal great-grandmother. It's Irish and means strong, virtuous, and honorable."

Chris squeezed my hand. "She must have been quite a woman."

I shrugged. "According to my father, she was a scoundrel."

Twenty minutes later, we parked. Ron and Chris pulled lawn chairs and a small cooler from Ron's trunk, before following a line of people moving toward a seating area.

Mystery batted her lashes at Ron before looking at the massive, up-lit Saturn V Rocket that poked the sky at the entrance to the museum. "Is that rocket the real deal?"

I rolled my eyes. *Good grief, she's a Huntsville native. She knows better.*

Ron paused. "No, this one is a mock-up. The authentic one is inside the Davidson Center for Space Exploration on the other side of this building. It's cool because it's suspended from the ceiling."

"According to Mr. C, the Space and Rocket Center owns one of only three authentic Saturn V's," I said, patting the moisture from my face with a tissue. The night felt like a steamy bathroom after a long shower. To make matters worse, there wasn't much of a breeze.

"I'd like to come back and tour the Davidson Center's exhibits and see the new interactive planetarium someday soon. It sounds interesting," Mystery said with a "hint, hint" tone.

Ron flashed a bright smile. "Let's go together."

Looking pleased, Mystery said, "I'd like that."

Chris and I exchanged glances. He winked, took my hand, and squeezed. "We should visit those, too."

"I'd love to, if we can coordinate the time," I said. Dating a homicide detective is a hit-and-miss situation since his schedule is so erratic. To further complicate the situation, I often do clearings at night.

Ron stopped in the middle of the seating area and looked around. "This looks like a good spot with an unimpeded view. The fireworks are set up over there, so we shouldn't get showered with debris."

"Suits us," Chris said and proceeded to set up our chairs.

We sank into our seats, groaning like four people stuffed to our eyeballs from a large meal. That last bite of the trifle almost pushed me over the edge of satiation.

Soon, a sea of people surrounded us, arranging chairs, blankets and coolers.

Ron opened the cooler and handed each of us a bottle of cold water.

I wanted to slip mine down the front of my dress but resisted the unladylike act.

"Thanks, Sugar. It's a tad warm tonight." Mystery held her frosty bottle to her cheek.

Ron flashed a toothy smile that crinkled the skin around his expressive brown eyes. "You're welcome. Mystery, you're looking lovely tonight. I like the dress."

"Thanks."

Mystery looked ready to ignite from the heat, but she did look attractive in her sundress covered with giant yellow sunflowers.

I pulled a folding fan from my purse and whipped up a breeze while we talked and people-watched. The number of people sporting outfits with patriotic colors was considerable.

Ron reached over and took Mystery's hand. "I'm glad you came with me tonight."

Before she could answer, a tall, slender blonde wearing a white tee shirt sprinkled with red and blue stars stopped beside Ron. A huge man who looked like an out-of-shape former football tackle accompanied her.

The blonde placed her left hand on Ron's shoulder. At least two carats of diamonds sparkled. "Hey there. How have you been?"

Ron stiffened before looking up. His eyes widened with surprise before he smiled. "Sarah!" He stood and hugged the woman. "You're looking good. It must be all the TLC that Jack's been giving you."

Jack reached across to shake Ron's hand.

Sarah did an exaggerated roll of her blue eyes and patted her companion's belly that lapped over his belt. "You mean that I'm giving him."

We all stood while Ron introduced the Shaffers. Jack offered a jovial smile, but Sarah gave Mystery a speculative up and down.

Waves of suspicion and disapproval flowed off her. I wondered, *What's with her? Did she date Ron in the past?*

Looking uncomfortable, Ron took a step to his left to create more distance between him and Mystery. "Sarah was Carol's best friend. I don't know how I would've survived without these two."

Sarah's eyes brimmed with tears. "I've been missing her more lately. The anniversary of her death is tomorrow." Her tone said, *I hope you remembered.*

Ron nodded, shoulders slumping. "I know."

I smoothed the front of my pink sundress. *So that's why Sarah's checking Mystery out.*

Jack tossed his sandy hair off his forehead before moving closer to punch Ron's shoulder. "Ol' Ron and I played football for Huntsville High School. That's how I met Sarah. She and Carol were cheerleaders."

Ron punched him back. "Who're you calling old?"

My, my, there's so much we don't know about this man. I pasted on a pleasant smile and turned to face Ron. "You never told us you played football. What position?"

"Quarterback," he said, standing taller.

Jack rose on his toes and scowled. Pointing past us, he asked, "Isn't that Rosa Lopez?" Anger laced his tone. "I think she's been spying on us."

We all turned toward where Jack pointed.

"Over there." Jack barreled his way through the crowd.

Who is Rosa Lopez, and why is she watching us? I caught a brief glance of a petite Latina before she whirled around, her long dark curls flying. She disappeared into the crowd.

Ron shifted from foot to foot, avoiding eye contact with anyone.

Sarah's expression shifted from surprised to glacial.

Within minutes, Jack returned, red-faced and sweating. "She got away."

Sarah clenched her fists before pointing her index finger within an inch of Ron's chest. Her angry energy shot out like a multitude of arrows, and some were striking me. I raised my shield enough to blunt the impact.

"I don't care what you said Ron. I'm convinced that woman hastened Carol's death, and we both know why." Sarah turned on her heels and stomped away.

Jack gave an apologetic shrug and said, "See you later, man. Gotta take care of Sarah." He loped after his wife.

Mystery's widening eyes showed alarm. "Who was the woman

that Jack was chasing?"

"Sorry about all that," Ron said, looking down. "Sarah's high-strung, and Jack will do anything necessary to protect her."

"What the heck is going on?" I asked, planting a hand on my hip. "You didn't answer Mystery's question."

Before he could respond, patriotic music blared from a speaker as the fireworks exploded in the sky. Both rendered any conversation impossible.

Ron pointed toward the sky, gave a helpless shrug, and sat.

Mystery plopped into her chair and crossed her arms.

Curious and frustrated, I put in my earplugs and tapped the arm of the chair with a manicured nail while watching the magic of pyrotechnics. Chris reached over, took my hand, and gave it a gentle squeeze. I smiled, but my brain asked, *Who was that woman, and why was Sarah so angry?* The trace of a headache from my earlier vision sent a shiver sliding down my spine. I pushed away the memory and focused on the fireworks above me and the warm safe feeling of Chris holding my hand.

CHAPTER 2: BRIANNA

Early the following day, I followed Mystery's blue Prius into the south entrance of the Maple Hill Cemetery. I pulled my red Tesla Model 3 that I'd named Hot Stuff to the curb. We were near the bronze plaque Mr. Craft had asked me to photograph during dinner.

After leashing our dogs, we walked toward the large plaque attached to a sturdy metal pole.

> "MAPLE HILL CEMETERY
> ESTABLISHED 1818
> OLDEST AND LARGEST MUNICIPAL CEMETERY
> IN CONTINUOUS OPERATION IN THE SOUTH."

"I knew Maple Hill was old, but not that old. That's a long time for a cemetery to stay open for business," Mystery said.

I framed the image on my phone camera. "It's still in operation because it's so large. Mr. C told me it's around a hundred acres, so there's still plenty of room left for burials." I paused to adjust the angle of my photo. "There's a lot of history in this cemetery."

Mystery looked around. "I didn't realize it was this big. None of my folks are buried here. They're all in Glenwood Cemetery. When I was growing up, this was considered strictly a white folks cemetery." She looked around. "I wonder if it's the largest in the

South?"

I shook my head before taking several more photos from different angles. "When I visited Mom in Savannah last year, I took a tour of the Bonaventure Cemetery. The guide told me it was about one hundred and sixty acres."

"That's huge! Sugar, I hope it wasn't a walking tour."

"They have some of those, but I took a motorized one to see more of the cemetery." I chuckled and gave her a knowing wink. "The tour buses seemed to be the main entertainment for the long-term residents, if you know what I mean."

"Were there as many haints in that cemetery as here?"

"More." I put away my phone. "Savannah claims to be one of the most haunted cities in the South."

We struggled to untangle the dogs' leashes.

Mystery harrumphed. "I believe these little rascals make a game of doing this to frustrate us."

I knew Phoebe's former owner had trained her to obey commands and had often walked her without a leash. On the other hand, Prissy is obedient but has a passion for chasing squirrels and chipmunks. If she spots one, no amount of yelling brings her to heel until she's cornered the fluffy rodent.

"Mr. Craft told me the cemetery may soon ban dogs due to inconsiderate owners not picking up after them."

"That's a shame. It's an interesting place to stroll and look at old tombstones," Mystery said, stopping to read an older stone.

I decided to broach the subject. "While we're here, I want to check out Carol Jeffery's grave."

Mystery stopped. Her eyes widened. "Why?"

"I want to make sure Ron's wife crossed over," I said, untangling the leashes again. "You don't need any unnecessary complications like a jealous spirit making your life miserable."

Mystery looked alarmed. "It never entered my mind."

"Speaking of Mr. Tall, Dark, and Adorable, how were the fireworks after the fireworks?" I shot her an exaggerated, bawdy wink.

Looking pleased and embarrassed, she said, "Nice." She ran a hand through her short curls. "Lordy, I don't know how to date anymore."

I nudged her with an elbow and grinned. "You know what I

mean."

She sighed with annoyance. "There's definite chemistry. Other than a foot-bopping good-night kiss, Ron was a perfect gentleman. On one hand, I felt relieved."

"On the other hand?"

"Disappointed."

I gave her a quick, reassuring hug. "Slow is always better. Come on, Ron's late wife is buried in Section 35."

Mystery chuckled. "How do you know?"

Grinning, I said, "I looked it up online. Let's leave the cars here and walk." I pointed north. "It's that way."

The sun slanted through the trees, creating dappled shady areas across the grass and tombstones. Polished stones gleamed in the radiant light of the open spaces. The newer section consisted mainly of granite tombstones, which were less interesting than the marble ones in the historic area near the west entrance on California Street.

I smiled when the scent of honeysuckle flirted with my senses before drifting past.

While we passed through a sun-drenched area, I noticed our shadows gliding beside us. "When I was a kid and first noticed my shadow, I thought it was a ghost. So, I ran to my dad and told him to make it stop following me."

"Yeah? What did he do?"

I smiled at the memory. "He dropped to one knee and gave a complete engineering explanation about shadows, most of which went right over my head." I hitched a shoulder. "What else could I expect from an aerospace engineer? But then, Mom intervened and told me the shadow was my best friend during sunny times and assured me it wasn't a ghost."

"Smart woman, your mother." Mystery tugged Phoebe away from a floral tribute.

"What did your parents tell you about your shadow?" I asked.

"Daddy was a physics professor, so I bet his explanation was similar to Sean's. Mama saved the day like Olivia."

"Where did Lucille teach?" I asked. She had already retired when I met Mystery.

"Same place as Daddy, Alabama A & M University."

I chuckled. "Did Lucille make you read the classics?"

Mystery rolled her eyes. "Goodness, yes. After all, she was an English professor."

I struggled to untangle the dogs' leashes once again. The furry tykes kept crossing back and forth.

"If my mother hadn't been psychic and able to guide me through those early years, I don't think I would've survived."

Mystery stopped and swept her hand to indicate the cemetery. "I wish you'd say something when you see the local haints. How am I supposed to know they're here if you ignore them?"

"I've warned you before, when you give attention to ghosts, it fuels them and encourages them to attach to you as a power source. That's why I don't acknowledge an earthbound spirit unless I'm trying to help them cross over or they invade my space." I gave her one of my this-is-important looks. "Ghosts often have poor boundaries and require a firm hand."

Mystery shuddered as a haint passed near her. "I have so much to learn."

I placed an arm around her shoulders and gave a quick squeeze. "You're doing great. We're a team, right?"

"Absolutely."

Both dogs stopped and sniffed the air.

Oh, great. Here we go again. I looked around for a squirrel or chipmunk, expecting Prissy to bolt at any minute.

As predicted, Prissy dug in her claws and began dragging me to the left. Phoebe followed.

"What's going on?" Mystery asked, holding tight to Phoebe's leash. "Are these dogs going berserk?"

"Not sure. You know about Prissy's squirrel fixation." I would've commanded her to heel or sit or something, but nothing works when she's in pursuit of the fluffy-tailed varmints.

Prissy towed me east, facing into the sun. I raised a hand to block the blinding rays. It was then that I noticed a gathering of ghosts surrounding a prominent gravestone with a carved angel draped over it. "Wonder what's happening over there?"

The vision flashed through my mind. *Six ghosts!*

"Over where?" Mystery asked. "I don't know what you're talking about, but Phoebe seems intent on following Prissy to find out."

The dogs stopped, dropped to their bellies and whined, not

wanting to approach the earthbound spirits.

The large, granite headstone with a carved angel draped over the top hid all but a woman's tan arm, the hand lying palm up. The nails were painted fuchsia. Engraved on the headstone were the words, *You are my Angel*.

Mystery and I stopped and stared.

A jolt of recognition zinged through me. *The angel. The fuchsia nails. My vision. This can't be good.*

"Do you think she fainted?" Mystery asked sounding concerned.

"Let's find out." I made a parting-of-the Red-Sea motion and said with a commanding tone, "Back away. We need to check for signs of life."

When the spooks had drifted out of range, Mystery followed me around to the front of the headstone. A Latina woman with long black curls lay on her back, her head turned to one side. She didn't look to be breathing.

A bloody gash on her temple and her pallor were the first things to catch my attention. I looked up to see a smear of blood on the gravestone. *Did she fall and hit her head?*

I took a step back and covered my mouth to stop the bile inching up my esophagus. *I don't know her, but she looks familiar. Where have I seen her before?* Try as I might, the memory wouldn't surface.

When I had control of my stomach, I said, "It looks like she hit her head." I stepped forward, crouched, and checked for a pulse.

"Please tell me she's alive. I don't want to find any more dead folks," Mystery said, rubbing her arms.

I shook my head, unable to speak past the sudden lump in my throat. Standing, I backed away, being careful to retrace my steps.

"Dead?" Mystery looked like shock had punched her in the solar plexus, stealing her breath. She stumbled back a step. "Are you sure?"

I swallowed hard. "She hasn't been dead long. She's still warm." I knew I had to do something to distract Mystery before she started to hyperventilate, so I put my hands on my hips and scowled. "Mystery Lucille Jones, you're becoming a dead body magnet."

Her mouth dropped open. "It's not my fault. I don't enjoy

finding dead folks. I don't even like 'em." She crossed her arms and jutted her chin. "Besides, it's not like it's a habit or anything. This is only the second one." She pointed her long acrylic-nailed forefinger at me. "In case you forgot, you were also there for the first one."

"As Lucille would say, 'That's neither here nor there,'" I said with a dismissive wave of my hand.

My stomach was still flipping like a rollercoaster doing a loop. *I hate the sight of blood.* Closing my eyes, I took a deep calming breath. I opened them and stepped back several more paces, so I could no longer see the body.

After grabbing my phone from my back pocket, I took another deep, cleansing breath and called Chris. "Mystery and I came across a dead body in Maple Hill Cemetery."

"How do you know it's dead?" he asked, sounding every bit like a homicide detective.

"*She's* not breathing and doesn't have a pulse. That's how I know she's dead." I flipped my hair over a shoulder, annoyed by his referral to the poor woman as "it." The heat creeping up my neck didn't improve my mood.

"Describe the scene. I'm taking notes," he said.

I started to describe the body and scene in detail and stopped. "I'll send you a photo." I snapped a pic on my phone and texted it to him. I heard the ping signaling a text arrival on his phone.

He grunted like I'd done something wrong. "This murder is the second one. Y'all will develop a bad reputation with the department if you two keep this up."

Striving to ignore the implication, I said, "I know this is the second one. I can count. Finding dead bodies isn't my idea of fun." I gave him directions to locate the grave.

"A uniform will arrive before we can get there. Try to stay calm. Is Mystery okay?"

"She's hanging in there. No panic attacks like the last time. At least not yet. I hope to see you soon." After disconnecting the call, I turned away from the victim. "Mystery, he irks me when he goes into cop mode." I rubbed my arms to dispel the chill from shock, despite the July heat.

"Cop mode is the least of our worries," Mystery said, trying to breathe slow and deep.

I stepped back into a ghost. The icy, electrified sensation made me shudder and feel even more nauseated. When I turned, I recognized the dead woman's ghost as she reeled away.

"It's her!" I pointed. "The dead woman's spirit."

Before I could ask what happened to her, the specter dispersed into a mist, disappearing like fog in bright sunlight.

"Dang, she's gone," I said, feeling disappointed at the missed opportunity.

"Where did she go?" Mystery asked, looking around. "Did she cross over?"

"She's a new earthbound spirit. When I backed into her, it drained her energy. If she sticks around, she'll need some time to recharge." I led Prissy farther away from the death scene.

Mystery followed with Phoebe. "You make it sound like haints are paranormal battery packs."

"In some aspects, they are. They receive a boost of energy from emotions, both theirs and ours. Strong ones like love, hate, and fear work best for their needs. Maybe that's why they try to scare people? When they do things, they expel energy and need to recharge," I said.

She nodded. "Sugar, I'll never forget the show Victoria Spellman put on at her funeral. I've never seen a church clear out so fast." She cocked her head to the side. "What did Chris say that made you look so fired up?"

I repeated Chris' smart-alecky remark.

She flung her hands in the air with frustration. "It's not our fault. If you want to get technical, Prissy found both bodies."

Prissy's ears twitched at the sound of her name.

I handed her Prissy's leash and walked back toward the body. I noticed that one of the ghosts had stuck her thumbs in her ears and wiggled her fingers while sticking her tongue out at the barking dogs.

"What's wrong with our fur babies?" Mystery asked while struggling to hold both leashes.

"Ghosts," I said.

I sent a push of energy at the troublemaker.

The female spirit flew backward, looking shocked.

"Sugar, what are you doing?"

"Taking care of the ghost and looking for clues about what

happened." I circled the area and leaned closer. "This is interesting."

Mystery inched closer and gawked. "Sweet Baby Jesus!"

The tombstone belonged to Carol Jeffery, Ron's wife. A pot of fresh flowers, looking a bit battered, peeked from beneath the body. I hadn't noticed them from where I'd stood earlier.

"Take a photo of those flowers, Bree. Maybe we can find the florist."

I pulled out my phone and took the photo before facing her. "Are we investigating this as a murder?"

"Chris would hate that," Mystery said, looking unsure.

The memory of our first murder case formed icicles down my spine. *Should we do this?* I looked back at the body. *She could have tripped and hit her head on the headstone. That would make it an accidental death.*

Something about the wide-eyed look of terror on the woman's face made me think this wasn't the case.

Then, there was the vision I had in Lucille's sunroom.

Mystery and I locked gazes.

"Investigating hauntings doesn't qualify us to be homicide detectives. We got lucky on the previous one. What do you think?" I asked.

Mystery crossed her arms and cocked a hip. "Maybe we shouldn't. The killer did try to murder you the last time we stuck our noses into a homicide investigation."

I shuddered, remembering my efforts to avoid the deranged woman who had tried to gut me. "True. If we do, we'll need to be more careful." I paused. "There's another reason I think we should investigate." I told her about my vision.

Her eyes widened. "You've never mentioned your visions."

"I've only had a grand total of five."

I could tell by her frown that Mystery was considering the situation. "Since the body is on Ron's late wife's grave, and there's an earthbound spirit, I think we should investigate. The vision seals the deal." She looked back at the body. "Won't this haint need our help to cross over?"

I nodded. "My guess is, yes."

"Count me in, but don't mention it to Mama."

"Roger that."

CHAPTER 3: BRIANNA

A blue and white SUV with "POLICE" written on the side was the first to arrive. A muscle-bound cop stepped out and flexed his biceps, straining the stitches on his uniform shirt. After looking around, he ran his hand over his military-style haircut and swaggered to where we stood.

Prissy and Phoebe showed their teeth and emitted low growls.

He stopped short. "I'm Officer Jackson. Where's the body?"

I pointed toward the gravestone. My hand was steadier than my still-racing heart.

After a brief nod, he walked back to the vehicle's rear to pull out a roll of yellow crime scene tape. He approached the body, being careful about where he stepped, and then stopped. He pointed the roll of bright yellow tape at me. "You." He jerked his head to hail me. "I need you to hold this end for me."

"Sure," I said, handing Mystery my dog's leash. I took the end of the proffered tape, and with a sardonic smile, said, "You're welcome," to Jackson's retreating back.

He used surrounding tombstones to hold the makeshift barrier in place. When he completed the circuit and reached me, he wrapped it once around the nearest monument and tied it off.

"That should do it." He returned the tape to the rear of the vehicle and then opened the driver's door.

"Is he leaving?" Mystery whispered.

Before I could respond, he pulled a metal clipboard from the interior and a pen from his pocket. He did a body-builder stride back to us. It reminded me of how diaper-wearing toddlers walk. From his expression, I could tell he thought he looked formidable.

The dogs growled again, raising their hackles.

"If they don't like him, he's probably not a nice guy. Prissy is an astute judge of character," I whispered to Mystery.

Mystery adopted Phoebe three months ago. In general, she seemed the type to lick a burglar to death. This made her reaction more disturbing.

Jackson cast a brief glare at the dogs. Then, after narrowing his gaze, he focused on me. "Ma'am, tell me what happened here."

I began explaining, leaving out the part about the ghosts. With growing amusement, I eyed a female specter that looked over his shoulder while he wrote notes.

Jackson shuddered and wheeled around to confront nothing—at least that he could see.

I covered my mouth, trying to suppress the laugh gurgling to the surface.

He turned back to face me. His heavy brows formed a V before he said, "You think there's something funny about a dead body?" He stepped forward, making jabbing motions toward my chest with his pen that forced me backward. "Why are y'all at this cemetery?" Jab. "At this time in the morning?" Jab. "At this particular grave?" Jab.

Prissy strained to reach him, barking. Phoebe showed her teeth, but Mystery held tight to the leashes.

I shot him a squinty-eyed glare. I felt my temper rise, ready to spread destruction like the fire-breathing dragon in the painting above my fireplace.

Jackson again glared down at the dogs before stomping his large, booted foot in their direction.

Both dogs lunged instead of fleeing.

Face flaming with anger, I took a step forward. "Back off! You're upsetting the dogs."

Mystery cocked her head toward me. "Do you realize you're yelling at Detective Chris Haddington's lady friend?"

I raised my chin and crossed my arms.

Jackson's eyes widened just a fraction before he took several steps back.

I exchanged glances with Mystery. "I'll continue to explain from here, if it's okay with you?"

She swept a hand toward the cordoned-off crime scene. "Be my guest."

I cleared my throat and took a deep breath. "I was taking photos for an elderly gentleman who is researching for the historical society. While we were here, my friend and I decided to exercise the dogs."

And to help Mystery avoid a bubble butt, I thought.

I paused a moment, before continuing with my haughtiest tone that I reserve for rude idiots. "The dogs pulled us over here. I can only guess that their keen sense of smell alerted them to the body."

A dark sedan approached, winding its way to our location, followed by a white van sporting the logo of a local funeral home. In Huntsville, the Coroner is an elected office, often held by one of the local funeral directors.

I heaved a sigh of relief. "As Lucille would say, 'the cavalry has arrived.'"

Jackson glanced over his shoulder.

I moved closer and whispered to Mystery, "Oh, no. It's Tony Ricci, and the area's crawling with ghosts. The last time we spoke, he's seeing ghosts on a regular basis now. If we don't get them out of here, he may have what Dr. Stone would call a phasmophobic-induced panic attack."

Mystery had had a few panic attacks during her late husband Tyree's funeral, and they didn't look fun.

Dr. Charlene "Charlie" Stone is a local psychologist who has a private practice and works part-time as a forensic profiler for the Huntsville Police Department. She can also see and hear ghosts, but this is only known by a few friends.

Mystery whispered back, "Last night, Chris told me Ricci had agreed to start therapy about his haint phobia. Heck, he may even be over it by now."

I shielded my eyes from the sun to better see his reaction. "I doubt it, but we'll soon find out."

Tony and Chris exited the car.

Tony looked in our direction and ground to a sudden halt. The pallor that crept over his Mediterranean complexion indicated he hadn't yet conquered the fear of earth-bound spirits.

"He's not over it yet," I said.

"Do something! Haints listen to you," Mystery said with a forceful whisper.

He may faint if I don't run them off soon. Using a commanding tone and expansive sweeping motions with my arms, I bellowed, "Get out of here! Go on. Move it!"

Jackson's eyes bulged before he turned to see who I told to leave.

Most of the specters scattered, shooting sullen looks at me.

I took several steps forward, advancing toward the muscle-bound cop who stood between me and the remaining spirits. Making shooing motions, I said, "Go on. *Move it!*"

Jackson retreated several feet, looking even more bug-eyed. His hand hovered over his pistol.

Unknown to him, the rest of the ghosts drifted away. I would be the next murder victim if the intensity of their looks could spear me.

I shook my head. *This must be more entertaining than the usual funerals.*

Tony's shoulders lowered. He gave an appreciative nod to me before walking toward us. His complexion returned to its normal, tanned tone, which contrasted against his starched white shirt. Today's tie selection featured Wiley Coyote.

I couldn't help but grin while eyeing his neckwear. When I first met him, he wore a Tinker Bell tie. "Which grandchild gave you that one?"

Tony's ears reddened. He smoothed the tie with a palm and said, "Ricky."

I nodded. "I've always liked that cartoon."

He scanned the murder scene before directing Officer Jackson to keep lookie-loos away and direct the forensics van to the scene. He nodded toward the clipboard in Jackson's hands. "We'll take over from here. I want that initial report in the system before the end of your shift."

Jackson said, "Yes, sir." He cast a wary look toward Chris before leaving.

When Jackson was out of hearing range, Chris asked, "Did No-Neck get sick?"

No-Neck? I shook my head. "Why?"

"He's got a reputation for tossing his cookies at messy murder scenes."

I watched the broad retreating back. "Maybe this one wasn't disgusting enough to make him sick."

Mystery shot a spiky look at Chris. "He was rude and a total jerk. You need to talk with Officer No-Neck about poking his pen toward a woman's chest while raising his voice in a threatening manner." She cut her eyes toward me.

Chris' eyes narrowed. His gaze shifted to me.

I nodded.

His jaw tightened. "I'll take care of that later."

The two detectives interviewed Mystery and me for the next thirty minutes. I couldn't speak for her, but I was efficient at laying out the facts, despite my rumbling stomach.

While I answered questions, I studied the haints loitering in the distance but failed to see the one attached to the dead woman. *I wonder if she's crossed over? I haven't seen the light. She probably hasn't recharged yet. If she'd stuck around, I could've asked her what happened.*

CHAPTER 4: BRIANNA

I cringed at the sound of squealing brakes. Heaving an annoyed sigh, I slid shut a display case full of wedding garters and stood in time to see Tiffany Blake's white Volvo make an abrupt halt in front of my store.

Kaya Mendez rushed into the retail area. "Was there a wreck, or was it Tiffany?"

Kaya, a petite Mexican-American, works part-time for me. A University of Alabama Huntsville student, she wears her long dark hair in a swishy pony tail most of the time. Her most attractive feature is her doe-like brown eyes.

I grumbled, "She's gonna get herself killed one of these days. How that woman passed a driving test is beyond me."

"Me, too," Kaya said before returning to the back.

Tiffany flew into the store causing the door alert to bing. The hot breeze followed her inside, distributing her distinct floral scent across the room. A huge smile covered her face.

I frowned at her while tapping my index finger on the counter. "Tiffany, how many wrecks have you had in the last five years?"

"None." Her smile faded. "There have been lots around me." She shrugged. "I guess I attract idiot drivers."

I gaped at her a moment before shaking my head in amazement. "Girl, you drive like a maniac on meth. You need to slow down and pay attention."

Kaya picked that moment to walk back into the retail area holding several hangers with support garments. "Pay attention to what?"

"How she drives."

Kaya lowered the hangers. "Tiffany, I pray every day that you won't have a wreck."

"That's what people keep telling me." She lifted her chin, a defiant gleam in her Kewpie doll eyes. Then, using a brusque tone, she said, "I don't know why? I have a perfect driving record." She walked to the counter. She took in a deep breath, paused, and her smile returned. In a sing-song tone, she said, "Can you come next door for a few minutes? I have good news."

I glanced over at Kaya.

"I'm good. Go ahead. I'm ready to put out some of our new stock." She made a shooing motion.

I followed Tiffany to Mystery's store.

Mystery looked up from writing on a sheet of paper. "Well, I thought I heard your squealing brake arrival." She smiled. "Wow, Tiffany, you certainly look professional. Nice blue suit."

"I've been working today."

Tiffany's long blonde hair was pulled up into a bun, changing her appearance from a blue-eyed bombshell in her early forties to a serious businesswoman.

"That's because I've been scaring up business for us." She winked. "Pun intended."

Tiffany placed her leather Michael Kors case on a stool and opened it. After pulling out some papers, she waved them with glee. "I signed up two defense contractors for background checks today."

Huntsville, Alabama, the security clearance mecca of the South, employs a league of engineers, scientists, and computer geeks who work for Redstone Arsenal, NASA, and a slew of defense contractors.

"When I explained how they could save thousands, the owners signed on the dotted line."

"Good work." Mystery took the contracts and glanced through them. "It's a win-win for both them and us. I'm hoping this will provide a steadier income source. Paranormal investigations are hit and miss, if you know what I mean."

Mystery had bought the store from Vera Plunk, her former boss, who was a private investigator. All the programs to do background searches, plus some spy equipment, and a cabinet full of disguises and wigs were included in the sale.

"I'm psyched! It's good to be back in the game and using my marketing degree." Tiffany's expression sobered. "It also helps to get out of the house. I've been ruminating like an old heifer over the Jason and Sierra fiasco. Detective Ricci told me it could be a year before Sierra comes to trial."

Sierra Locke had conspired with Tiffany's late husband, Jason, to murder her to inherit her wealth.

Mystery reached over and gave her hand a comforting pat. "Sugar, a two-toed sloth moves faster than the court system." She grinned. "On the bright side, you don't have to file for a divorce, and we recovered the missing funds Jason moved offshore before he died."

Tiffany tucked a loose tendril of hair behind her ear. "That's true. I'll focus on the positive. Brianna, I'm also working on some contracts for haunted houses."

"That's good. Did Mystery tell you about the murder in the cemetery?" I asked.

"No." Tiffany directed a shocked glance my way and then looked at Mystery. "Did you find *another* dead body?"

Mystery huffed with indignation. "It's bad enough that Bree called me a 'dead body magnet' without you implying it." She crossed her arms. "Besides, Prissy and Phoebe found her."

I moved closer. "If Prissy keeps this up, we can hire her out to the homicide squad to find missing victims."

Mystery and I tag teamed while relaying the story to Tiffany.

"So, the police decided it was a murder, not an accident?" Tiffany asked.

"Based on preliminary evidence. It won't be official until after the autopsy." I leaned against the counter and crossed my arms. "Chris won't tell me why it's not an accident, but I'll find out." I winked. "I think he enjoys making me wheedle every tidbit of information out of him."

"Are y'all going to investigate this murder, too? Do y'all want me to do some snooping?" Tiffany set her case on the floor and sat on the stool. "Ron lives in the Twickenham Historic District. I can check out the rumors circulating on the Camellia Express."

"That would be great," I said.

The Camellia Express is the high-speed gossip network in the historic district. I knew not all the information would be accurate, but some tidbits might lead us to some suspects.

"Do we know the identity of the victim?" Mystery asked before sitting on a nearby stool.

"No, but I saw her ghost," I said, twirling my hair. "She looked familiar for some reason."

"Sugar, maybe all ghosts start looking alike," Mystery said.

I frowned, aggravated by my memory block. "Not really. Disembodied spirits each look like themselves. The weaker ones are more translucent, and the more powerful ones appear more solid with vibrant coloring."

"Why didn't you ask the ghost who killed her?" Tiffany asked, squirming to adjust her skirt.

"Newly dead spirits are weak, so I drained her power when I accidentally backed into her. She evaporated before I had a chance. That's why any information you can discover will be helpful," I said.

"I'll see what I can find out." Tiffany picked up her phone. "I've set the appointment for Mr. Craft to tell us about his haunted furniture. I love this new scheduling system that Jasmine created." She pulled a sheet of paper from her bag. "I almost forgot, here's Mr. Craft's contract. I need to return a copy to him."

Mystery accepted it and scanned the contents. "Good. When do we learn more?"

"He plans to come to our staff meeting to discuss it."

Mystery's assistant, Jasmine Williams, came in from the rear. She swung her backpack with a University of Alabama-Huntsville emblem onto a counter and waved. "I finished tweaking those cameras from last week's install at Ron's business. There must be something hinky going on because he wants a camera focused on one of his new hires."

"Interesting," Mystery said. "I'll ask him about it."

A saucy grin spread across Jasmine's face as she did a hip wiggle. "Met a hot guy in class today. Said he'd text me later."

I looked toward heaven. *Lord, let this one be a good one.*

Jasmine's attractive exterior hides a wicked brilliant mind about computers and anything electronic. She has often wowed her professors with her programming feats. Yet, she's inherited a defective gene from her mom when it comes to picking a decent man.

"Please tell me this one doesn't have a police record," Mystery said with a hardy dose of sarcasm.

Tiffany shot a disapproving frown her way. "Give her a break. This gentleman could be different."

"Hope so," Jasmine said. "Ms. Lucille said I should run a background check on every guy I consider dating."

"I don't always agree with everything Mama suggests, but I do this time. Are you still enjoying your new apartment?"

Lucille had renovated her detached garage into an adorable furnished apartment that she has rented to Jasmine at a reduced rate in exchange for help with outdoor tasks.

Jasmine's face brightened. "Yes. Ms. Lucille has me over to the main house for cooking lessons. Yesterday she gave me a Julia Child cookbook. She called it the 'bible of cooking.' It's the thickest book I've ever owned." Jasmine stepped closer and with an excited tone said, "After we fix supper, we eat together, like a real family." She looked down. "Didn't realize how much normal life I've missed until I stopped living with Mom." She paused. "Heck, I'm not sure I knew what normal meant."

Mystery patted her shoulder in an understanding way. "As Mama would say, better late than never. Speaking of Chantel, how did your Independence Day meal go?"

"Yeah, we missed you at the July Fourth feast," I said.

Jasmine hitched one shoulder. "The usual." She rolled her eyes as only Jasmine could. "She's hooked up with another loser. Made me happy I'm out on my own. On the bright side, Ms. Lucille saved me some of the leftovers."

Mystery attended middle and high school with Chantel and knows her ways. She told me once that Chantel was boy crazy back then and man crazy now.

Wanting to redirect the discussion, I said, "Mystery and I'll have to come by and sample your cooking."

A flash of panic filled Jasmine's eyes. "Give me a few more weeks to work out my culinary kinks."

"Sugar, if you're like me, you'll be working out your 'culinary kinks' for the rest of your life. I didn't inherit Mama's cooking gene. That's why it bothers me that she guards her cookbook like it's gold-plated."

You mean Gertie's cookbook, I thought.

Tiffany nudged me. "Tell Jasmine about the body y'all found."

"You two found *another* corpse? This is becoming a habit," Jasmine said, a curious gleam in her brown eyes.

Tiffany crossed her arms and cocked her head in my direction. "That's what I told them."

I threw my hands into the air. Emphasizing each word, I said, "It's. Not. Our. Fault. It was Prissy."

"And Phoebe!" Mystery crossed her arms. "You should have seen our little girls defending us from that, that..."

Jasmine grinned and raised a finger. "Remember the bad habit jar."

To help Jasmine develop to her full potential, Mystery started the bad habit jar. Every time Jasmine mispronounces a word, uses poor grammar, or curses, she has to pay the jar a dollar. To make it fair, Mystery agreed to the same rules and allowed Jasmine to pick the charity that receives the proceeds. She chose the homeless shelter.

Mystery took a deep breath. "Mean cop."

I told Jasmine the details of finding the homicide victim. Her eyes grew wider as the story progressed.

Mystery pointed at me. "I thought she would deck that big cop for poking his pen at her. I swear that man was a human bull with no neck."

"There's more," I said. "The grave where we found the body was Carol Jeffery's resting place."

"Do you mean our customer, Ron Jeffery's late wife?" Jasmine asked with an amazed tone.

I nodded. "The very one."

"Ms. Lucille would say it's a small world," Jasmine said, nodding. "Did you notice someone is moving into the gift shop that closed last month?"

We all exchanged interested glances.

"Do you want to go welcome the new shop owner at lunch?" I asked. "Kaya isn't going to lunch until one."

"Sugar, I'm game now that Jasmine's here."

Tiffany held up both hands. "Sorry, ladies, I have a hair appointment." She glanced at her watch. "Well, diddly, I need to get on the ball, or I'll be late." She waved and rushed through the door, sending the bell jingling.

We all cringed when Tiffany backed out without looking and sped down the street.

With a disbelieving look, Mystery said, "She must have a super vigilant guardian angel. This is why I made a stipulation in her contract that she never drive a company vehicle."

"I don't blame you," I said, shaking my head.

Jasmine looked around the shop. "What do you want me to do next?"

Mystery retrieved the new contracts from a drawer and waved them. "Tiffany scared up some work for you. Your contact person is on the paperwork. These background checks should keep you busy, but first, I want you to see if you can use your new software program to enlarge a photo of a bouquet."

"What am I looking for exactly?" Jasmine asked, curiosity lacing her tone.

"Anything that might identify the florist." I pulled out my phone. "I'll send you the photo."

Jasmine grinned. "Good, I need the extra hours. Textbooks are expensive."

"Sugar, do you have everything you need to start graduate school next month?"

"Pretty much. The scholarship helps." She shifted from foot to foot. "To be truthful, I'm a little nervous. Never thought I'd make it this far."

Mystery squeezed her shoulder. "Sugar, your genius will blow those professors out of their seats."

Jasmine's face flushed. "Thanks. Hope so."

"Before you start on those things, I want to pop next door with Bree." Mystery imitated Jasmine's little signature wiggle. "I need to replace my granny panties with something pretty. I have a date with Ron Jeffery tonight."

"You wear granny panties?" Jasmine did her neck thing.

I rubbed my neck. *If I tried that motion, I'd be heading to a chiropractor.*

Mystery narrowed her eyes. "Sugar, must I remind you that I

was a widow for two years and had no need for pretty underwear."

"Glad you're finally *venturing* out," Jasmine said, looking smug.

I asked, "Is that your word of the day?"

"Yep."

When Jasmine turned twenty-one in April, Mystery's present was a vocabulary calendar. It's become a game to see how many times Jasmine can use each daily word in her conversations.

"In that case, I'll *venture* next door," Mystery said before waving goodbye.

We passed under the pink and black awning that shades my store and opened the door.

The moment we entered, Mystery looked dreamy-eyed. I feared she would swoon from the rich, tempting smell of her favorite food group.

Kaya looked up and exchanged pleasantries before strolling to the back.

I walked over to the four glass display counters that formed a barrier in the center of the rectangular retail section of the store. I operate my register from here. The smallest one displayed a selection of bridal garters; the rest held chocolates from all over the world. I knelt to lock away my purse in a drawer and stood, ready to transform Mystery into a sex goddess.

"Bree, this place smells like a giant chocolate bar. I want some more of that tasty dark chocolate with almonds. The stress from solving Tiffany's case has almost depleted my Girl Scout Thin Mint cookie supply."

I gaped at her. "It was a stressful time for me, too." Then, donning a mischievous expression, I peeked over the counter. "You might want to ease up on the sweets. You don't want a Thin Mint bubble butt now that you're dating."

Looking offended, she rose to her full five-foot-seven and thrust her ample bosom forward. "I'll have you know dark chocolate and almonds are healthy foods. With the two combined, that makes them twice as healthy."

I flipped my hair over a shoulder before bending to pull a box of chocolate bars from the case. "If you say so." I set them on the counter. "How many bars?"

She tapped her chin with an index finger. "Twenty ought to do it."

My brows shot up. *"Twenty?"*

I could feel Mystery's emotions whirl while she searched for an excuse for the large purchase. "I, uh, don't want to make extra trips."

"I'm located next door!" I gathered the chocolate. "Lady, you can rationalize better than anybody I know. Anything else? I have a new shipment of chocolate from Ecuador."

She ignored the rationalization remark since it was true. "That's enough goodies, but I do need some pretty lady things."

I rubbed my hands together with an air of excited anticipation. "I've been waiting years for this day."

"Now, don't you be going overboard on me. I'm not wearing those tiny stretchy things that barely cover anything!"

I threw my head back and did a deep belly laugh. When I gained control, I swiped away laugh tears. "Trust me. I have a good idea of what will look best on you." I held up my right hand as if swearing an oath. "No tiny stretchy things. I promise."

Inspired by Mystery's shop, I'd installed Formica-topped counters with drawers underneath along three walls. Baskets of panties sat on top of these counters with signs displaying the sizes. Racks of bras, slips, sleepwear, and other lingerie items covered the space between the display cases and the counters.

We were looking at an array of colorful lace brassieres when I asked, "Do you still miss Tyree?"

"Of course, I do. I was married to the man for ten years." She fingered a lavender lace bra before choosing her size. "I'll admit, I finally feel at peace now. As Mama would say, 'That chapter of my life is complete. It's time to turn the page.'"

Chuckling, I said, "Lucille has a saying for every occasion." I handed her a dark purple bra and matching panties. "Ron is a catch. He's not only good-looking but his accounting firm is rumored to be quite successful. From what I've heard, many single women in Huntsville have an eye on him." I paused, feeling sad. "I heard it was too late when they discovered his wife's breast cancer. Bless her heart, she never had a chance."

"I just hope he's worked through his grief. It took me two years to get past mine." Mystery fingered the soft lace. "Bree, I'm worried he's hiding something. You were there. Remember how he didn't answer our questions about that woman Jack was chasing? And what was Sarah accusing him of doing?"

At that moment, the memory clicked into place. "Ye gods and little fishes!"

"What?" Mystery's eyes rounded.

"Our murder victim at Carol's grave was the woman at the fireworks. What was her name?"

Mystery's brow furrowed. "Rosa, something."

"Lopez!" I said, happy to solve the mystery niggling at the edge of my mind. "Anything else bothering you about Ron?"

"He's conservative. I'm afraid he won't accept the paranormal part of my business."

Confused, I asked, "Why?"

"Ron raised his eyebrows and looked shocked when Mama chided us for our paranormal work." She crossed her arms. "It's not like what my business does isn't painted on the shop's windows."

"I was too busy watching Lucille building up to one of her classic hissy fits. Do you think she'll ever understand that we're serving a spiritual purpose when we help these earth-bound souls?"

"Probably not." She sighed with frustration. "You know how narrow-minded and stubborn Mama can be."

"Has Ron said anything about the paranormal to you?"

"No, not yet," she said while checking out a lavender panty that matched the bra she'd chosen earlier. "It will be nice to have some pretty things to wear instead of just black."

After she made some choices, I found the correct sizes in several matching sets and carried them to a dressing room. "I'm sure you'll find something you'll like. Meanwhile, I'll look for some sleepwear that will be both pretty and comfortable."

Thirty minutes later, she checked out with everything she'd need for several perfect romantic interludes. Despite the twenty-percent discount I gave her, she still took a deep swallow when she saw the final tally. A swirl of doubt emanated from her. She straightened her shoulders and handed me a credit card.

When we returned to the Mystery Shop to put away her purchases, Jasmine came out of the computer room, followed by Phoebe. "I found your florist."

"Good, I'll check it out after Kaya returns from lunch," I said, my stomach rumbling.

CHAPTER 5: BRIANNA

Mystery and I walked toward the new store on the other side of Craft's Antiques.

"Whoever owns this place will have more customer parking problems because it's next door to Garuda. I know it hurt the previous gift shop and might be why they closed," Mystery said.

"That and their exorbitant prices," I added.

The Thai restaurant, Garuda, is a blessing and a curse. The patrons of its lunch and dinner meals gobble up the limited parking of the rest of the stores in our strip mall.

On the positive side, those same customers sometimes drop in to shop after leaving the busy restaurant.

We stopped and looked up at the new bright blue awning with white lettering that read, Herbal Healing Solutions.

"Sounds New Age. My kinda place," I said, beaming a pleased smile.

We peered through the window at a woman in her early forties, who was dressed in a long multi-colored skirt and a coordinating turquoise top. Her long black hair was pulled back into a French braid. Dangling turquoise earrings swung as she moved about, placing items on different shelves.

I knocked on the door to gain her attention.

The woman looked up, her almost black eyes rounded with surprise.

We smiled and waved.

The woman walked to the door and said through the glass, "Sorry, I'm not open yet."

I gestured at Mystery and myself. "We're shop owners, too. We wanted to welcome you and treat you to lunch, if you have time."

Surprise once again flashed across her tanned face before she assumed a neutral expression. She nodded and raised her index finger. "One moment." She walked behind a counter, grabbed something, and returned carrying a large colorful purse. After opening the door, she stepped out and locked it. "I'm Theodosia Bosswell." She extended a tanned hand. "Call me Dosi."

Her energy felt calm and steady.

She pulled her hand back and studied me a moment. Her intense look made me feel laid bare.

After the introductions, we strolled to Garuda and claimed a booth in a corner. Mystery and I shared one side, and we piled all the purses onto the other with Dosi.

The light from the restaurant's wall of windows made it easy to see the large photos of Thailand spread along the opposite wall. A loud drone of voices beat against my ears like waves of cicada song. The heady scent of spices filled the air, triggering my mouth to water.

After we had ordered, we settled down to talk.

Mystery told Dosi about her shop's paranormal investigations and ghost tours.

Dosi listened but didn't respond one way or another.

When I explained what my shop sold, Dosi's expression brightened.

"Do you carry brassieres in my size?" Dosi asked, her tone full of hope.

Being well-endowed myself, I could understand why she might have trouble finding underwear that fit correctly and was comfortable.

After gazing at her with a measuring eye, I said, "Yes. Stop by when you have an opportunity." Pleased to have a new potential customer, I smiled and said, "Tell us about your store," while placing my napkin across my lap.

"I'm an herbalist who specializes in healing remedies."

I wondered, *Is she a hedge witch?* I'd heard of their magic with

43

natural remedies but had never met one.

The waiter served up a pleasant smile along with our sweet iced teas. He did a tiny bow before leaving.

Like most Southerners I love robust sweet tea. There's nothing like the caffeine and sugar shock to propel me through an afternoon slump.

Dosi sipped from her glass before continuing with a cautious tone. "What type of paranormal wares do you sell, Mystery? I hope we aren't duplicating items."

Mystery and I exchanged wary glances.

"Mainly ghost hunting equipment, both kits and the more expensive items. I recently began carrying books about ghosts and ghost hunting guides. The rest is security and spy equipment, conceal-carry purses, magic kits, and some self-defense items. What do you plan to sell?"

"Herbs and spices, of course." Dosi unwrapped her utensils and placed the napkin in her lap. "I'll also carry tarot cards, rune stones, and healing stones."

"I'll come by and check those out," I said.

"Will you carry any books?" Mystery asked.

Dosi nodded. "Books about supernatural powers, palm reading, and guides to using herbs for healing. We should compare our inventories, so we offer different options to our customers. I don't have any books involving ghosts, and I'll avoid ordering any in the future."

"Thanks. That's a wonderful idea," Mystery agreed.

My stomach growled when I saw the waiter coming our way.

After the salads arrived, we focused on them for a few bites.

"I love this ginger dressing." I swallowed and dabbed some off my mouth. "How did you become an herbalist? Is there a school for that occupation?"

Dosi gave a wry smile. "I'm Roma, so I learned it from my grandmother and mother."

"What's Roma?" I asked, hoping I hadn't misheard.

"My family comes from Romania. Have you heard of Gypsies?"

"Yes."

"The Romany people prefer to be called Roma. My family was nomadic until my mother immigrated here when I was twelve. She wanted a more stable life for me after my father's death."

"Sugar, it must've been hard to lose a parent when you were so young," Mystery said.

Her face assumed a flat expression before she offered a tight nod.

She doesn't want to discuss how her dad died. Best I leave that alone for now, since we just met. I leaned forward and asked, "Did your mother teach you any other skills?"

"The women in my family also instructed me in the art of reading palms, tarot cards, and the runes."

I shifted forward. "You can read palms?"

Dosi held out her hand. "Would you like for me to read yours?"

My face flushed with heat. I offered my hand across the table.

Dosi turned it palm up and swept several fingers down my wrist to coax it to open. She fished inside her purse with her free hand and pulled out reading glasses. After perching them on her nose, she stared at my palm.

I could feel an intense flare of her energy field.

She looked up with a bug-eyed expression I can only describe as amazement. "You're gifted with great power over the dead."

I stiffened and pulled my hand away. Glancing around, I lowered my voice. "How did you know?"

"It's in your palm. I sensed that you have other powers, but that's the main one." Her brow furrowed. "Beware, too much knowledge about special powers can be dangerous."

Good grief, what does "special powers over the dead" mean? The mere words sent a shiver running down my nerve endings. Sensing Mystery's curiosity, I decided to change the subject. "Dosi, have you met Mr. Craft yet? He owns the antique shop between ours."

Still staring at me with an amazed expression, she said, "Not yet. Is he the older gentleman who guards his parking slots with the zeal of a soldier at war?"

Mystery chuckled at her accurate description. "That's Mr. C. Poor soul, his arthritis has been acting up more. Do you think you can help him?"

Dosi turned to study Mystery, then me with her intense dark eyes. "I sense the two of you care a great deal about people." She smiled. "Yes, I can help."

"I'm so glad. I'll send Mr. C your way. When do you open?" I asked.

"Friday, but tell your Mr. Craft to come today. No need for him to suffer until Friday. Pain drains the spirit."

"Thank you. I'll tell him," I said.

Dosi paused and put down her fork to eye Mystery with a laser-like focus. "I sense your destiny is to help Brianna with her work."

"I do my best to keep her out of the weeds." Mystery leaned closer and lowered her voice. "It isn't always easy."

"I am fortunate to have met you both. I felt guided to open my shop in this location. I've been adrift since my mother died in March." She sighed. "It is lonely when people don't understand your gifts."

I nodded. "Believe me, we understand."

Our main dishes arrived. We sat back, giving the waiter room to place them on the table.

I lifted my fork and said, "Eat up, ladies. I have a shipment to unpack. Someone," I nodded at Mystery, "recently bought out my entire supply of dark chocolate with almonds."

CHAPTER 6: BRIANNA

Later that afternoon, I stood outside Blooms for You trying to decide how to wheedle the information I wanted from the clerk inside. I took a deep breath to calm my roiling stomach. *Too much coffee. I need to cut back.*

A chime sounded when I entered the shop. An array of floral scents bombarded me, and I fought off the urge to sneeze.

The shop owner had used numerous creative ideas to display various plants and dish gardens at varying levels in the small shop. Several colorful metallic balloons with messages ranging from "Get well" to "Happy birthday" bobbed in the breeze from a nearby vent. Brightly lit cooler cases held a colorful array of cut flowers across one wall. Everything about the place lifted my mood.

"May I help you?" a gray-haired matron asked while wrapping floral tape around the base of a corsage. She placed it in a clear plastic container sitting on the counter and sealed it with a pop.

"Yes. I'd like to know who purchased this mixed flower arrangement." I pulled the photo up on my phone and showed it to her.

She took the glasses hanging by a chain around her neck, perched them on her nose, and squinted at the photo. Her brows rose. Frowning, she said with a hint of suspicion, "You're the second person today to ask me about this bouquet."

Surprised, I took a step back. "Who else?"

The woman opened a drawer, fished out a card, and handed it to me.

Darn, Chris beat me here. I stared at the card a moment. *Maybe that's better. If I'd gotten here first, this woman would've told him I was here asking about the same flowers. Tony will have a hissy fit if he thinks I'm interfering in one of his cases again, especially since the last one nearly got me stabbed while he was running to save me.*

The woman pursed her lips and tapped an index finger on the counter while staring over the top of her reading glasses. "Who are you, and why are you asking?"

I explained, even revealing that Mystery and I had found the victim.

The woman's expression softened. "I'm Betty Bloom." She waved a hand in a dismissive gesture. "I've heard all the cute remarks, so spare me."

I chuckled while handing her my business card.

Betty moved the card back and forth until she hit the perfect reading range. Her eyes crinkled when she smiled. "Chocolates and lingerie, an interesting combination." Her expression sobered. "Ron Jeffery bought the bouquet. Do you know him?"

I gave a brief nod, not wanting to reveal that he was dating my best friend.

"I made it at his request. It's a combination of Carol's favorite flowers."

"Did he say why he wanted the bouquet?"

Betty took off her glasses and rubbed one eye. "Bless her heart, Carol died last July fifth. I did the flowers for her funeral."

I knew from watching Mystery how gut-wrenching the death anniversary could be. "When did he pick up the flowers?"

"Around six-forty-five. I usually come in around six-thirty if I have events. I have three funerals today, so I started on the orders before the shop opened." She rested her forearms on the counter and clasped her hands. "Ron wanted to visit Carol's grave before he went to work, so I told him to show up before seven." Her sad smile widened. "That sweet man bought her a fresh flower arrangement weekly while she was ill."

Several thoughts and feelings crowded my awareness. First, the story was touching and sad—a life lost to such a horrid disease. But it also triggered a disturbing thought. Did Ron kill the woman we discovered at the cemetery? I remembered Sarah's accusations and anger at Ron at the fireworks display. *All the pieces don't fit. Wait until Mystery hears this.*

CHAPTER 7: MYSTERY

For our second date, Ron promised to cook dinner at his home. I felt a tingle of excitement and, to be truthful, a smidge of anxiety. Bree called me last night. Her latest suspicion that he was a potential murder suspect made my stomach tumble like a gymnast. I found it difficult to resolve that a man who gave Carol a weekly bouquet of her favorite flowers could murder a woman on his wife's grave on the anniversary of her death. Brianna was equally spooked, so she made me promise to call when I got home.

I drove to the Twickenham Historic District located near downtown Huntsville. I admired the homes on Adams Street before reaching the street where Ron's house was located.

The brick Georgian-style home had a beige portico and brown shutters. The property was surrounded by a three-foot black wrought iron fence.

I pulled to a stop in front of the ornamental gate and checked the car's navigation system to verify my location. *Yep, this is it. Ron must be doing well to afford this house in such a pricey neighborhood.*

After stepping out of out of my blue Prius that I named Sweetie Pie, I glanced around before pulling the leopard skin top down to cover my backside. I couldn't shake the feeling that I was being watched. *I wish Bree was here.*

Once I was past the gate, I meandered down the long brick

walk, admired Ron's verdant lawn, and wondered how he kept it perfect. I hesitated a moment before ringing the doorbell. *Calm down. You're a grown woman.*

Ron opened the door wide, smiling his welcome as his gaze traveled over me. "Wow! You look great. I hope you like grilled steaks."

I placed a hand on my hip and returned his smile. "What Southern lady doesn't?"

He chuckled. "The vegetarian ones."

He looks tired.

The square foyer opened to three areas. The living room on the left was full of furniture with clean lines and muted tones. On the right, a formal dining room contained a gorgeous crystal chandelier hanging over a cherry dining table. The matching cabinet displayed crystal and fine china.

Ron led me straight ahead, past a stairway, and down a hall leading to the house's rear. I couldn't help but notice how his tight jeans fit while following him. The hallway opened to a den with a stone fireplace and windows that offered a sweeping view of a brick-walled back garden.

I stepped forward and rested a hand on a beige leather sofa. "This is beautiful!"

"Thanks. I can't take credit for the inside because Carol did it. I'm responsible for the back garden. Let me get you a mojito."

"What's in it?"

"White rum, lime, and tons of mint. It's refreshing on a hot day. I grow the mint in my garden."

He set about making my drink at the kitchen counter.

"This is a nice modern kitchen for a home in a historic neighborhood." I ran a hand across the cold gray granite.

"It was so dated that we had it modernized." He scrunched his face. "The kitchen had harvest gold appliances with Formica countertops."

Surprised, I raised both brows. "I don't think I've ever seen appliances that color."

Ron handed me the mojito and led me outside to a large screened porch with white wicker furniture topped with cushions printed with varying shades of green tropical foliage.

Reminds me of Mama's sunroom.

He held the squeaky screen door open for me before casting an embarrassed look at the hinge. "I keep meaning to oil that thing."

"I wouldn't if I were you."

"Why?"

I spoke in my instructing-a-customer tone. "It's an alarm to warn you that someone has entered your porch."

He cocked his head to squint at the hinge. "Hadn't thought of it that way, but you're right."

I stepped onto a stone patio shaded by a pergola covered with clematis and honeysuckle.

"What a wonderful aroma!"

Ron put his arm across my shoulders. "The flowers or the steaks?"

I gave him a playful elbow nudge. "Both."

"How do you like your steak?" Ron asked, picking up a long tong with a wooden handle.

"Medium."

"Me, too. Why don't you wander around the garden while I check the grill?"

I felt drawn to a small landscaped waterfall that emptied into a pond about twice the size of my car. Koi flitted around and came to the surface, mouths open, ready to be fed.

"They sensed the vibrations from your footsteps," Ron said.

Startled, I whirled to find him standing behind me. *Calm down. His presence at the cemetery doesn't mean he killed anyone.* My pounding heart wasn't listening.

He handed me a plastic container full of pellets. "It's dinner time for them. Give them a handful. They'll try to convince you they're starving and need more, but ignore the act."

I placed the mojito in the center of a nearby table and opened the container. "What will happen if I overfeed the fish?"

"They'll get constipated," Ron said and winked before returning to the grill.

Constipated! Is he pulling my leg? I'll Google it later. "Okay, guys, don't you be looking at me that way. I'm not going to contribute to any colon malfunctions." *Do fish even have colons? I'll check that, too.*

I sat on a chair close to the pond and sprinkled the food in a bit at a time. The sound of water cascading over the rocks and the dance of the red and gold bodies of the fish maneuvering for their share of the pellets relaxed me. I noticed my stomach felt normal. Better yet, my neck no longer felt stiff like a telephone pole.

I need a pond in my backyard. I wonder how much maintenance there is to something like this? A vision of Phoebe jumping into the water to chase the fish erased the pond from my mental to-do list.

Ron strode over, wrapped his arms around me, and nuzzled my neck.

It tickled, causing me to giggle. Things were happening to my body that I hadn't felt in a long time. My defenses lowered as I relaxed into the sensation, sighing with pleasure.

My mojito shot across the table and smashed onto the tile. The glittering shards sparkled in a shaft of sunlight.

We froze.

The combined aromas of rum, lime, and mint assailed my nose as I stared at the mess. "Sweet Baby Jesus!"

Ron had gone tense. He stepped away from me and looked around, his brow creased. But there was no visible culprit.

A chill ran over me, one I recognized from my paranormal investigations.

What's happening?

My mind sought logical explanations but found none.

We weren't anywhere near that table and there was no wind. Is it a haint? If Bree were here, she would know what to do.

Ron ran a trembling hand through his hair. "No worries. I'll clean it up and make you a new one. Stay away from the glass." He glanced around with a panicked expression before breaking into a full sprint toward the house. He was behaving like a man wearing gasoline-soaked boxers being chased by an invisible maniac carrying a flame thrower.

I squinted in the bright light, trying to see what I sensed. The air around me became even colder, and I shivered.

Bree once told me not all spirits choose to manifest, and some don't have the power to manage the task.

Still, if a ghost can slide a drink to the ground, it should be able to show itself.

I stood and walked closer to the table and whispered with a sing-song tone, "Come out, come out, wherever you are."

A cold blast staggered me. I instantly felt nauseated. Rubbing the chill bumps from my arms, I backed away.

I knew the feeling well. A ghost had roared through me.

Ron appeared, holding a fresh drink. "Are you cold?"

"Just a bit. Let's walk in the sunshine." *Anywhere away from here.*

I followed him to the grill and held out my hands to warm them.

Ron nudged me. "We're about ready to eat. Grab a chair, and I'll serve."

We sat in dappled shade on the patio.

I cut into my tender, juicy steak. A baked sweet potato and salad completed the meal.

Hummingbirds dashed from flower to flower, offering a glint of iridescent color when they paused to feed. The buzz of their wings filled the air.

I glanced around, looking for anything supernatural, before taking a bite and chewing with appreciation. "My steak is cooked perfect—just the way I like it."

Ron looked delighted. "I aim to make you happy."

I returned a saucy smile. "That's what you keep telling me."

"Then maybe you'll believe me."

"Oh, I almost forgot. Jasmine wanted me to ask how her adjustment to your security camera is working out? If it's still not right, she'll try again."

Ron washed down a bite of sweet potato with his drink before saying, "It's perfect. I have a new office worker, so I want to see her entire work area."

"Is there a problem?" I asked, cutting the crisp lettuce of my salad into smaller bites.

"Some of the employees have said she's always using her phone. I never know if a report is an attempt to run off a new employee or if it's true."

I nodded. "This way, you'll have evidence."

Ron sliced into his steak. "How many employees do you have now?"

I set my fork on the plate. "Jasmine does a bit of everything but is primarily the Queen of the Machine. She's a whiz on computers. Then there's my new clerk, Clay Wilkes. He'll work the retail area and create and maintain my soon-to-be web site." I sipped my drink, enjoying the fresh minty concoction. "I think you've already met Zach Stanner, my installation technician. They're all students and work part-time."

"What about the rest?"

"Bree and Tiffany work on commission."

Ron eyed me while tapping his index finger on the table. "Amazing. I have all these full-time folks with all the trouble and expense that goes with it. Maybe I need to reconsider my business model."

I gave his hand a reassuring pat. "You're running a different type of business."

"True."

I eyed him with concern. The dark circles under his eyes made him look exhausted. "You look tired. Is everything okay at work?"

"The usual. Anytime you own a business, there's always something."

So true. "Are you feeling all right?"

He shrugged off my concern. "I'm fine. Just a few sleepless nights."

I thought with a shiver, *I can guess why.*

With a guilty tone, I said, "Ron, I need to tell you something."

His mouth turned down into a frown. "From the look on your face, it must be serious."

I told him about finding the murder victim on Carol's grave. I didn't want him to find out through the Camellia Express. Despite the flash of anger in his eyes, I also added that Bree discovered that he'd put the flowers at the tombstone base that morning.

His expression hardened into ice. "What were you doing at Carol's grave?"

Feelings of guilt heated my face. "Bree and I had made plans to walk in the cemetery after taking a photo for Mr. Craft. Remember, he asked us to do it that night at Mama's?"

He paused, a contemplative expression on his face. "Sorry, I'd forgotten."

Since he didn't ask how I knew about the flowers, I asked, "Did you see anyone in the area after placing the flowers on your wife's grave?"

Ron looked away toward the pond. "Um, no."

He doesn't lie worth a darn. Mama would say he's clear as a crystal vase.

"Are you finished?" He nodded toward my empty plate and stood.

"Yes. It was delicious." *Why won't you tell me what you saw at the cemetery?*

He stacked the dishes and carried them into the kitchen.

Feeling confused by his reaction, I grabbed the glasses and followed him. After setting them in the sink, I reached to turn on the faucet.

Ron stayed my hand with a gentle touch.

A sensual feeling zinged up my arm. My desires were shoving caution aside.

"Leave that mess. I'll clean up later. Besides, most of it will go in the dishwasher." He put his arm around my waist and led me toward the sofa in the den.

"I'm serious, Ron. Please tell me if you saw something or know something about the murder."

He kissed my forehead. "There's nothing to tell. If it's all right with you, I don't want to discuss Carol or the topic of murder while on our date."

Once we were seated, he picked up the remote and turned on the TV. "There are some cool movies on Prime Video." He started rubbing the back of my neck, sending waves of pleasure over me. I didn't know I was so touch deprived. *I want more. I need more.*

I pasted on my sexiest smile and wiggled closer to him.

I'm wearing new sexy undies, so my mind isn't on a movie.

I traced his earlobe with a finger and blew a gentle breath across it. "I could think of better things to do." *It's been such a long time.*

Ron's brows rose, then a seductive smile curved his lips. He eased me down on the sofa, covering my mouth with his. "I've been waiting for this moment since I bought the surveillance system from you in April." He licked my earlobe. "You're so beautiful."

We kissed, longing building with each exploration. All of my thoughts about the murder evaporated in the heat of passion.

The crash of breaking plates and glasses from the kitchen separated us like teens caught in the act by our parents.

Round-eyed, Ron jumped up, hair askew and shirt unbuttoned. "What in the world?" He held up a hand and said, "Stay here." He ran toward the kitchen.

Ignoring his order, I followed while buttoning my blouse over my pretty lavender bra. I suspected a stack of plates balanced on the counter's edge had toppled to the floor. *No biggie. Right?*

When I reached the kitchen, I drew in a shocked breath. It looked like a raving manic had thrown a temper tantrum. The plates and glasses were smashed to smithereens across the floor. Gasping for breath, I said, "What happened in here?"

Ron ran a hand through his hair, looking defeated.

I took a few steps forward. "Sugar, let me help you clean up this mess."

Ron shook his head and held up both hands. "Stay back! You might cut yourself."

"What's going on here?" I asked. It was so cold that a mist formed with each word. I looked for the entity that caused the upheaval, but none manifested. I can't see ghosts like Bree, but it never keeps me from trying.

Ron shook his head again. "Can we call it a night? We'll talk later."

"But, Sugar—"

He sliced the air with his hand. Then with a pleading look, he said, "Please leave. It's for your own safety."

CHAPTER 8: BRIANNA

Chris had caught another murder case, so I'd opted for take-out pizza tonight from D.J.'s Pizza and a glass of Dark Horse Rosé. Now that my stomach was full, Prissy and I snuggled in my recliner while I read a murder mystery.

"Respect" by Aretha Franklin blared on my phone. I answered and put it on speaker.

I heard laughing, and then Mystery said, "Daft dog!"

"What has Phoebe done now?"

Mystery chuckled. "The little tyke planted her paws on my chest and kissed my nose."

I glanced at the clock on the wall. "Mystery, where are you? Are you already back from your big date with Ron?"

"Yes." One word, yet her uneven tone said volumes.

"It's only nine o'clock. What happened?" I felt concerned and curious at the same time.

I heard the clunk of a footrest popping into place and deduced that Mystery was in her recliner in the living room. She let loose a frustration sigh. Mystery is a chronic sigher and has a range of them to cover different emotions.

"Bree, remember I told you Ron looked uncomfortable when the paranormal side of the business came up during dinner on the Fourth of July?"

"Yes. What does this have to do with your date tonight?"

"I think Ron's house is haunted."

I sucked in a breath. "You're kidding!" I thought a minute. "He does live in an older house, so it's possible."

She gave a brief synopsis of the ghostly shenanigans.

"You're right. It sounds haunted to me."

"Bree, I kept wishing you were there. You could've seen who is haunting him."

"Let me think." After a long pause, I said, "Do you think it could be Carol?"

"Maybe."

"Don't jump to conclusions. It could also be another ghost attached to his home." I considered other factors. "Did you say he had made improvements on his backyard? Sometimes existing spirits don't like changes."

There was a long pause.

"I don't think these changes were recent." Her tone suggested uncertainty.

"We'll just have to wait and see what happens unless you plan to sign him up for ghost debugging. It's Ron's reaction that puzzles me the most. Is he confused about what's happening, or is he in denial?"

"Probably both. I think Ron knows something, because he told me I needed to leave for safety reasons."

"It doesn't add up," I said. "The only spirit I can guess who would haunt his house is his deceased wife, unless it was a previous tenant. This doesn't make sense to me because everything I've heard about Carol was positive.

"All I know is the entity is jealous," she said.

Prissy's sweet face and soft snores were somehow comforting, soothing my concern about the situation. Her paws twitched, triggering me to smile.

"Why do you think Ron's unwelcome guest is the jealous green-eyed monster?"

"She acts out every time he puts his hands on me. That's not all. I confronted him about the flowers."

I sat straighter. "What did Ron say?"

"He went on the offensive, demanding to know why I was at his wife's grave." She paused. "I have to admit, I wasn't expecting that reaction."

I chuckled. "I can't wait to hear how you explained the

situation."

"Sugar, I told him what you told the police about the sign and walking the dogs."

"Did he accept the answer?"

"Seemed to. Besides, he was too busy sidestepping my questions. I think he knows something that he isn't telling me. Something weird is going on, and you know how I am."

I chuckled. "We both can't stand an unsolved mystery."

CHAPTER 9: BRIANNA

A box of doughnuts sat on the Mystery Shop's conference table. The aroma of freshly brewed coffee and the sugary scent of the treats permeated the air and made my senses jump to attention.

Mystery, Tiffany, Jasmine, and I, along with Zach and Clay, gathered around the table for our nine o'clock Wednesday morning staff meeting.

After everyone was seated, I raised a Boston cream in a salute to Clay Wilkes, who slouched in his chair across the table. "Thanks again for picking these up on the way into the office."

He smiled and nodded.

Mystery placed her mug of java on the table before lifting out a chocolate-glazed beauty. "I'll pay you for them out of petty cash."

Clay did a mock salute. "No worries."

A tall UAH graduate student, Clay has Alabama clay-colored hair and a sprinkle of freckles covering his nose and pale cheeks. He'd met the staff while attending a newcomer meeting of the Rocket City Paranormal Society. He, Tiffany, and Jasmine were now members of the organization. Like Jasmine, he studies computer science.

Zach Stanner seemed to have grown another inch since I last saw him. His lean frame, long skinny legs, and spiky blond hair reminded me of a mix between a cockatoo and a giraffe. Despite his elongated appearance, he's a technical wizard who likes to pick up spending money by installing cameras and security systems. Since he's a sophomore in the mechanical engineering program at UAH, I suspect Mystery will have him as an employee until he graduates.

"Let's start," Mystery said, ensuring she had everyone's attention. "I'll make it quick. First, congrats to Tiffany for bringing in two background investigation contracts. It's a nice start. I plan to use these contracts to fill in the bare spots between equipment sales, paranormal investigations, and the ghost tours."

Tiffany flushed and grinned. "It's always a good idea to have multiple sources of income. I have more appointments to pitch our services over the next couple of weeks."

I clapped. "Way to go. Have you scared up any paranormal investigations yet?"

"Yes, Mr. Craft is coming to talk to us"—Tiffany glanced at her watch—"in about ten minutes."

"How's the website coming?" Mystery asked while taking notes.

Clay raised his hand. "I'm taking the lead on the website, since my training focuses more on that area than Jasmine's does." He looked over at Jasmine, all doe-eyed. "She's more the Queen of Security. Tiffany and I are coordinating on this, but we need to meet with you later to clarify the parameters of what you want."

I shook my head. *Good lord, how does she find all these brainiacs?*

"That's great." Mystery's enthusiasm poked out in all directions, lighting up her energy field. "We'll talk after the meeting." She wiped sticky sugar from her hands before picking up a pen to write another note. "As Mama would say, let's get this show on the road. We're working on another murder. We need to limit our time on this because Ricci will get his boxers in a wad if he thinks we're interfering in a police investigation."

"And we're not getting paid for this one," I said, holding a glazed doughnut with a napkin. "At least not yet." I grinned. "I have some news that I wheedled out of Chris during our last phone conversation."

Mystery's energy fluoresced even more. "Tell us everything."

"The victim has been confirmed through dental records as Rosa Lopez. The suspected cause of death is head trauma, at least until the autopsy is completed. The manner of death is homicide."

"How do they know it's homicide?" Mystery asked.

My shoulders tensed. "I don't know. Chris is being chintzy with the information."

"Jasmine, find out everything you can about her," Mystery said before licking chocolate off her lip.

Jasmine thumbed something into her phone and said, "I'm on it."

Clay flashed Jasmine a bright smile before fishing out another doughnut from the box. "If you need any help, let me know."

He's smitten with Jasmine. She seems to like him, too. I'd like to see that girl hooked up with a nice guy with a future that leads somewhere other than prison.

Mystery and I had drafted our employee handbooks together. Unless she had added an addendum, there were no rules about fraternization in the workplace.

I wonder if we both should add some. Office romances could become awkward if there's a breakup.

Banging on the back door caused us to jump in our seats.

Tiffany looked at her watch. "Mr. Craft is punctual as usual."

"I'll let him in." I stood, turned left into the fluorescent-lit hall, and hurried past the restroom, Mystery's office, and the computer room. I knew her shop like the back of my hand since both of our stores have the same layout.

After looking through the peephole, I opened the heavy steel door and smiled.

Dapper as usual in a suit and tie, Mr. Craft stood leaning on a cane. "Good morning, Brianna. My dear, you look lovely today."

My cheeks flushed hot. "Thanks, Mr. C. Get yourself in here and outta that heat. The humidity is high enough to wilt a starched shirt. We're in the conference room."

The distinctive scent of mothballs and Old Spice cologne hit my nose when he passed. *Is it my imagination, or is he walking better today?*

When Mr. Craft reached the conference room, he stopped in the doorway, blocking it.

I tamped down my impatience. *Lucille does the same thing. Drives me crazy.*

Mystery stood and pulled out the chair next to her. "Come sit by me, Mr. C."

He made his way to the chair, where he part-lowered, part-fell into the seat. "Dang chairs seem to be getting lower every day."

Jasmine poured him a cup of black coffee. She placed it in front of him and handed him a napkin. "You're looking spry today."

"I visited Dosi, and she started me on one of her herbal remedies. I haven't felt this good in years."

"Glad to hear it," I said before introducing Clay to Mr. Craft.

Clay sat straighter and gaped. "You're the Tow Master!"

Jasmine screwed up her face. "Say what?"

"This man is infamous. He must have the record for having the most vehicles towed in one year." Clay's tone was one of admiration. He looked like he might stand and bow at any moment.

Fearful Mr. C might feel insulted, I gave Clay *the look,* the one my mother claims could stop a charging bull elephant. "If people were more considerate about not parking in his spots to go eat at the restaurant, Mr. Craft wouldn't have to tow their cars. The signs are posted."

Clay shrank into his chair. "Sorry."

I felt a little bad for chastising Clay in front of everyone during Mystery's staff meeting. Mr. Craft is like a grandfather to me, so I feel protective toward him.

Prissy pranced over, tail wagging to greet the older gentleman. Phoebe followed.

Mr. Craft smiled and reached down to rub Prissy's ears. Soon he had both hands busy, a dog seeking attention on each side of his chair. His contented smile indicated he couldn't be more pleased.

Once everyone was settled, Mystery said, "You mentioned during Mama's dinner that you're having a problem. Could you fill in some of the details for those who weren't there?"

Mr. Craft folded his gnarled hands on the table before peering at us from under his caterpillar brows. He looked at Clay and said, "When you sell antiques, it's not unusual to get a spirit freeloader from time to time." His gaze traveled from face to face stopping at mine. "I've purchased a lovely secretary writing desk and the area around it stays cold. So, I'd like for y'all to check for a ghost. If I do have one attached to the desk, it needs to cross over so I can sell it. I'd hoped the problem would resolve itself since I first mentioned it on Independence Day, but it hasn't."

Mystery nodded and checked the clock on the wall. "We all need to open our stores in about ten minutes. Can we come over to evaluate the situation after closing tonight?"

"Seven-fifteen is fine with me," Mr. Craft said. "Don't forget to bring Prissy and Phoebe with you. They're always welcome."

Prissy yipped and jumped into his lap. Phoebe looked up, tongue lolling.

Mr. Craft's eyes crinkled with delight as he scratched their necks.

"Wish I could come," Jasmine said with a downward turn of her mouth.

"I know you hate to miss out on any paranormal assignments," I said.

"Why can't you?" Tiffany asked, while returning a notebook to her case.

"I have a date." Jasmine shot Mystery a sideways look.

I noticed Clay's smile drooped along with his shoulders.

Mystery harrumphed. "Is it that guy you met in class? The one who said he'd text you?"

Jasmine nodded.

"Did you take Mama's advice?" Mystery asked, raising her chin.

Jasmine did her neck thing. "As Ms. Lucille would say, he's 'clean as a whistle.'"

"Good." Mystery lowered her chin. "Keep in mind that lack of a criminal record doesn't mean he's not bad news. Be careful." She paused as if thinking. "Text me when you get home."

Jasmine rolled her eyes the way only she could. "Okay," came out like an exasperated sigh.

I compressed my lips to hide a grin. I knew in truth that Jasmine loves when we play mother hen. Jasmine's mom, Chantel, neglected her during her childhood, being more interested in the latest man in her life. As a result of this dysfunctional upbringing, Jasmine seems much older on some matters and somewhat immature on others.

Mystery reached for another doughnut.

I cleared my throat and whispered, "If you plan to add walking days to avoid a doughnut-induced bubble butt, you'll need to contact the manager of Krispy Kreme and have him send over one of his employees."

She paused to glare at me before biting into it. The chocolate icing coated her lips like Goth lipstick.

Clay turned to Mr. Craft. "Wish I could come, but I have a class tonight."

"Come over this morning," Mr. Craft said with a jovial smile.

Clay's eyes widened. "Can I bring my ghost meter? I haven't had much chance to use it, so that would be great."

Mr. Craft nodded. "That would be fine." He winked. "You can tell me the details of how I became infamous."

Tiffany, Bree, and I agreed to meet at Craft's Antiques after regular business hours.

Mystery said, "Sounds good. Meeting's adjourned."

Tiffany reached over and laid a hand on Mr. Craft's arm. "Wait right here, Mr. C. I'll bring you a copy of your contract."

His broad smile crinkled the corners of his eyes. "Tiffany, could you push that box of pastries closer before you leave?"

Tiffany laughed. "I'll do better than that, Mr. C. I'll bring you a fresh cup of java to go with it."

CHAPTER 10: MYSTERY

As noon approached, I strolled down the sidewalk to Hardees because I was in the mood for a burger and fries. To be honest, I was surprised I had any appetite after all the doughnuts. Traffic on Andrew Jackson Way zoomed by, stirring the gas fumes in the humid air.

I reached Hardee's and was about to enter when the song, "Let's Get It On" by Marvin Gaye played on my phone.

A warm feeling stirred me. I stepped inside, hoping to hear better. Once there, I stopped to sniff the tantalizing aroma of fries. It triggered my stomach to jump with the joy that only carbs, grease, and salt can provide.

I answered the phone with a throaty, "Sugar, how long did it take you to clean up that mess Friday night?"

"I finished about midnight," Ron said.

"You sound exhausted. Are you sleeping well?" I asked while moving aside to let a couple enter the restaurant.

"Some. I'm having a bout of insomnia."

"Bless your heart. Anything I can do?" If Mama could hear my seductive tone, I'd get her famous, act-like-a-lady lecture.

He gave a deep-throated chuckle. "Maybe. I'm not getting enough exercise."

I arched a brow. "What type of exercise did you have in mind?" I asked with a drawl. *He better not mean jogging because I don't jog.*

"Mattress aerobics."

After giggling like a fifteen-year-old, I looked around to make sure no one heard me. "Never heard of it. Is it a new Olympic sport?"

"If it was, everyone would buy a ticket to see the event."

"Maybe you can teach me the rules," I said, fanning my face with my free hand.

"My pleasure. We might even play a few rounds," Ron said.

"Oooh! Your place or mine?" I asked, my body zinging with anticipation.

"I was thinking about Ted's Bar-B-Q."

Say what? Did this conversation take a left turn without signaling first? "That sounds a bit too kinky for me."

He gave a hearty laugh. "I have a yearning for some good barbecue. Unfortunately, that's the best I can manage time-wise this week. I'm afraid I'll have to put the mattress aerobics on hold."

"And here I thought you had a yearning for me."

"That, too."

Feeling miffed, I said, "Barbecue will have to wait until tomorrow. I'm booked tonight."

"Anyone I know?" He sounded upset.

"Yes. He's an older, distinguished gentleman."

"Do I know him?"

I grinned. "Yes siree!"

"Do I have competition?" he asked, his voice gruff.

"It's work. We're checking out Mr. Craft's haunted furniture tonight."

"Oh, yeah. He mentioned that at your mother's house. I remember because she gave him a scalding look. I'm surprised he didn't have third-degree burns." He paused. "I guess you have to work nights on occasion." His tone was conciliatory. "You must know a lot about ghosts."

"Not as much as Bree."

After we worked out the details for the lunch date, I strode with a massive grin toward the counter. All I could think about was mattress aerobics and hot salty fries.

CHAPTER 11: BRIANNA

Mystery, Tiffany, and I gathered outside the rear door of Craft's Antiques, waiting for Mr. C to let us in. The vapor light above the door shoved the shadows into the corners of the alley, making the area feel less creepy. Phoebe nosed about until she found some scraggly grass and squatted. Prissy came behind her and christened the spot, claiming the territory as hers.

I shook my head after witnessing the squat for power. *Prissy is going to make sure Phoebe knows who's the top dog.*

I had worried that Phoebe might decline due to missing her deceased owner, but she had adjusted better than I expected. I'm no pet psychologist, but Prissy's companionship seemed to be a significant factor.

Tiffany scrunched her nose. In a nasal-sounding voice, she asked, "How often do they empty the dumpster?"

"Mr. C pays for it. He knows the schedule," I said, breathing through my mouth.

Mystery eyed Tiffany with suspicion. "I didn't want to bring it up in the meeting, but do you remember our agreement that all paranormal investigations are not in your job description, therefore off the clock?"

Tiffany waved her hand in front of her nose. "I know. I'm fascinated by this ghost business. Besides, I have an hour to blow before meeting an old school buddy passing through town."

The metal door creaked open before I could ask if the friend was male or female.

Adam Craft peeked out. "Timely as usual. Ladies, come in out of the heat."

We piled in before he closed and locked the door. The back of his store consisted of a small office, a work area for repairs and refinishing, and a storage space. The faint odor of varnish filled the air.

I reached down and picked up Prissy.

Mystery picked up Phoebe and rubbed her chin across the top of the Yorkie's head.

Stepping closer, Mr. Craft petted the two little dogs while crooning sweet words. "You can put them in my office while you work."

"Sure thing, Mr. C." I placed Prissy on the office floor and removed her leash.

Mystery did the same with Phoebe.

Before closing the office door, I noticed the old man had purchased a large pet bed, water and food bowls, and two chew toys for our dogs. Each bowl held a small Greenie pet treat. When I rejoined the group, I gave him a big hug. "I saw the doggie goodies. Thank you, Mr. C."

Mystery kissed his cheek. "You're such a sweet man."

His eyes popped wide before a smile spread across his face. "You're welcome. They can come to visit their Uncle Adam anytime."

I rubbed my hands together. "Let's get started." I took a deep breath and lowered my shields to begin my work.

Mr. Craft pointed across the room. "It's over there."

We all walked closer to the antique secretary. I could see the specter standing next to it with her hands clasped in front of her. Her eyes darted to each of our faces.

Mr. Craft shuddered. "That corner feels like the frozen food aisle at the grocery. This morning, I walked over to dust and felt a strange tingling sensation followed by a dizzy feeling. I felt nauseated afterward." He turned his concerned gaze toward me. "Do you think I had a stroke?"

I patted his shoulder. "I'm sure you're fine. You walked through the spirit's energy field. I know first-hand that it's not a pleasant sensation. Let's get to work. I haven't eaten yet, and my innards are trying to gnaw their way to food."

"I second the food part," Mystery said.

I motioned toward the ghost and spoke for the benefit of the rest. "The lady's dress is light gray and from a different century."

Mr. Craft hobbled forward. "I wish I had your gift to see and hear the dead."

"You may think that, Mr. C, but it's not always good," I said. I pulled my abundant hair into a scrunchy, ready to get down to the nitty-gritty. I'm never quite sure what will happen, so I eliminate anything that could interfere with my need to act.

"Describe her clothes," he said. "I may be able to determine the century by her dress. The secretary is from the seventeenth century, but that doesn't mean she is."

I could probably just ask her, but she was wringing her hands and looking anxious. I didn't want her to leave. Since ghosts are typically curious, I thought I'd let her eavesdrop and become more comfortable with the situation.

I shifted my position for a better look. "Our Gray Lady appears to have been wealthy."

He leaned closer, cocking his right ear toward me. "How do you know, my dear?"

"She's wearing fancy clothes. Her knitted socks have a design on the side."

Mr. Craft produced a knowing smile. "Those designs are called clocks."

Tiffany's mouth popped open. "I thought clocks told the time."

I nudged her. "Shhh! The shoes are buckled, and she's wearing a slew of petticoats." I moved a bit closer and waved. "She's clearer now. Goodness, she waved back." I glanced over my shoulder and noticed Mystery easing closer. I held up a hand. "I don't want to spook the spook."

"Go on," Mystery said, leaning closer despite the warning.

I nodded. "Mr. C, she appears to be wearing a corset and something to poof her skirts around her hips and backside."

He leaned on his cane and smiled. "Sounds like she's wearing a padded bum roll."

"A bum roll?" Mystery shook her head with disbelief.

Moving to the side, I gained a better angle on the enhancing device.

Mystery plopped a hand on her hip. "Heck, here I'm trying to make my hips and bootie look as small as possible, and she's padding hers?"

The Gray Lady cocked her head and gave me a confused look.

From the way she's looking at me, I bet she has no idea what a bootie is or why Mystery wants hers smaller.

I laughed. "I guess they didn't have Thin Mint cookies back then."

The ghost shook her head, appearing even more confused.

Mystery glared at me. "Watch it, or I won't go eat dinner with you."

I gestured for her to calm down. "Changes happen in clothing styles all the time. Women back then must have wanted big hips and tiny waists, so they wore corsets and bum rolls."

I noticed that Mystery cringed at the mention of corsets.

"I hate girdles or anything like them." She shivered. "Mama forced me to put on a girdle once for a special occasion. I almost had a panic attack trying to fight my way out of the dang thing."

I chuckled. *I'd have given anything to see the contortion act.*

"If Mama hadn't been there to wedge me out of the that torture device, I might have perished."

A headline flashed across my mind's eye. *After a week stuck in a girdle, a woman was found smothered to death.*

"Corsets were pure torture devices designed by men to keep women frail and obedient. I'm surprised they could take a decent breath. No wonder fainting couches were so popular." Mystery jutted her jaw forward.

"Our ghost seems to agree with you if her nods are any indication," I said.

"Girdles weren't any better. Mama wore one of those when she was younger, and let me tell you, nothing jiggled. A 6.5 earthquake wouldn't have produced any movement."

Tiffany giggled.

"Today, we have Spanx. I sell them in my store," I added.

Mr. Craft's sallow complexion pinkened. "Ladies, please. Technically, the corset was called a stay. It also served as a brassiere."

Mystery huffed and crossed her arms. "With all those clothes, it's a wonder there was any baby-making going on."

Mr. Craft produced a low chuckle, and with a twinkle in his blue eyes, he said, "They wore no undergarments."

The spirit lowered her eyes, looking uncomfortable. *I'm sure she'd be in a high flush if she were alive.*

We all turned to gawk at him and then looked at each other.

I shifted my gaze back to the specter. *Bless her heart, she looks embarrassed. During her century, ladies' undergarments would never be discussed publicly, especially in front of a man.*

I cleared my throat and focused back on the Gray Lady. "Enough! We've embarrassed our specter. There's a scarf over her shoulders, and she has it crossed over her chest."

"That, my dear, is called a kerchief. I bet the Gray Lady is also wearing a day cap and an apron."

I turned to look at Mr. Craft with wide-eyed amazement. "She is, and both are delicate looking. How do you know about all this old stuff?"

He shifted his position to better lean on his cane. "I'm an old man, whose hobby is history, who is in a business dealing with old things. My guess is that she's from the sixteen-hundreds, which is the same era as the furniture."

"Okay, it's time to see if she'll talk to me. Ghosts communicate using telepathy, but I'll ask the questions out loud for y'all's benefit."

Moving closer to be in a normal conversational range, I first introduced myself, then the rest. "I can see and hear you, but the others can't." Since I wasn't sure if she spoke English, I asked, "Can you understand me?"

"Yes," the Gray Lady said. Her voice had a soft lilt.

"What is your name?"

I scooted closer for a better look at her face. *Goodness, she looks young, maybe in her early twenties, younger than me. I wonder how she died?*

The ghost answered, "Felicity Abbot." She had an upper-crust English accent.

Mr. Craft shuffled forward, cocking his better ear toward me.

I pulled out a notebook and pen and handed them to Mystery so she could take notes. "Is that Abbot with two 'bs'?"

Felicity nodded, a shy smile quirking the corners of her full lips.

"Where are you from, Felicity?" I asked.

"My family is from Essex, England."

Mystery took notes for the next twenty minutes while I repeated Felicity's tale.

"As I expected, she is earthbound because of unfinished business," I said.

Tiffany asked, "What business?"

"Felicity died of food poisoning in her early twenties while her husband was away on business," I said.

"I've read food poisoning was common during that time," Mystery said, scribbling her notes.

"Quite true," Mr. Craft agreed.

I rubbed the goosebumps on my arms. "Felicity hid her mother's brooch in the secretary for safekeeping because she suspected one of the domestics was stealing objects that could be tucked into a pocket. She wanted her daughter to have the jewelry. Unfortunately, she died before she could reveal the location."

"That's so sad," Tiffany said.

Mr. Craft nodded his agreement.

"Felicity wants the brooch to be passed on. It originally belonged to her grandmother," I explained.

Mr. Craft gave a sage nod. "It sounds like she's been attached to this piece of furniture for centuries trying to fulfill her mission."

I shook my head. "It's not the furniture. She won't leave the jewelry that's hidden in the furniture."

"Why didn't your husband search the secret compartment?" I asked.

"The secretary was a gift from my grandmother. He didn't know a secret compartment existed," she said, looking down as if guilty for hiding the secret.

I thanked Felicity and suggested we meet in Mr. Craft's office.

*

Once the door was closed, Mystery said, "As I see it, this is a three-stage mission. First, we need to find the secret hiding place and secure the brooch."

"What's the second stage?" Mr. Craft asked, peering from beneath his caterpillar brows.

Mystery looked up from her notes. "Get Jasmine to locate a family member to take possession of the jewelry. She's great at researching these types of things."

I released my copper waves from the scrunchy and finger-combed them. "In stage three, Felicity needs to find the light and cross over. That's my specialty."

Mr. Craft tapped his cane on the floor to gain our attention. "You ladies forgot stage four."

Mystery, Tiffany, and I looked at each other and shrugged.

"I need to sell this lovely antique and find it a happy home."

CHAPTER 12: BRIANNA

Mr. Craft wanted to stay to complete some paperwork. Mystery and I left the dogs to visit with him and walked to Garuda to eat. The plan was to bring Mr. Craft a to-go order after we finished our meal, and then pick up our dogs before heading home.

Tiffany waved and headed toward her Volvo. I never did find out if her "old buddy" was male or female.

*

Mystery poked at her cashew chicken with a fork while telling me more details about her last date with Ron.

"To clarify, your drink flew off the table, and neither of you was near it?" I asked, cocking a brow.

"Yep." She stuffed a forkful of the spicy dish into her mouth and chewed while frowning.

"And you didn't see anything?"

She swallowed with effort and followed it with sweet tea. "No." She wiped her mouth and leaned closer. "The drink toppling wasn't as weird as Ron's reaction."

"Oh?"

"Before the incident, he had his arms wrapped around me and was nuzzling my neck. Then, when all the glass hit the pavement, he let go of me like I was molten lava and looked around. He seemed kinda spooked."

Mystery looked around to make sure no one was listening.

"Then later, when we got passionate in his den, things started crashing in the kitchen. At first, I thought a plate toppled to the floor."

"You never told me exactly what happened in the kitchen." I took a bite of my fried rice and smiled. *Mmm!*

"I'm not sure, but it looked like a temperamental French chef threw a temper tantrum of epic proportions and wrecked the place."

"That is strange," I said, alarm tingling my senses. "Ron could be in danger."

"Lordy, I hope not," Mystery said, her eyes widening.

"I was sure that would be a romantic night for y'all and… you know." Heat flooded my face.

Mystery sighed her disappointment. "Me, too. I was ready. I even wore my new French undergarments."

I rubbed my cheek. "I wonder?"

She put down the fork and gave me her full attention. "What?"

"If his wife, Carol, is still on this plane of existence."

CHAPTER 13: MYSTERY

The next day, I frowned while scrubbing handprints off my shop's glass door. *Lordy, did the culprit who left these prints have glue on their hands?*

I'm a sunny, blue skies kinda lady, and this wasn't that kinda day. The wind outside whipped through nearby trees, tearing leaves from the branches, and whirling them in the air until they fell to skitter across the pavement. The heavy cloud cover darkened the day along with my mood.

I need chocolate!

Jasmine, who'd been unloading a new shipment of merchandise, popped into the front of the shop. "Anything you need me to do before I start background checks on this next round of job candidates? I've unloaded everything, so you can decide on the pricing."

"Cover the front while I go to lunch," I said.

"Sure, no problem." She cocked her head. "Isn't today your lunch date with Ron?"

"Yep."

"Looks like a storm is brewing." She walked toward the window and squinted up at the sky. "Those bulging clouds look nine months pregnant and ready to give birth."

I grabbed my purse and umbrella, rushed out the door, and hurried down the block to Ted's Bar-B-Q. With one eye on the clouds, I thought, *Lord, don't let it rain before I get back.*

Pink heat lightning flashed in the distance. *Better yet, don't let me get struck by lightning.*

Ron stood inside the door, waiting for me. "You look awesome today." He bent and kissed my cheek.

His lips were warm and he smelled of Polo cologne.

I wanted to close my eyes, snuggle, and inhale his maleness for a while. Instead, I adjusted the knot on his smooth silk tie. "My, don't you look official today. I don't often see you gussied up in a suit."

He chuckled. "That's not an expression I hear every day. Sounds like something your mother would say."

I nodded, resisting the urge to roll my eyes. "It's a Lucille Miller favorite. She has a ton of them."

"I'm 'gussied up' because I'm meeting with the head of a small engineering firm after lunch. I hope to become their accounting firm."

"Best of luck, Sugar."

He put his arm around me and led me to the counter to order. The aroma of smoked pork and tangy sauce made my mouth water.

A bored-looking blonde sporting an inch of dark roots leaned on the counter. She smacked her gum and asked, "Whacha want?"

I scanned the menu and said, "A pork sandwich with chips."

"Ya want slaw on that?"

"Yes."

"What kinda chips?"

I debated the choice. "Plain."

"Anything to drink?"

"A Dr. Pepper, please." I stepped to the side so Ron could order.

Ron leaned forward and said, "I'll have the same."

It looked like the weather would hold, so we decided to dine outside, where it would be quieter. The breeze and clouds made the temperature bearable despite the humidity.

Once we'd eaten some of our sandwiches, I said, "Thanks for lunch."

"The least I could do." He sent a mischievous wink my way. "I haven't given up on the mattress aerobics."

I put down the sandwich and wiped my hands. "About our last date, what came over you?"

Ron lowered his gaze and took a large bite of his sandwich. Chipmunk-cheeked, he took his time chewing.

Chew away, Ron. I want answers. "You didn't answer my question."

He gulped down a swallow. "I, uh, felt bad that your drink smashed to the floor." He shifted in his seat. "But I thought the steaks turned out well."

Frustrated, I ran a hand through my curls. "The steak was delicious. About the Mojito—"

"I thought we might go bowling this weekend." Ron picked up his soda. "Haven't been in years. What do you think?"

Ignoring his conversational detour, I said, "After the drink fell, you acted differently toward me. Why?"

Ron swallowed his last bite and glanced at his watch. He stood. "Gotta go. Don't want to be late and make a bad impression. Think about bowling."

Before I could take a breath, he was gone. I stewed with frustration while consuming my bag of chips. They seemed tasteless. Still fuming, I gathered the trash that kept trying to blow away and deposited it in the bin.

The entire way back to the shop I pondered what Ron could be hiding.

Phoebe greeted me at the front door of my shop.

Jasmine produced a wide grin. "That little dog sat looking out the window waiting for you. She even acted worried."

"That's my girl," I said, hooking a leash on Phoebe's collar. "Let's go out back, so you can do your business before it rains."

Using mincing steps, Mr. Craft made his way to the green dumpster and tossed a box inside. Then, peering at me from under his bushy brows, he asked, "How's the search going for Felicity's family? If this keeps up much longer, I'll have that piece of furniture moved to the center of the backroom and turn off the window unit. Free air conditioning."

"Jasmine's working on it today. We'll call you when we know something."

I took Phoebe back inside and removed the leash. A boom of thunder shook the building, followed by rain slashing sideways to the ground. Phoebe scooted toward my office like a wild animal was chasing her.

I gazed at the torrent of rain. *As Mama would say, "made it in the nick of time."* When I passed my office, I heard lapping sounds.

If there was one thing, I've never been able to tolerate, it's an unsolved mystery. *What is he hiding? Do I need to cut my losses and run?*

Frustrated, I backtracked and stomped into Jasmine's small office.

Jasmine turned. "You'll love this. Our background check will save one of our new clients mucho bucks."

I flopped into a nearby chair, desperate for good news.

Jasmine cocked a brow, her expression curious. She opened a drawer and handed me a bite-sized chocolate bar, and then continued her report. "One of these applicants was fired twice before, but he left it off his resume."

"Bet he thought no one would check." I popped the candy into my mouth and chewed.

Jasmine clicked her mouse. "The second bad boy resigned after several sexual harassment charges were made against him."

I harrumphed. "I think our client is better off without those two bad boys. Good work. Anything on our ghost investigation? Mr. C just asked me about it in the alley."

Jasmine's face brightened. "Yes. The ancestry program I finished writing last month for one of my school projects found a Felicity Abbot who lived in Essex, England. Mr. Craft was on the money about the time frame. I've managed to track her family around the UK. My next task is to find her descendants who live here in the States."

"How do you know they've migrated here?" I asked, shifting to relieve a twinge in my lower back.

"I'm assuming they moved here. How else did the furniture end up in Mr. Craft's store? If we're not too busy in the shop, I plan to continue to try to pin down any living relatives."

"Good luck, Sugar. Remember, sometimes dealers purchase antiques from families and then ship them over to shops in the States."

Jasmine's brows drew together. "I hadn't considered that possibility. If that's the case, Felicity's family could still be in the

UK or Europe. It could make returning the brooch more difficult." Jasmine seemed to ponder the situation before her lips stretched into a radiant smile. "If that's the case, I'm willing to deliver the jewelry overseas if Mr. Craft foots the bill."

I laughed. "In your dreams. How soon can you get me the report on Rosa Lopez? Bree and I need to start interviewing suspects."

The bell jingled.

I turned to the monitor and saw a man in a business suit walk to the counter. "I'll take this customer, Sugar. You keep searching."

CHAPTER 14: BRIANNA

I opened Mystery's shop door and walked inside.

Pierre ghosted through the window. "I have missed my time with you, ma chérie."

I burped my burger-and-fries lunch. "Excuse me." I patted my mouth.

He chuckled. "Un tel petit rot de dame."

I shook my head while working through the translation of "Such a lady-like little burp."

Mystery stood behind a glass display case and watched me with her head cocked to the side.

"Pierre's here. I was trying to work my way through a weird translation."

"Oh! Bonjour, Pierre."

He gave a courtly bow.

"Kaya's at the wheel, so I thought I'd check to see if we have any more information on our two cases."

Hearing an excited squeal, Mystery and I looked toward the back.

Jasmine bounded into the retail area sparking with enthusiasm.

Tingles of electrical charges peppered my skin, forcing me to raise my shields. I held up both hands. "Tone it down! You're about to fry my nerve endings."

Jasmine stepped back. "Sorry. I'm stoked." She took some deep breaths. "Okay, I'm calmer now."

I lowered my shields and found the energy level to be acceptable.

Pierre chuckled. "Elle est like a puppy, bouncing with delight."

Jasmine continued, "I found a relative of Felicity Abbot." Still a bit breathless, she inhaled before saying, "One of Felicity's folks lives in the Birmingham area! You'll never guess." She paused for effect. "Her first name is Felicity."

"Quel nom charmant! It means un grand bonheur," Pierre said

"Pierre says Felicity means great happiness."

Eyes twinkling, Jasmine said, "Pierre's here? Great!" She gave an exuberant wave.

I found it necessary to raise my shields once more to block her electrifying excitement.

My grimace shifted into a smile. "Your progress on the search is wonderful. How did you manage such a feat? Did you go on Ancestry.com?"

Jasmine's mood shifted from exhilarated puppy to bristling porcupine. Her neck gyrations said it all.

Mystery spoke up. "Jasmine wrote her own search program as a school project."

I patted Jasmine on the shoulder. "That's great. Are you going to market it?"

Jasmine's shoulders lowered a little. "I might."

Mystery asked, "How should we handle this?"

"Let's ask Mr. Craft. After all, he's footing the bill for the search and clearing," I said.

The look of discomfort contorting Mystery's face caught my attention. "What's wrong? Are you in pain?"

She shifted her weight from one foot to the other. "I wish I'd worn more comfortable shoes." She stepped from behind the counter. "I wore these sexy high-heels trying to impress Ron. I didn't think about the walk to the restaurant and back."

Pierre looked at her shoes and smiled. "Tell her those shoes are indeed sexy."

I passed on the message, which produced a smile.

"Where is Pierre now?" Jasmine asked.

Swallowing a smile, I nodded toward the door.

"Oh!" She turned and waved in the correct direction. "There's more."

Pierre shook his head. "At least she did not spear me with her compteur fantôme this time."

I laughed. "Jasmine might pull out her ghost meter any second. Don't hold your breath, Pierre."

Jasmine chuckled. "Ghosts don't breathe."

"Let's go to the conference room and sit. My feet are tuckered out," Mystery said, rubbing her lower back.

Pierre floated near the refreshment table, appreciatively inhaling the scent of fresh-brewed coffee. *It seems like torture to be able to smell food and drink and not be able to consume them.*

Once we were seated with steaming cups of java, Jasmine gave her report about the murder case, using animated gestures. "Rosa Lopez was a nurse who worked with a local home-nursing service. I found out she worked for Ron while his wife was ill. It was her third job in the past four years, and her finances weren't in good order."

I pulled my hair up and released it to fall over my shoulders. "Is that it? We knew Rosa occasionally stayed with Carol."

"You don't get it," Jasmine said. "Rosa worked five days a week as the night nurse for months, until Carol died."

Mystery leaned forward. "That means she was there most of the time when Ron was off from work."

Jasmine nodded. "Rosa was also between relationships. She'd divorced a guy named Ricky Lopez, a construction worker. He has a history of drunk driving and several domestic violence charges."

"Good work," I said. "That makes him a primary suspect. He may have been jealous. Do you know where to find Ricky? I have time to talk to him today."

"I'll text you the information," Jasmine said.

"Be careful," Mystery said, her brow wrinkled. "I'd go with you, but Jasmine is leaving for class soon."

"I will. I'll take Prissy for protection."

Pierre puffed out his chest and placed his fist over his heart. "I will protect you, ma chérie."

I knew he'd do his best.

Jasmine said, "Don't find any more dead bodies."

CHAPTER 15: BRIANNA

I pulled into a parking area of an apartment complex that had seen better days. Two buildings sat within twelve feet of each other and shared a paved parking lot that was devoid of trees. Each building was a two-story, eight-unit affair with beige siding that needed a good pressure washing. A hallway located in the middle of each one had metal stairs and offered access to the apartment doors. The baking asphalt parking lot was almost empty, but the few cars still present indicated a paycheck-to-paycheck existence. Ricky Lopez's last known address was 3B. The building on the right was marked B.

Pierre and I exited Hot Stuff.

"I don't understand how you manage to stay in the car while it's moving," I said,

Pierre's brow furrowed. "I do not know how to explain, but to say it is a force of will and energy."

I leashed Prissy and looked around. "All I need is for you to see a squirrel and take off. Or worse yet, find another murder victim."

Prissy's ears twitched when she heard the word squirrel. When Pierre drew closer, she curled her upper lip revealing her canines, and snarled.

Pierre held up his hands. "Okay, petite chienne."

While approaching the hallway, I noticed the "manager" sign on the door of 1B, located on my left.

The walkway between the apartments held a faint odor of cat urine, which sent Prissy's nose into a twitch fest. Once she located the offensive site, she resolved the issue to her satisfaction by washing the spot with a generous spray of her urine.

"Prissy! Stop." I pulled her away from the puddle, but not in time to avoid the combined reek. I waved my hand in front of my nose in a vain attempt to dissipate it. "That didn't help a thing, young lady."

Pierre one-upped Prissy by turning his back to me and doing a ghostly christening.

Ghosts can urinate! I looked closer and saw a puddle of ectoplasm. "I can't believe you did that. Gross!"

Growling, Prissy marched over and rewet the same area.

I held up a hand. "Stop. This isn't a pissing contest!"

After searching for a nonexistent doorbell at apartment 3B, I took a deep breath, which I regretted due to the stench, and knocked.

Silence.

After waiting a bit, I put my ear near the door and listened.

Nothing.

I pounded harder and yelled, "Mr. Lopez."

"What's all the ruckus about?" a female voice demanded from behind me.

I leaped away from the door and whirled, heart pounding.

A stooped, gray-haired woman with spectacles stepped outside of 1B and frowned. "You a bill collector? If so, you're out of luck because Ricky will pay me first, or I'll evict him."

I moved closer and introduced myself and Prissy.

The woman looked down. Her eyes crinkled when she gave my dog a wide smile. "Well, ain't you a cutie? You need to stick around and run off that dang cat that keeps using my hallway like it's a litter box."

Pierre had the decency to look guilty.

Prissy walked forward, tail wagging.

After stroking Prissy's ears, the woman looked up at me. "I'm Helen Petty, the manager. What's this all about?"

I handed her a business card. "I'm helping a friend investigate the murder of Rosa Lopez."

Helen's eyes widened. "What?" She swayed a little, alerting me that she could faint. "Rosa's dead?" She leaned against the door jamb, tears welling in her eyes. "What in tarnation happened to her?"

I explained what little I knew about the murder, without mentioning any of the supernatural parts.

Helen shook her head. "I was always afraid that fool would kill her someday."

A chill slithered down my spine like an icy snake. "You think Ricky did it?"

"Once he found out she was in love with someone else, he started drinking more. That man has a nasty temper when he's drunk. I had to call the police several times when they were arguing. After Rosa left and the divorce went through, I thought things had settled down."

"Where is Ricky now?" I asked.

"At work. I was hassling him yesterday to pay the rent. He assured me that he was working on a patio home near the Toyota plant in Madison." She shook her head. "He promised me money when he gets paid on Friday."

"Thanks for the information."

I returned to my car and phoned Jasmine for help.

"You caught me before I left. I'll try to locate the construction site," Jasmine said and disconnected the call.

Ten minutes later, she texted two viable options. I pressed a button on Hot Stuff's steering wheel and told the car to navigate to the first address. Within twenty minutes, I was at the construction site.

I left Prissy in the car and set the Tesla climate control on "dog mode" to keep her comfortable.

Pierre glided beside me. "This Ricky does not sound like un homme gentil."

I huffed. "This from a ghost who entered a pissing contest with my dog."

He grinned. "I won."

I rolled my eyes. "No, you didn't."

After picking my way across scattered building debris, I saw a worker carrying a pail come to the front door of a unit.

"Excuse me, I'm looking for Ricky Lopez. Am I at the right place?"

The man looked me up and down with too much interest for my liking.

"You're not my type," I said with a matter-of-fact tone.

Pierre frowned and said, "Il te regarde comme s'il faisait du lèche-vitrine."

It took me a moment to translate that the construction worker looked at me like he was window shopping.

"Hey, Ricky, there's una mujer hermosa out here who wants to see you." He turned and disappeared inside.

Pierre took off after the man.

A broad Latino man about five-foot-seven inches came to the doorway. He smiled, teeth dazzling white against his construction worker tan and his thick black hair shone in the bright sunlight. He walked across a board that created a bridge from the house to the ground.

I heard a cry of alarm from inside the unit.

I was pretty sure Pierre was responsible for that exclamation.

"Hey, pretty lady. You looking for me?" He pulled a rag from the back pocket of his jeans and wiped his hands.

I introduced myself but didn't offer my hand. Instead, I decided on a straightforward approach. "I wanted to talk to you about your ex-wife, Rosa."

"What about her?" He looked at me through slitted eyes. "Whatever that puta said, I didn't do it."

I took a step back out of the range of his clenched fists. "Rosa can't say anything about you, because she's dead."

He stopped mid-step and looked sucker-punched. Crossing himself, he looked up at the sky and muttered, "Santa Madre de Dios." With a hoarse voice, he asked, "What happened? Did that guy kill her?"

My spine stiffened. "Which guy?" I intentionally used "which" instead of "what" to see his response. I'd learned the trick from Vera, Mystery's former boss, who was a private detective before she retired to move out west.

Ricky's eyes widened. "There was more than one?"

Ignoring the question, I asked, "What was his name?"

He swiped at his eyes with a sweaty forearm. "I don't know?" He shrugged like it no longer mattered. "She was all moon-eyed over some guy whose wife was dying." He ran his hand through his hair and swore softly in Spanish. "We got in an argument, and I was arrested. She moved out and served me divorce papers while I was in jail."

"Where were you Monday morning?"

"Are you the police?"

"No." I handed him a business card with only my name and the store's number. "I'm helping a friend investigate her murder."

He wiped the sweat from his brow with the dirty rag while reading. "Why does this matter to you?"

"My friend and I found her body in Maple Hill Cemetery."

He looked up with a stunned expression. "What was my Rosa doing there?"

The phrase "my Rosa" caught my attention.

A few minutes ago, you were calling her names and now you're acting like she's your long-lost love. A psychologist friend once told me abusive men are often possessive, jealous, and treat the women in their lives like possessions.

"I don't know. That's why I'm here talking to you."

Ricky jerked a thumb over his shoulder. "I was here. We start work at six." He turned and yelled, "José, come talk to this lady."

The man with the pail reappeared at the door rubbing his knee.

Pierre floated over to me.

"Tell her about Monday morning," Ricky said.

José looked confused, but shrugged and said, "I picked Ricky up for work at five-thirty, we got breakfast at McDonald's, and we started work at six. We started framing right after we got here." His brow furrowed. "The boss checking on us?"

I shook my head.

Looking shaken, Ricky said, "I lost my license after my last DUI, so José drives me to work every day."

So, Ricky has an alibi from five-thirty through the entire morning. Mystery and I found the body about seven-fifteen and she was still warm to the touch. "Thank you for your time."

"Do you think the police will show up to question me?" Ricky asked, sticking his hands in the pockets of his jeans.

"Probably."

He said a word that would have cost him a dollar donation to the Bad Habit Jar if he'd worked for Mystery.

CHAPTER 16: BRIANNA

Prissy and I closed my store at seven that night.

After setting her alarm and locking the rear door, Mystery joined me, leading Phoebe. The two dogs greeted each other with wagging tails. We walked through the back alley, past the dumpster that still smelled like rotten bananas, to Mr. Craft's antique shop. He stood at the door, waiting for us. After giving us a slight bow, he ushered us inside before closing the door.

I picked up Prissy and asked, "I hope it's still okay that we brought the dogs."

With a crinkly-eyed smile, Mr. Craft reached for Prissy, who greeted him with doggie kisses and tail-wagging delight. He rubbed his cheek on the top of her head. "Goodness, her kisses are the only ones I get these days. Prissy is always welcome." Next, he reached to pet Phoebe, who snuggled in Mystery's arms. His smile widened when she licked his hand. "So is Phoebe. Two adoring females." He winked. "I'm a lucky man."

A knock on the back door announced Jasmine's arrival.

Mystery exchanged glances with us. "That girl is so jazzed that her computer program located Felicity's relative that she can't wait to tell Felicity all about it."

I said, "I'll let her in, Mr. C."

Jasmine breezed inside, crackling with excitement.

"Whoa! Tone it down," I warned. "Your energy is zinging my

nerve endings again. You're up to bee-stinging volume today."

I raised my shields and let out my breath with relief when I felt the instant protection.

"Sorry." Jasmine shifted from foot to foot. "I've been waiting all day to share my good news."

We all moved closer to the furniture in the corner. Prissy started to bristle and growl in my arms.

"May I put the dogs in your office again until we're finished? They're sensitive to spirits."

Mr. Craft smiled. "Certainly, my dear. Those little bundles of fur are expert spook detectors."

Mystery and I put the dogs down in the small room. I pointed a finger and said, "Behave."

Prissy gave a defiant yip.

I spun on my heels. "Don't you be sassing me, Young Lady!" I closed the door.

Mystery giggled. "You sound like Mama."

Ignoring the comparison, I said, "Let's get to work. I'd like to go home sometime soon."

We all faced the antique secretary.

I closed my eyes, took a deep breath, and adjusted my shields until I could see Felicity without being flattened by Jasmine's energy. Then I opened my eyes.

There she stood. "Hello, Felicity. We have good news."

Jasmine took a step forward, unsure where to look.

I pointed to the left corner of the furniture.

Jasmine nodded. "Um, hi. I'm Jasmine. Sorry I didn't meet you the other night, but I had a date, which was a total bummer."

Felicity cocked her head to the side and frowned.

I nudged Jasmine. "She doesn't know what 'total bummer' means. Stop confusing her with your love life and get on with it."

Jasmine cleared her throat. "Using a computer, a machine that didn't exist during your time, I've managed to find one of your descendants."

I chuckled, feeling pleased. "Felicity's smiling and crying at the same time. Tell her the rest."

"Her name is also Felicity, and she lives in Vestavia Hills in the Birmingham area, a city only a couple of hours away by car. That's another invention that wasn't around when you lived."

"She says she's so grateful." I patted Jasmine on the back. "This young lady has worked hard to find her. How do you want us to handle this from here?"

Mr. Craft sported a pleased-looking smile.

I listened for several minutes and frowned.

I crossed my arms and said, "She wants one of us to bring her relative here, so she can see her. She'll only tell her namesake how to open the secret compartment to retrieve the brooch."

"It would be easier if we took the brooch to her, since you're in the spirit realm," Mr. Craft said.

I laughed at the ghost's reaction. "Mr. C, she crossed her arms and said, 'no.' This one is stubborn."

Mystery exhaled an aggravated sigh. "I'll see what I can manage."

CHAPTER 17: MYSTERY

The next morning, I phoned from home to set up a meeting with Felicity's descendant. I'd drawn the short straw on this part of the investigation. But, to be fair, Kaya had classes, so Bree had to work.

"Hi, I'm Mystery Jones, owner of the Mystery Shop in Huntsville, Alabama. I'm looking for Felicity Ortega?"

"This is Felicity." Her tone was part curiosity, part suspicion.

"This isn't a spam call. Please don't hang up." I then partially explained the reason I wanted to visit her today.

To my relief, she agreed to meet with me.

*

Two hours later, I sat in my Prius outside Felicity's white two-story home on Southwood Road. The house backed up to the Vestavia Hills Golf Club. To improve the curbside appeal, Felicity had removed some of the original landscaping and replaced it with smaller shrubs.

I mentally rehearsed my cover story, took a deep breath, and exited the car. My reluctance to complete this task made the short journey up the sidewalk seem miles long.

I touched the black iron railing and yanked back my hand. It felt tacky and the smell of wet paint hung in the humid air. I climbed the three steps to the red door and paused on the porch. I was tempted to retrace my steps and leave but instead pressed the doorbell.

A petite blonde with a perky ponytail and a pixie face smiled up at me.

"I'm Mystery Jones, owner of the Mystery Shop."

"I'm Felicity Ortega. I know your place, it's in Five Points. I sometimes eat lunch at the Thai place when I visit the area."

I smiled my approval of her choice of restaurant. "I love their lunch specials."

"Me too. Come in. Your call intrigued me," Felicity said while stepping back to let me enter a split entry foyer. I followed Felicity up steep carpeted stairs. I reached the top and blinked when I saw the living room decorated in bright colors. One wall was sunflower yellow, another lime green, and the third bright blue. The blue one continued into the attached dining area. This abundance of color was in complete contrast to the traditional white exterior of the home.

I turned in a circle to see it all.

Felicity laughed. "My husband, Julio, and I like bright colors."

"I see. Can't get depressed in this room," I said and chuckled.

"My mother hates the décor." Felicity scrunched her pert nose. "She's a subdued antique lover. Can I offer you something to drink?"

My throat felt like sandpaper. "Water, please."

Felicity returned with two glasses of ice water and handed me one. She pointed toward a blue sofa topped with different colored decorative throw pillows. "Have a seat."

I sat, looked around, and thought, *I need to add more colorful accents to my décor. Maybe some throw pillows, to brighten things up a bit.*

I gulped down some water and cleared my throat. "I'm here to discuss a piece of furniture."

Felicity looked confused. "Furniture?"

"I'm sure you've noticed Craft's Antiques next to my shop. My business often does investigative work on the provenance of certain antiques for Adam Craft."

"I've been in there. My mother can't resist shopping there when we're in town visiting her sister. My Aunt Susie lives in the nearby Old Town District." Felicity sipped her water and nodded for me to continue.

"Well...we discovered something about an antique secretary. We believe it belonged to Felicity Abbot, who lived in Essex, England, during the seventeen hundreds. My assistant wrote a computer program to trace lineages. During her search, she followed the trail of Felicity's descendants from England, to New York, to Tennessee, and eventually down to Alabama. Jasmine believes you are a direct descendant."

Felicity's eyes widened, and she crossed herself. "Stay here. I'll be back." She rose and disappeared down a hall.

Well, that wasn't the reaction I expected. I drank more water. Feeling calmer, I picked up a red throw pillow and felt the nubby fabric. *Love the color, but this fabric is too textured for my liking.* I put it down.

Next, I tried one with orange, yellow, and red swirls. The smooth fabric brought a smile to my lips.

Felicity bustled in carrying a large leather-bound book and a box. She sat next to me.

Startled, I put the pillow down, feeling guilty for touching her things.

"This is my family album. My mom is big-time into genealogy. It drives my dad over the edge when she drags him to cemeteries to do rubbings of the tombstones." She opened a book that seemed to smell of ages past and flipped through some pages. She stopped and pointed. "This is Felicity Abbot, my namesake."

I peered at a photo of a painting. A blonde woman with hair pinned away from her pixie face wore a prim smile. *So that's what she looks like. She's wearing the same dress with a lace collar and cuffs that Bree described.* A brooch was pinned at her neckline. "Sweet baby Jesus, she's wearing the brooch she told us about." I reached for the album and peered at the jewelry. "She was beautiful. You look so much like her."

Felicity slid away from me. With a suspicious tone, she asked, "What do you mean, 'the brooch she told you about?' Who are you talking about?"

Oops. "The, um, reason Mr. Craft hired our business to investigate the piece of furniture is because it has a haint attached."

Felicity's mouth dropped open. She shifted away another couple of inches.

"The Mystery Shop does paranormal investigations. A contract employee of mine is a psychic who can see and talk to ghosts. Mr. Craft hires us to clear any spirits attached to antiques he buys, so the ghosts can have peace and the new owners aren't haunted by restless spirits."

Felicity closed her mouth. Her eyes narrowed with skepticism.

Sensing future problems, I blundered on. "Felicity Abbot was described by my psychic as looking just like this photo. Her haint is attached because she died due to food poisoning while her husband was out of town." I tapped the photo with my index finger. "She hid the brooch in a secret place in the secretary. She suspected some of the help was stealing from her. Unfortunately, she died before she could retrieve it or tell her husband where it was stashed."

Shaking her head with disbelief, Felicity held up a hand. She lifted the box on the coffee table, set it on her lap, and removed the lid.

The inside smelled of mold. I tried to avoid the sneeze tickling my nose by rubbing it.

Felicity lifted out a leather-bound book the size of a paperback. She turned the pages and read for several minutes. "Oh my gosh."

"What?" I leaned closer despite the foul smell.

"This is Clarence Abbot's journal. He was Felicity's husband." She read aloud.

"I received word from a messenger that Felicity was ill. When I returned home, I was too late. My loving wife had passed. We buried her in the family crypt, but I still feel her presence in the parlor near the secretary, where she labored over the household accounts."

A chill ran over me like a cluster of icy spider feet. *Mama would say someone just walked over my grave.*

Felicity closed the journal, placed it back in the box, and closed it. "So, you think my great, great, great grandmother's spirit is not at rest because she could not pass down her brooch?"

"Sugar, that's what she told my psychic. She refused to reveal the location of the brooch or to cross over to the next level until we produce a family member to take possession of the jewelry. Mr. Craft would like to sell the piece without a spirit-freeloader. He's reluctant to look for the jewelry because he doesn't want to upset the haint or damage the furniture."

Felicity's eyes twinkled with interest. "What's the next step?"

"We need you to come to Craft's Antiques, meet your, um, deceased relative, and claim the brooch. After that's achieved, my psychic can help the spirit with her journey."

"Can I bring my mom? She's such a genealogy hound. She'd love to meet Felicity and ask some questions."

"I guess so. It will need to be at seven in the evening. Is that acceptable? Our businesses will need to be closed, so customers won't interfere. If your mom has questions, this could take longer."

"I'm sure that will be fine. Give me your number. I'll call Mom to find out when we can go."

I shook hands and managed to walk down the stairs in my new strappy sandals without incident. I drove the two and a half hours back to the shop, wondering when I'd hear from Felicity and what Bree and my next steps would be to find Rosa's killer. But first, I needed to decide what to wear tonight to go bowling with Ron.

CHAPTER 18: MYSTERY

I tried one outfit after another. Each one failed to camouflage my bootie to my satisfaction. Usually, this wasn't such an issue, but bowling meant bending over, exposing my generous backside to the full view of Ron and the entire bowling alley.

I settled on a pair of skinny jeans and a long top. I posed in front of a full-length mirror in the bedroom, turning to see every angle.

Phoebe whined and cocked her head. She probably wondered why I was contorting this way and that.

"Phoebe, if he can't appreciate my bodacious lusciousness, the heck with him."

She yipped.

I reached down and petted her. "Glad you agree with me. Your food and water bowls are full, so everything will be fine until I get back."

The doorbell rang.

Phoebe took off like a furry rocket, sounding the alarm.

I grabbed my purse and hurried to greet Ron. Once there, I shooed the dog away and opened the door.

Ron stepped inside, grinning with delight. "Hey, there, Phoebe girl. You sounded ferocious, like a Doberman."

I closed the door. My fur baby licked him while he petted her squirming furry body.

Lifting my chin, I said. "She's my first round of protection." I chuckled. "At least that's what Bree calls her."

Ron's grin widened. "I see. Does she lick the burglar to death?"

I crossed my arms and shot him my best stink-eyed look.

Ron swallowed his smile and cleared his throat. "Are you ready?"

"Yep. Let me set the alarm." I keyed in the code and locked the door.

We drove to the bowling alley in Ron's black Porsche.

"When will you ditch this gas guzzler and buy electric or at least a hybrid?"

Ron's jaw tightened. "It's not that bad. I get twenty-one miles per gallon in the city and twenty-eight on the highway. Besides, I plan to drive the wheels off this baby."

Fifteen minutes later, we pulled into the parking lot of Stars and Strikes.

I peered through the bug-spotted windshield at the sign. "Is this place new?"

"It's newer than the other bowling alleys in Huntsville. Not sure when it opened. One of my employees recommended it."

We walked into a cacophony of sounds from a sea of arcade machines spread across a hideous purple, blue, and pink diamond patterned carpet. There were other attractions past the arcades that I couldn't make out. To the right, a small restaurant emanated the scents of spicy, savory, and hops.

"Wow! This is a keep-your-kids-busy-for-hours kinda place," I said.

An expanse of wood flooring led up a ramp.

Ron pointed. "The sign says the counter up there is where we go for bowling."

He placed a warm hand on my lower back and guided me to the correct spot. The heat spread like tiny waves through my body.

A pimply teen trying to grow a wispy goatee asked, "Can I help you folks?"

Still on sensory overload, I asked, "How many activities do y'all have in this place?"

The guy looked up at the ceiling and counted on his fingers. "There's the arcade, laser tag, escapology, bumper cars, virtual reality, and bowling."

"We want a lane for two," Ron said.

"Need shoes?"

"Yes." Ron pulled out his wallet and handed over his credit card. "Mystery, let's get the special that allows us to play longer."

"Sounds good," I said, my stomach growling.

"Somebody's hungry," the clerk said with a knowing grin. "The Grille will bring your order to your lane, so you can eat and bowl."

"Works for me. Let's go find a ball," Ron said, sliding his receipt into his wallet.

I frowned at the selection of balls. I have large hands, so the finger holes in the pretty ones were too small. The ugly ones with larger holes were too heavy.

Ron called, "What's taking so long?" He was already tying his bowling shoes.

"I'm trying to find one that fits my fingers but won't send me to a chiropractor," I said.

After poking my fingers into several bowling balls, I settled on a blue one that was only a tad tight and about the right weight. I muttered, "If he plans to do this often, I'm buying my own ball."

I carted the ball over to our lane and put it on the track. I'd finished tying the laces on the rented bowling shoes when a perky teen with fuchsia hair handed us a menu.

We stopped and studied the selections.

"Anything to drink?" she asked, looking at her order pad.

"I'll have a Heineken. What do you want, Mystery?"

"Is your chardonnay woody?"

"Um…" She looked confused by the question.

"Just bring me a glass of chardonnay."

"Any food?"

My growling stomach answered that question. While I was curious about the restaurant's wings, I couldn't imagine bowling with sticky fingers. We both settled on burgers with an order of fries.

Ron stood and rubbed his hands together with anticipation. "Let's get going. Ladies first." He bowed and swept his hand toward the lane.

I approached the ball, wiggled in my fingers, and hefted it into my hands. I was once a decent bowler but hadn't done it in over ten years. I prayed I'd be able to straighten my back tomorrow morning. Tyree taught me the sport, so his words dropped from my memory into my mind. *Line up on the black marks on the lane. Right, left, right, and slide.*

I took a deep breath to steady my pounding heart, found a spotter mark I liked, and stepped forward. On the slide, I bent and slung the ball as hard as possible. It stuck briefly to my sweaty fingers and lofted, landing with a bang. I straightened and frantically tried to wave the ball in the correct direction. I knew this didn't work, but I couldn't help myself. It hit the gutter and jumped onto the lane to my right. I wanted to cover my eyes and pretend I hadn't invaded my neighbor's territory, but I couldn't take my gaze off the ball. As if by a miracle, it corrected its course in the neighboring lane.

"Strike!" I sucked in a breath and covered my mouth with my hands before releasing a whoop.

The Hawaiian-shirted guy waiting to bowl to my right looked over at me slack-jawed and said, "Thanks, lady."

Ron guffawed.

I turned to find him sprawled across two seats, red-faced and holding his stomach. His reaction drew the attention of the folks in surrounding lanes.

My face sizzled with embarrassment. I wanted to run to the ladies' room and hide in a stall. Instead, Mama's voice from my childhood chided me. *Baby Girl, you get yourself up there and try again!*

I set my jaw and glared at Ron.

He wiped laugh tears from his eyes.

By pure will and Christian upbringing, I didn't swat him.

Grabbing the ball, I walked to the correct spot. I approached and set the ball on the lane with less force this time.

The ball did a perfect curve and hit the pocket.

"Strike!" I jumped up and down before doing a victory dance.

Ron leaped from his seat and hugged me. "Technically, it's a spare. That was your second shot."

I pointed at the X on the automatic scoreboard. "Tell the machine. If you want to get technical, I had two strikes. Not everyone can get one on the next lane."

Ron threw up his hands and shrugged. "I can't argue against that logic."

Our food arrived, permeating the space with the smell of steaming salty fries. Ron paid the waitress and gave her a generous tip.

"Oh, good, my stomach thinks someone cut my throat."

Ron frowned. "What a grim way to express it."

"Another Mama saying." I took a bite of the cheeseburger. The mingled flavors and textures of lettuce, tomato, meat, cheese, and condiments fought for my attention. I sipped my wine and found it to be good.

When we'd finished our meal, Ron wiped his hands and slid over to the seat next to mine. He looped an arm around my shoulders and rubbed his stomach. "That was good food for a bowling alley."

"It was delicious."

He winked at me. "My turn for a strike."

Ron strode with confidence to the ball holder and hefted the black orb into his hands. After taking his place on the lane, he took position and paused. He moved with grace and executed a perfect release that didn't sound as it touched the polished wood. The ball curved in an arc heading for the pocket between the one and three pins. The impact caused a blur of white pins. A pin slid toward the ten-pin in the back rear corner and nudged it.

It rocked left.

Ron leaned left.

It teetered to the right.

He tilted in the same direction.

When the dang-blasted thing settled in an upright position, his shoulders drooped. Poor Ron was left with the bane of every bowler, a classic 7-10 split.

He scraped his fingers through his hair, stomped one foot, and swore under his breath.

Hawaiian Shirt Guy said, "It happens to the best of us."

Ron nodded but avoided eye contact. When the ball returned, he picked it up and moved into position. After standing for several minutes, he eyed his options. He once again made a beautiful delivery sending the ball toward the ten-pin.

I inhaled, trying to mentally pray the ball to the correct position to clip the outside right edge, so it would slide across into the seven-pin for a spare.

The ball dropped into the gutter just short of the pin. No spare.

I exhaled my pent-up breath.

"Good try," Hawaiian Shirt Guy said with a sympathetic look.

Ron nodded again and walked back to his seat, looking at the floor the whole time.

Men have such delicate egos. I bet if I laughed the way he did when I messed up, he'd have a man fit. I wasn't sure what to say or do, so I decided to pat his shoulder as I passed to bowl again.

My following approach was much smoother. I hit another strike. After my mini victory dance, I turned to see the open-mouthed shock on Ron's face.

Hawaiian Shirt Guy nudged Ron over the seat. "Lucky shot."

My jaw tightened. *If Ron had bowled that strike, you'd say it was due to his expertise, not luck. Men!*

Ron shut his mouth. His jaw tightened, the muscle moving up and down like mini pushups. He stood and gave a quick nod as he passed me. He took a deep breath, squared his shoulders, and grabbed the ball. After a flawless approach, he rolled the ball. "Strike!" He punched the air with his fist.

I stood and clapped, even though he only nodded when I got a strike.

The game continued, but despite his best efforts, Ron was still behind.

I bowled a spare on the tenth frame, which gave me an additional shot. While I prepared, I could feel Ron's and the Hawaiian Shirt Guy's gazes boring holes through me. Mama's words reverberated in my mind. *You're as good as any man. Don't ever let me see you throw a game to make a man look good. Do you hear me? You learn a lot about a man by the way he handles defeat.* I doubled down on my resolve and took deep breaths to hone my focus.

The release of the ball felt good. The graceful arc put my blue orb into the pocket. A strike! I victory danced my way back to my seat.

Hawaiian Shirt Guy frowned at me before telling Ron, "Show that woman what you've got."

I was having unkind thoughts toward Hawaiian Shirt Guy.

Like hot grease sliding in a pan, Ron's ball shot down the lane and hit the pins with a loud crack. He leaped in the air. "Strike!"

I jumped to my feet and clapped, yelling, "Woohoo."

"Do another one," Hawaiian Shirt Guy said.

Because Ron bowled a strike in the tenth frame, he was allowed two extra throws.

After careful deliberation, he sent the ball in a graceful curve that overshot the pocket to hit between the one and two pins. However, due to the force of the throw and the backward spin, he still managed to get a strike.

Ron pumped his fist and did a comical little dance. He turned and shot me an I'm-going-to-win wink.

I gave him a you-haven't-won-yet smirk.

After grabbing his ball, he stalked like a panther into position. He paused and rocketed the orb toward the pins. It curved into the pocket, sending pins flying every which way. Only number ten wobbled in place.

I held my breath.

Ron stomped the floor with his right foot.

The pin fell.

Hawaiian Shirt Guy exploded to his feet, yelling, "Three strikes in a row on the last frame. You got a turkey!"

The two men chest bumped and clapped each other on the back.

When Ron completed his male bonding with a complete stranger, he plopped on the seat next to me. Before I could chide him for cheating with the foot stomp, he locked gazes, pulled me close, and kissed me. It was a long, lingering winner-take-all kiss.

Blam!

"Holy Toledo!" Hawaiian Shirt Guy yelled, "Look."

We jumped apart and turned to see him backing away while pointing at my bowling ball. It zipped across the floor, zoomed off the edge, and rammed my foot.

"Ouch." I hopped up and searched the area around me, suspecting the jealous ghost was responsible for my attack.

Pale and wild-eyed, Hawaiian Shirt Guy blurted, "It jumped off the rack and hit the floor. I never touched it. Honest!"

Ron's eyes widened with fright. He glanced around before heading to the rack to find a reason for the phenomenon.

I sat and reached for the ball. "Ow!" It zinged me when I touched it.

Ron turned to face me, a sheen of perspiration covering his face.

"What happened?"

I shook my hand to dissipate the stinging sensation. "It shocked me. It felt like a giant static charge." Puffs of condensation formed while I spoke. The sudden cold caused goosebumps to spread across my bare arms.

Ron sat beside me, took my hand, and examined it. "Mystery, I'm so sorry."

"For what? It wasn't your fault." *Unless you're not telling me something about this haint.*

The Hawaiian Shirt Guy continued to tell anyone who would listen about the ball leaping to the floor where it attacked me.

A crowd began to gather. People were pointing at the bowling ball near my feet.

Ron reached for the ball and yelped, jumping back. "It zapped me, too."

I touched his arm. "Sugar, can we leave? Everyone's staring at us." I nodded toward Hawaiian Shirt Guy. "Your buddy over there is drawing quite a crowd."

"Sure."

We rushed to change shoes and left the ball where it stopped. The other bowlers watched us go, still talking and pointing toward the ball.

Ron kept his distance on the way to the car. He opened the door for me before getting in on his side. After a few miles, he turned on the radio to fill the silence.

The sequence of events ran through my mind. *Bree isn't going to believe this.*

When we turned onto my street, I said, "You're not going to tell me what's happening, are you?"

Ron ran his fingers through his hair. With a shaky voice, he said, "It's complicated. I need time."

Ron pulled into my drive and stopped. He stared straight ahead, tapping his fingers on the steering wheel.

When it was clear he had no intention of kissing me goodnight or talking this through, I opened the car door and exited. Leaning back in, I said, "Sugar, take all the time you need. When you're ready to tell me what the heck is happening, call me." I slammed the door and walked with rigid-spine dignity toward my house.

CHAPTER 19: MYSTERY

I yawned, then reached for a pod to place in the Keurig. I only use the Mr. Coffee when more people are around, and today was Jasmine's off day. I'm not a fan of working Saturday mornings, and this one seemed worse than usual. After the bowling alley incident last night, I'd had trouble falling asleep and was plagued with nightmares of flying bowling balls zapping me with electricity until my short curls stood out with static frizz. I wasn't sure what was worse, the zapping or the frizz.

After doctoring the brew, I sat in front of my desktop screen, determined to do some bookkeeping. This task has taken more of my time since Tiffany came onboard.

With an ear tuned to the bell on the door, I smiled as Phoebe pranced to her dog's bed. She circled it several times before collapsing with a contented-sounding release of breath.

Opening QuickBooks Pro, I cracked my knuckles and reached for a pile of receipts.

The phone rang.

"The Mystery Shop," I answered with what I considered to be professional enthusiasm.

A gruff, masculine voice said, "Let me speak to Mystery Jones."

"Speaking. How may I help you, Sugar?"

Silence.

"Hello?"

"I'm not your Sugar. This is Max Flanker, and I want to know what kind of scheme you're trying to pull?"

I wondered if Bree was trying to prank me with a call. *Nah, she's not that good.* I looked at the phone. *Scheme? Who is this guy?* "I'm not sure what you're talking about, Mr., um…."

"Flanker," he bellowed. "You came to my daughter's home talking about ghosts, long-lost relatives, and a ruby brooch." His voice dropped to a threatening octave. "I won't let you scam my family for money. We worked hard for what we have."

My heart felt like a trigger-happy roofer, nail-gunning shingles in place. I fought for control over my emotions. With a voice sounding calmer than I felt, I said, "Mr. Flanker, I assure you there is no scam. Adam Craft, the owner of Craft's Antiques, has hired me to find the descendants of the original owner of a piece of furniture that contains an item that needs to be claimed. He's paying for my services. There is no charge for your daughter. She only needs to claim the brooch."

More silence.

"What's all this hullabaloo about a ghost?" he asked, sounding less aggressive.

I pondered how to answer this question. Nothing I could say would alleviate this Flanker guy's suspicions if he didn't believe in haints. "The original owner of the seventeenth-century piece was Felicity Abbot."

"I still don't see what this has to do with a spook."

I rubbed the spot on my forehead where pain began to throb. "Felicity Abbot is the spirit attached to the brooch hidden in the furniture." There, I said it. I cringed, waiting for his next biting comment.

He harrumphed. "Why don't you recover the brooch and deliver it to Felicity? Why does my daughter have to go to Huntsville?"

I slid down in the chair. *Why me?* "Because the haint in question will only reveal the location to her namesake. Mr. Craft doesn't want to damage the valuable secretary while trying to find it."

I didn't say, *Is it too much to ask her to come to claim a valuable brooch?*

He yelled with a threatening tone, "Leave my family alone. You

108

hear?" He severed the connection.

I put down the phone and rubbed my temples. *I'm too tired to deal with this right now.* I stared at the computer. *I'm also too far gone for bookkeeping.*

An hour, one customer, and two cups of java later, I phoned Mr. Craft.

"Mr. C, there's a problem with the ghost and your furniture."

"Oh, my. I hope it's nothing serious," he said.

I took a deep breath and exhaled red-hot frustration before sharing my conversation with Mr. Flanker.

"He doesn't sound like a pleasant person. Although I can't blame him for trying to protect his daughter."

I nodded. "Every time I mention the word haint, communication crashes. I'm sorry. Do you want me to try talking to Felicity Ortega again?"

"No, my dear. Let's give it a few days to see what happens. The best we can do at this time is tell Mrs. Abbott that her relative's father isn't willing to believe us. I'll go tell her when we finish talking. I'm sure she won't be pleased."

"Do you want Bree to do it?" I asked.

"I hate to bother her. It will be fine," he said.

Still boiling with frustration, I sat on a stool behind one of the counters, watching the rain drip off the store's black and white awning. The calming, consistent drip had almost lulled me into a hypnotic state when the bell on the door rang.

Looking sheepish, Ron slunk into the shop.

I sat straight before crossing my arms. *If Ron Jeffery thinks he can skulk in here without telling me what the heck is going on, he has another thought coming.*

"Sorry about last night. Can we talk?" he asked.

I managed an indifferent shrug. *Not good enough.* "Sugar, are you ready to tell me what's happening?"

Ron shook his head and jutted his jaw. "Can't we just be together while I work this out?" He managed to make it sound like I was the one being unreasonable.

Part of me wanted things to work out between us, but the situation was unsafe. Images of flying bowling balls and shooting spears of lighting lashed across my mind's eye, along with Rosa Lopez's body sprawled across the grave.

"Sorry, Ron. I think you're a wonderful guy, but you need to figure this out or tell me the truth."

Ron stood there, his jaw muscle flexing, and stared at the top of the glass case.

I decided on a direct approach. "Sugar, I think you're being haunted. Bree and I can help. We assist earthbound spirits in crossing over."

He rubbed the back of his neck and shook his head before taking a step back. He never met my gaze.

"Is it Carol?"

He didn't answer.

With a tone dripping with finality, I said, "Come see me when you're willing to share your secret and accept some help."

"I understand." Both shoulders slumped before he turned and left.

I wiped away a tear. "This is the Saturday from Hell." I stood. "Where did I hide those Thin Mint Girl Scout cookies?"

CHAPTER 20: BRIANNA

When the door pinged, I looked up to find Ron Jeffery coming into the shop. He hesitated once inside, as if gathering his resolve before stepping forward.

I closed my mouth and tried to cover my surprise. I knew Ron had had a date with Mystery last night but hadn't heard anything about it yet.

He looked—haunted.

"Hey. You here to buy some chocolates for Mystery?"

He shook his head. "Can I talk to you and Mystery? Today?"

The urgency flowing off of him caused me to glance at my watch. "It's almost noon. I'll close for lunch." I locked my register, put up the closed-for-lunch sign, and locked the front door behind us. I could now feel panic emanating from Ron. I didn't initiate further conversation until we were inside Mystery's store.

Mystery glanced up and did a double-take. "When you left this morning, I thought you would take your secret to the grave."

He wiped a hand down his face and looked at her with a haunted expression. "I need your and Brianna's help."

"What's going on between you two? Did something happen?" I asked.

Mystery told me what had happened during their bowling date.

Alarm sent adrenaline racing through my body. I held up a hand. "Ron, is this about the ghost or something else?"

Ron rubbed a hand over his face. "I just left the police station."

Mystery sucked in a breath. "The police station!"

"Detective Ricci thinks I killed Rosa Lopez. He brought me in for questioning. I called Jack. If it weren't for him, I'd be in jail by now."

I froze as if a sudden arctic blast had turned me into ice. *Jail!* "Why would Tony think you killed her?" My mind raced to the image of the flowers on the grave.

"Because I was there that morning. I swear, I didn't kill Rosa." He flung his hands in the air. "It's a long, complicated story." His pleading eyes locked on Mystery's.

I frowned and asked, "And who is Jack? Is he your attorney?"

"He is for this situation. You met Jack and Sarah at the fireworks display, remember?"

I tried to resolve the image of the pot-bellied man wearing jeans and a tee-shirt with my expectations of a well-dressed attorney. The two didn't merge.

Ron rubbed his mouth. "According to rumors circulating around the Camellia Express, you two solved Victoria Spellman's murder. I need y'all to solve this one, so…."

He had my full attention. "So what?"

His face darkened. He looked down, swallowed, and looked back up. "So I won't go to prison for something I didn't do?"

Mystery tilted her head. "Anything else?"

"And to stop this ghost from stalking me."

"Does she stalk you all the time?" I asked.

He shrugged. "I don't know."

I tried to hide my surprise that he finally admitted it. I tapped my chin while squinting to study his demeanor. *So, he's not sure who his ghost is either.* I waited for further explanation.

"Can we sit down?" He ran his hand across the back of his neck. "This could take a while."

"Sure." Mystery turned her open sign to closed and locked the front door.

Ron walked with slumped shoulders to the conference room. It was as if he'd already lost hope.

Mystery gestured for him to sit at the conference table, and asked,

"Want any coffee, tea, or water?"

"Water."

She headed to the fridge in the corner.

I need a cup of java for this. Without thinking, I picked up a yellow happy-face mug, decided it was not the best choice under the circumstances, and put it back. The one with the Ghost Busters emblem imprinted on its white surface was also not a great option, so I grabbed a plain white one.

The comforting smell of the brewed coffee seemed to wrap me in a warm blanket of soothing scent, which helped to calm my nerves.

Mystery grabbed a water bottle from the fridge, placed it in front of Ron, and sat across from him.

After fortifying myself with a sip, I inhaled a deep breath to prepare myself for what I might hear; but first, I wanted to correct any of his misperceptions. "Before you tell us more, you should know the Spellman case was a fluke. We got lucky. Besides, we're not private detectives."

Mystery nodded. "She's correct."

"We hunt troubled spirits and try to help them cross over," I said, watching for his reaction.

Ron rubbed one hand over the knuckles of the other. His leg bounced against the table leg, causing ripples across the surface of my coffee. For some reason, it reminded me of the ripples in the water glass in the movie Jurassic Park.

I held my lower lip between my teeth to stop myself from saying, *Come on! Spit it out.* I admit I could've been more patient, but his reticence had put Mystery in danger twice.

He uncapped the water and gulped some before saying, "Rosa had been stalking me since my wife's funeral. She had this crazy idea that I would marry her."

I sat back. *Marry her?*

Mystery's jaw dropped. "Where did she get an idea like that? Did you propose?"

He shook his head and held up both hands. "No way. That woman was unstable. Two days after the funeral, she started calling me." He ran his hands through his hair. "Here I was trying to get my head around losing Carol, and Rosa started asking me out on dates. I couldn't believe it! I tried to be polite when I declined, but eventually, I had to be rude and tell her to never call me again."

"Did she stop?" I asked.

He shook his head. "That was when the hang-up calls started in the middle of the night."

During lunch one day, my psychologist friend, Dr. Stone, had told me stalkers obsess on their victims as love interests, but they change their fixation to punishment and revenge when their romantic overtures are rejected.

"Did you trace the calls?" I asked.

"I tried, but she used a burner phone. So, I had to disconnect my phones at night to get any sleep. Based on Jack's recommendation, I sent her a registered letter telling her I'd press charges for harassment and stalking if she didn't stop."

"Did that work?"

"For a while. Rosa stopped calling, but I'd see her almost everywhere I went. Then, when I tried to confront her, she'd disappear like she did at the fireworks."

"So that's why Jack took off after her?" Mystery asked in a what-else-have-you-not-told-me tone.

He nodded. "We've been best buds since high school. He has a big heart and has done his best to help me through this mess. I owe him a lot."

"For what?" I asked.

He shook his head and looked over my shoulder with a faraway expression. "I thought the entire Rosa mess was over, but things heated up when I started dating again. Every time I saw a lady, Rosa would sabotage things and punish me."

"Punish you how?" I asked, leaning closer.

"The worst one was when she keyed my car," he said, his face contorting in anger.

That man loves his Porsche. "Did you file a police report?"

"Yeah. It didn't do any good. I thought I had Rosa that time because the business had a camera pointed at the parking lot." He looked down and gave a can't-catch-a-break shake of his head. "It wasn't working."

He resumed rubbing the knuckles on his left hand. I wanted to place my hand over his to stop the annoying behavior and reassure him, but I didn't.

"Maybe it's best if I start at the beginning," he said.

No kidding. I reached for my coffee.

Mystery gave an encouraging nod.

"When the doctor diagnosed Carol with breast cancer, that tumor crashed into our cozy little world like an asteroid, obliterating all our plans. It was well into stage four and had already metastasized when they found it." He rubbed his face with both hands. "There wasn't much the doctors could do at that point. All I could do was watch her die. Do you know what that's like…to lose a little bit of someone you love every day? I felt helpless to do anything to save her."

"No, but I know what it's like to have Tyree yanked from my life without warning. At least you had a chance to say goodbye." Tears glistened in Mystery's eyes.

Ron looked like he wanted to reach out to her, but he didn't.

I drank from my cup to avoid watching the intimate moment.

He cleared his throat. "Rosa worked for the home nursing company and covered the night shift Monday through Friday." He paused again and drank the water like he'd just left the desert.

While I felt the heaviness of his distress, I was losing patience. "And…" I made a circular motion with my forefinger.

"Rosa and I'd sit in the kitchen sometimes and talk. The whole cancer experience was awful for me. Every single day, Carol seemed to be more removed from this world. She slept most of the time. I didn't realize it then, but in hindsight, I suspect Rosa was medicating Carol to make her fall asleep earlier as time passed." He raked his fingers through his hair and looked at Mystery with desperation.

Suspecting what I might hear, I gripped the warm cup in my hands tighter and waited.

"Rosa was kind and such a good listener. At first, I thought she was offering sympathy when she patted my hand or hugged me when I'd break down into tears." He looked embarrassed. "I was an emotional mess."

Unable to stand another moment of his dancing around the facts, I said, "Did you sleep with her?"

Ron looked down. His hands squeezed the bottle making the thin plastic crackle, before he gave a slow nod.

"So, y'all became lovers?" Mystery asked, her tone shrill.

Ron's head jerked up. "No! It was only one time. Rosa wanted it to be a love affair, but I was so appalled by what I'd done that I felt nauseated every time I looked at her. So, I suggested it was best for me to request someone else to stay with Carol at night."

"What did she say?" My stomach felt like I'd swallowed rancid grease. I put my hand over my mouth.

"Rosa said if I did, she'd tell the agency that I took advantage of her. Then she threatened to tell Carol I seduced her." He shook his head as if wondering how all this happened to him. "Rosa made it clear she wasn't leaving." He rubbed his red eyes. "Every night, I did my best to avoid her. I even had to install a lock on my bedroom door." He shuddered. "I woke one night to find her crawling into bed with me."

I wondered how he handled that situation but didn't ask. Instead, my memory replayed Sarah's words the night at the fireworks display. "I don't care what you say, Ron, I'm convinced that woman hastened Carol's death, and we both know why." I locked gazes with him. "Did Sarah know?" *And if she did, I wonder how she found out?*

"She suspected something was going on. I'm not good at hiding my emotions. Sarah kept giving Rosa the evil eye when out of Carol's view."

Well, that explains a good bit. "So who killed Rosa?"

"I've thought about it a good bit." He leaned an elbow on the table and cupped his chin. "My first guess would be her husband. She showed up a few times with bruises. Then, right before Carol passed, Rosa started talking about the life we'd have together after she divorced him." He shook his head with a look of disbelief. "Something was wrong with that woman. She wouldn't take no for an answer."

"I've already talked with her ex-husband. He had an alibi," I said.

"Maybe he paid someone," Ron said.

I shook my head. "The man is treading water to keep from drowning in debt. He can't even manage his rent. Anyone else?"

Ron sat straighter, his eyes popping wide. "I overheard her on the phone sweet-talking someone in Spanish. I took three years of Spanish in high school, so Rosa didn't know I could understand what she said."

"How do you know it wasn't her husband?" Mystery asked, her

expression flinty hard.

"She'd hung up after screaming at her husband and then dialed the other guy," he said.

"Mama would say you weren't the only rooster in the hen yard. Do you know the other guy's name?" Mystery asked.

He rubbed his mouth and shook his head.

Great! An unknown boyfriend. "Anyone else?" I asked, trying to hide my exasperation.

"Not off the top of my head. If Rosa had two of us on her leash, do you think she maybe had more?"

"It's possible. I suspect Rosa wanted a lifeboat handy before jumping off the wreck of her abusive marriage," I said.

He looked at me, then Mystery with brown puppy eyes. "Will you please help me?"

CHAPTER 21: MYSTERY

Dreading Monday morning, I carried Phoebe through the shop's back door. I kissed the top of her head, and inhaled her comforting puppy smell before placing her on the floor. "I'll be there in a minute to fill your bowls."

She offered her version of a tongue-lolling doggie smile and walked, tail twitching, toward my office.

I mumbled, "But not before I get a cup of coffee."

It'd been a day since my last talk with Ron. I hated to admit it, but I missed him. *To make matters worse, I can't stand an unsolved mystery. Mama has always told me I was like a cat, only I didn't have nine lives to lose due to my curiosity. Maybe I should heed her warning. After all, I'm not a detective.*

I exhaled my frustration. "I was just getting into this dating thing. Men are sometimes so difficult. Makes me wonder if they're worth the trouble."

After brewing my coffee, I carried the mug to my office. Phoebe sat looking up at me with beseeching brown eyes. "Stop looking at me like you're starving. You had breakfast earlier."

The minute her treat pinged into the ceramic bowl, Phoebe pushed her nose in, sniffed, and grabbed it.

I stood and rubbed my lower back, which reminded me of the bowling incident. Satisfied that everything was in order with my fur baby, I carried the mug to the retail area and unlocked the front door before plugging in my new "open" sign.

The ping signaling the opening of the backdoor startled me. Zach had installed the device Sunday while we were closed, and I'd forgotten it.

Jasmine called out to Phoebe and crooned baby talk.

I yelled with more gusto than I felt, "I'm in the front."

"I'll be there after getting a mug of go-go juice," Jasmine replied.

We settled on stools and looked out the front window on another dreary day. A fine mist of rain blurred the edges of reality and softened the world around us. The steady drip of rain off the awning had a mesmerizing effect.

I sipped the hot brew. "I hate it when it mists like this. I feel like a wuss if I use an umbrella and a fool if I don't."

Jasmine nodded. "It soaked me to the skin in no time flat. I put my outer shirt across a chair to dry in the back."

"What do you have lined up for today?" I asked.

"So far, three background checks."

"UPS delivered a shipment Saturday afternoon. We need to get it unpacked, priced, and merchandised."

Jasmine stood, snapped her heels together, and saluted.

I rolled my eyes, trying to imitate Jasmine, but no one can do it better than her.

"I almost forgot; Ms. Lucille is bringing lunch today."

I smiled, feeling my fate change to the positive. "That's great! What's she cooking?"

Shrugging, Jasmine said, "Told me it was a surprise. She wants you to invite Brianna, Tiffany, Ron, Mr. Craft, and the herbalist lady. What's her name?"

"Theodosia Bosswell, but she prefers Dosi."

"I think Ms. Lucille wants to check her out. I told her Zach, Clay, and Kaya had classes today."

I won't be inviting Ron. "Will do. Diners at Garuda won't have to worry about Mr. Craft calling a tow truck if he's eating with us."

"You'd think folks would've learned by now to not park in the two slots in front of his store." She pointed out the window. "There are signs posted." Jasmine perched on a stool again. "How many cars do you think he has towed each week?"

"Four or five at least. Mr. Craft stands out front like a hawk

119

ready to pounce and warns folks when they exit their vehicles." I fluffed my curls, which always misbehave in this type of weather. "I guess he feels they deserve to get towed if they ignore him."

Jasmine drained her cup. "I'm going to start unpacking Saturday's delivery first. It seems *imperative*."

I chuckled at her word usage. "Your word of the day?"

Jasmine nodded and slid off the stool.

"I think it's *imperative* to call everyone and invite them to lunch." I picked up the phone.

Jasmine waved before strolling toward the storeroom. She stopped and said, "Tell them it's imperative they arrive on time. Ms. Lucille hates for her food to get cold."

When I picked up the phone to call Bree, a mischievous thought crossed my mind. *I haven't made one of my prank calls to her in a while.* I ran through several options until one struck me as viable. *Another one of Jasmine's words of the day.* I dialed.

"Chocolates and Delights," Bree said with a perky lilt in her tone. "We have twenty percent off Fleur Du Mal lingerie today."

Using my best French accent, I said, "This is why I am phoning you. You do not have a license to sell Fleur Du Mal products in your establishment."

Silence.

I waited, wondering if she'd check into the situation or tell me where to stick my demands.

With a terse tone, she said, "I buy Fleur Du Mal through my distributor and have every right to sell their products in my store."

Even though she couldn't see me, I lifted my nose to dive deeper into my French alias. "You do not. Take all the Fleur Du Mal products off your shelves immediately." I imagined that Bree was red-faced and working herself into a full-blown hissy fit.

"I do so have a right to sell that lingerie."

I grinned to myself. "Do not."

"Do so!" she yelled.

"Do not."

"Let me tell you something, you little French—."

I couldn't help it. I laughed. I could've probably carried on for a while if I could only resist the urge to laugh.

"Mystery Lucille Jones! Shame on you."

She hung up.

I looked at the phone, surprised. I must've really upset her this time. I walked to the back and stuck my head in the storeroom. "Please watch the front a minute. I need to go over to Bree's and smooth things over."

Jasmine looked confused, then her eyes widened. "Did you do another prank call?"

I grinned, feeling downright naughty.

Jasmine shook her head before standing. "Got it covered."

Phoebe sensed I was about to leave, so she scampered around me.

Jasmine picked her up and kissed the top of her furry head. "It's best you stay here with me where it's safe."

I strode out the door sending the bell into a merry jingle. After opening the door to Bree's store, I stepped inside, stopped, and inhaled the luscious scent of chocolate. *Lordy, I could gain ten pounds simply by breathing.*

Something whacked me in the face.

"Ow!" I'd barely batted the object aside when I was hit again. "Stop! That hurts. Have you lost your ever-loving mind?" I ducked as a third UFO grazed my curls.

I took refuge behind a standing display of brassieres. Unsure what to do, I lifted a white D cup off the rack and waved it in the air.

"I surrender."

"Too bad. My aim was improving until you ducked," Bree said, sounding too pleased with herself.

I stood, wondering if she was through attacking me. She had a selection of bridal garters scattered on the glass cabinet in front of her. She'd been sling-shotting them at me. When I picked one up off the floor, I noticed it had little metal charms attached.

Bree came around the counter to get the rest of her arsenal. "I was ready to blow a heart valve over that call. That's one of my best-selling brands."

"Sorry. I couldn't help myself."

Bree stopped and gave me a dead-eyed shark stare.

I shivered involuntarily. "I came because Mama has invited you to lunch today at noon."

Her countenance brightened. "What's she cooking?"

I shrugged. "Mama told Jasmine it was a surprise."

"I'll be there."

I decided to leave on a positive note.

*

Just before noon, Bree held the door so Mr. Craft could enter. Bent over his cane, he peered out from his bushy brows while working his way to a nearby stool. Clutching the counter with knobby fingers, he hefted himself onto the seat. "Don't get old, ladies. All the seats become either too high or too low."

Phoebe tore out from the back of the shop as he spoke. Then, standing on her hind legs, she waved her paws while whining.

I reached down and held the wiggling dog so he could pet her. Bree did the same, so Prissy could join the lick fest. The old man chuckled.

"Have you considered getting a small dog, Mr. C?" Bree asked.

Sporting a delighted grin, he said, "Oh yes, but I'm not sure I could properly care for one." He dropped his gaze. "Or outlive one."

I wanted to disagree, but he was in his seventies, had arthritis, and was unsteady on his feet at times. A rambunctious dog could knock him off balance and cause him to break a bone. "If it's okay with you, I'm sure Prissy and Phoebe would love to come to visit more often. One could come one day and the other the next."

His eyes brightened. "I'd love it, my dear."

We turned when the bell jingled.

Dosi entered the store and looked around. She wore a patterned shirt over a purple skirt, with matching earrings dangling from her ears. Her neat French braid hung down her back.

I smiled my best welcome. "Glad you could make it, Dosi."

"It was kind of you to invite me. Mr. Craft, how is your arthritis?"

"Much better, but it always acts up on rainy days."

She eyed him in a diagnostic manner. "If it still bothers you, there's another remedy that may help."

A horn honked. We all turned to find Mama parked in front of the store.

"Time for lunch." I placed Phoebe on the floor.

Bree said, "Why don't you go wash your hands while us women folk get everything on the table?"

"Sounds like a plan." He eased off the stool, steadied himself on the cane, and headed toward the restroom, located in the rear.

"I've already set the table, so let's haul in the goodies," I said.

The squeal of brakes announced Tiffany's arrival. She left her Volvo and rushed toward Mama's Chrysler 300 to hug her. Their widowhood seemed to have formed a bond between them.

Mama stood tall while directing the efforts. Her graying braids circled her head like a crown. When she stepped around the car, her refined ensemble in peacock blue and green was color-coordinated from her earrings to her shoes.

Since everyone else was helping Mama, I held open the door. Covered platters, casserole dishes, and a cake carrier were carried past me. Once everyone was inside, I locked the door, flipped off the open sign, and hurried to the conference room. I stepped inside, closed my eyes, and sniffed. Chicken and dressing, carrots, green beans, and squash casserole. I opened them to confirm the menu.

Bree introduced Mama to Dosi. The two women appraised each other warily. In many ways, they were similar in personality. *Mama may have met her match with Dosi.*

"I heard you were a gypsy," Mama said.

"We prefer to be called Roma," Dosi said stiffly. "I suppose all people are sensitive to names people have placed on them over the years."

"So true," Mama conceded.

Mama had settled into her usual seat at the head of the table with Mr. Craft to her right. She patted his blue-veined hand while they conversed.

After all the covers were removed and serving utensils placed in each dish, the rest of us took our seats. Mama invited Dosi to sit to her left. Bree, Tiffany, Jasmine, and I grabbed the remaining seats.

Mama smiled the special one reserved for Mr. Craft and said, "Adam, would you please say the blessing?"

"My honor, Lucille."

We held each other's hands and bowed our heads.

"Dear Lord, bless this food before us. Please bless the cook and keep our businesses profitable."

"Amen," everyone intoned.

Tiffany looked down at the casserole dish in her hand. "What's this?"

"Goodness, child, haven't you ever eaten chicken and dressing?

It's one of those stick to your ribs concoctions." Mama's gaze traveled around the table. "Where's Ron?"

I looked down at my half-loaded plate. "I, um, Ron couldn't come." I could never lie to Mama with any success.

Her laser gaze lingered on me, melting all pretense. Then, pursing her lips, she asked, "Goodness gracious, is everything okay?" She used a frown I recognized.

Oh great, she thinks I've done something wrong.

Bree shifted in her seat and glanced over at me with a be-brave look.

"Everything's fine." I held a casserole aloft. "Y'all must have some of this squash casserole. Mama makes the best."

Mama cocked a brow, letting me know she knew what I was doing, before saying, "Thank you, Darlin'." She eyed the table before asking, "Did anyone bring in the sliced tomatoes? Jasmine and I grew them in our garden. That child sure does have a green thumb." Her tone held both pride and approval.

Unused to praise from a mother figure, Jasmine blushed and jumped to her feet. "Where in the car did you put the tomatoes?"

"The back floorboard," Mama said with an appreciative tone.

Jasmine headed toward the door. "Be back in a jiffy."

Bree looked at me. "Did our Jasmine say, 'back in a jiffy?'"

Looking confused, Mama said, "What's so unusual about that? I say it all the time."

I shot Bree a don't-go-there look.

Before more could be said, Jasmine carried in a platter full of ripe tomato slices.

Mama and Dosi seemed deep in conversation. I was curious, but they were speaking in low tones.

When the plate with tomatoes reached Tiffany, she speared a slice and said, "Ron needs to do some damage control, pronto. Rumors are sizzling sparks along the Camellia Express."

Mama stopped chewing and stared at Tiffany. She swallowed and dabbed at her mouth with a paper napkin. "Darlin', what is a Camellia Express, and what does it have to do with Ron?"

Mr. Craft looked up from his plate. "It's the gossip network in the historic district." His caterpillar brows wiggled up his forehead. "Is it true that Ron was arrested for killing his wife's former nurse? I can't remember the nurse's name. When you get my age, names fade like disappearing ink."

Jasmine said, "Rosa Lopez," between bites.

I took one look at Mama's face and sighed.

Her head swiveled in my direction, gaze fastening on me. Then, with a tone of pure disappointment, she said, "I'd hoped you would stop sighing like a deflating balloon when you reached adulthood." She looked over at Dosi, "That girl sighed and rolled her eyes her entire teen years." She then straightened her back as if preparing for a blow. "What's this about Ron murdering someone?"

Bree flicked me a you-are-in-for-it-now look before bringing Mama up to speed on Ron's woes and the investigation. She wisely left out any mention of haints.

With downcast eyes, Mama gave a sorrowful shake of her head and said, "I had such high hopes for that young man." She looked up at me, eyes narrowing. "Are you still seeing him?"

"No." *And that's all I'm saying about it. I can tell by how Mama's shaking her head that she's thinking about all the grandchildren that won't be born. I've seen it before.*

Not much was said during the rest of the meal. I was grateful since Mama had outdone herself once again. I only wish I'd inherited her culinary gene.

Jasmine's eyes gleamed when she opened the cake carrier and lifted out a homemade carrot cake with cream cheese icing.

Everyone clapped. It was a beautiful sight.

I stood. "I have vanilla ice cream in the freezer and the coffee should be ready."

Everyone except Mr. Craft and Mama scampered to distribute coffee, cake, and ice cream.

Mr. Craft savored his first bite and winked at Mama. "If I wasn't such a broken-down old man, I'd ask you to marry me."

Giggling like a teenager, Mama fanned her face with a napkin. Then, flushing, she pointed her fork at me. "See, I keep telling you the way to a man's heart is through his stomach. You need to learn to cook some special meals."

Bree cocked her head and arched a brow at me.

I ignored her. "Yes, Mama." There was no use arguing. Besides, I'd rather eat cake.

After dessert, everyone sat back and patted our distended bellies.

The mess was cleared. The leftovers were given to Mr. Craft, who beamed his appreciation.

Everyone left the conference room except Mama.

I was rinsing the coffee urn when Mama cornered me.

To throw her off the hunt for information, I asked, "What did you think of Dosi?"

She paused. "She's a strong, intelligent woman. I'm a little leery of what she does. Mr. Craft sang her praises. She invited me to come by her store when I finish here."

That should be interesting. I hope Mama doesn't run like the devil is chasing her out the door. If she doesn't like the paranormal, she won't like palm reading.

She interrupted my thoughts by asking, "Do you think Ron is innocent?"

Mama considers herself an excellent judge of character, so I knew this turn of events had dented her beliefs about him. I started to sigh but didn't want to be described as a deflating balloon again. "I don't know? Circumstantial evidence points toward him. He swears he's innocent and has asked for my help."

"Is this why y'all aren't together?"

That and a jealous ghost. I set the carafe in the rack to dry and faced her. "Mama. I'm so confused. He doesn't seem like the kinda man who could kill someone, yet...."

"Yet, what?"

"He's hiding something."

Mama picked up a towel and started drying the carafe. "Baby Girl, most men are hiding something from their past. Your grandmother always called them the weaker sex and said it had something to do with their hormones."

True. I thought back to my late husband, Tyree. "Honestly, I don't know if we'll ever date again, even if this gets straightened out." To my surprise, tears welled in my eyes.

Mama placed an arm across my shoulders and led me to a seat at the table. "Sit, Darlin'. Tell me all about it."

How can I tell her when she hates hearing about haints? I wiped my eyes with a nearby napkin. "Ron has something happening in his life. Whatever it is has interfered with our last two dates."

She gave a knowing nod. "I don't know why men keep

everything to themselves. That's why they have so many dadgum heart attacks!" The moment she'd said it, her eyes widened. "Sorry, Darlin'."

Tyree died of a heart attack.

I patted her shoulder. "I know you meant no harm."

"So, what're you going to do?" Mama asked.

"I told him we're no longer dating."

She patted my hand. "Probably a wise thing to do." She pursed her lips. "I have to admit I'm disappointed. He seemed like a nice gentleman." After screwing her face into a horrified look, she said, "Then again, so did that serial killer, Ted Bundy."

CHAPTER 22: MYSTERY

I yawned and stared at the QuickBooks file on my desktop computer. Procrastinating on this task was becoming a habit. A pile of receipts sat to the left, waiting to be entered, but Mama's abundant lunch made my eyelids feel weighted, causing them to flutter closed. I jerked awake.

Besides carb overload, the Ron situation had served as a distraction lately. Dosi popped into the front of my mind. Maybe she should tell my fortune with tarot cards. I could use some insight and clarification.

Phoebe was asleep in her basket

On impulse, I tip-toed out of my office and headed down the hall. When I reached Jasmine's office, she was hunched over the computer, deep in thought.

Popping my head in the door, I whispered, "I'm going to run over to Dosi's place. I'm sneaking out on Phoebe."

She didn't look up. "Okay. I'll keep an eye on things."

When I entered Dosi's store, a mixture of herbal scents flooded my senses. I stopped and scanned the area. Somehow, she had made the inside look ancient and mysterious, a completely different look from the gift shop that closed. Her rectangular store had attractive wooden shelves lined with books along the wall to the left. To the right, an elaborate illuminated glass case was full of attractive stones and sparkling crystals.

Bree would like those.

A nearby table displayed rune stones and their velvet bags. An interesting upright rotating contraption was full of a variety of tarot cards. Along the right wall, pegs held small plastic bags with herbs inside. Each was labeled and displayed in an orderly manner. I recognized some like turmeric and rosemary, but many more were foreign to me.

Nice! I like what she's done with the place.

A long, waist-high counter stretched across the back wall. Shelves of glass jars filled with what appeared to be herbs were stacked on custom shelves behind it. All the jars held identical labels, creating an orderly appearance.

I studied the jars. *Could be the eye of a newt in one of those, for all I know?*

Dosi stood behind the counter, grinding something with a mortar and pestle. She looked up and smiled. "Greetings! Please tell your mother she is an excellent cook."

"Thanks. I will."

Cocking her head to one side, she said. "Something troubles you."

She said it as a fact, not a question.

"Yes. I could use some insight. Will you do a tarot card reading for me?" I asked, feeling foolish.

"Certainly." She stopped her task and reached under the counter. A thick deck of cards in a yellow box was in her hand.

"Let's sit at the table." She gestured toward a nearby square table under a small decorative tent, nestled in a corner. It reminded me of a fortune teller's tent.

We settled into chairs on opposite sides of the table covered with royal blue velvet that draped to the floor.

While I watched Dosi take out the cards, I wondered if she could sense my anxiety.

Her voice was melodious and soothing, like the light lavender fragrance that she wore. "This is a Rider Tarot Deck." She gestured toward the display of cards to her left. "As you can see, there are many lovely decks, but I was taught on this one, so it is my favorite."

"Go with what you know," I said, sounding nervous, even to my ears.

Dosi handed me the deck and told me to shuffle them while thinking about the question or events for which I sought enlightenment.

I took the cards and paused, thinking. "What if I have more than one concern?"

"That is fine as long as it's not more than three. Think of them clearly in your mind," Dosi said, offering an encouraging smile.

I shuffled them and thought, *Will Bree and I solve this murder? What will be the outcome of my relationship with Ron Jeffery?* I swallowed down my fear. *Will my business survive?*

When I handed the deck back to her, she said, "I'm using a standard ten-card layout."

"What does that mean?" I asked.

"I don't usually use a chart because I can do this in my sleep, but I will this first time since you're a neophyte. It will help you understand the layout."

She placed the chart on the table, "I will explain as I place the cards face up from my perspective."

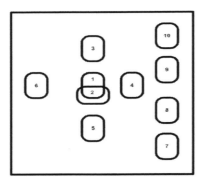

She placed the first card in the center of the table. It was a beautiful card of a woman in a flowing robe wearing a crown. The card said The Empress, and it landed upside down.

I reached to right it, so the lady's head would be up.

Dosi stayed my hand. "The cards land as intended."

I looked into her eyes. "What does that mean?"

"Each direction has a different meaning. This first position represents your present situation. You are dealing with learning the truth about complex matters."

True, but she already knew this.

"Card two crosses the first one and reveals obstacles and influences that lie ahead."

The Moon was written at the bottom of the card, with two dogs howling at a yellow moon. A red lobster crawled ashore.

I get the dogs, but what's with the lobster?

"It was upright before you turned it sideways, so that must be good," I said with a hopeful tone.

Dosi's lips thinned. "There are hidden enemies sowing deception. You could be in danger."

A chill drenched over me like a waterfall.

"This third one is your destiny card." Dosi placed it above the other two. It landed upright. A man sat on a bench, chiseling a pentacle on a round disc. Seven more hung on a wall. "It's the Eight of Pentacles. It shows skill in your craft and business." She smiled. "It will be successful on many levels."

"That's good news. I've been sorta worried since it has only been mine for a little over a year. I still struggle to meet payroll some months," I said.

Dosi nodded and gestured around her store. "I understand. I don't know how long before I see a profit." She placed a card to the immediate right of the first two cards. It landed upright. "This fourth card is your distant past, the one you harbor within you." She touched her heart. "It is the Nine of Swords."

A person sat up in bed, hands covering his face with nine swords hanging above.

"This card represents death and despair," Dosi said, looking concerned. "You are still grieving a loss?"

"My husband, Tyree, died a couple of years ago. Ron is the first man I've dated since then."

Dosi nodded. "It is hard to be alone."

"Yes." I wanted to say more, but the words wouldn't come.

"The fifth card represents recent events that are affecting your situation."

Dosi placed the next card below the two center cards.

Death!

An armored skeleton rode a white horse. A robed person offered a child to Death.

"The meaning of this one is clear. A recent death preceded your current situation."

"Rosa Lopez, the murder victim we found," I said.

Dosi's brows rose. "At lunch, someone said this involves Ron."

"Somehow, but it's not clear yet," I said. Dread filled my stomach like rotting meat, causing it to rebel. My hand unconsciously covered the painful area.

Dosi placed the sixth card to the left of the crossed center cards. "It's the four of pentacles." Her gaze met mine. "It's reversed."

I stared down at the red-robed figure, who sat with a pentacle above his crown, the second grasped in front of him, and the remaining two under his golden slippers.

"There will be delays, suspense, and possibly opposition in your near future," Dosi said.

I mumbled, "All I need is more suspense."

"Card seven represents your attitude when you arrived here today." Dosi placed it on the right side of the other cards toward the bottom. It landed upright and read, Wheel of Fortune.

"You came today with great hope to solve your situation," Dosi said.

"True."

"The eighth card represents environmental factors affecting you and those around you."

Dosi placed the card above the previous one. An armored knight carrying a golden chalice rode a gray steed.

Dosi's eyes widened. "The Knight of Cups reversed represents duplicity and fraud. You should beware."

Without waiting for me to comment, she placed card nine above eight. A bright sun reigned over sunflowers and a child riding a white horse.

"Ahh, The Sun, and it is in an upright position. It represents your hopes and desires." She shrugged. "Sometimes your fears."

"Which means?" I asked, feeling impatient.

She tapped the card and smiled. "You want contentment,

material worth, and a happy marriage."

"Doesn't everyone?" I asked. To be truthful, I was ready for this to be over. I was feeling more confused than when I started.

"The final card represents the outcome. It is The Lovers."

My stomach churned.

It was upside down.

"I guess Ron and I won't make it."

Dosi looked sad. "The future isn't concrete. On the bright side, your business is predicted to succeed."

"At least that's good news."

Dosi's brow creased as she scanned the cards. "Be careful. Two of the cards warn that you, and possibly Bree, could be in danger."

I took a deep breath and stood. "Thank you. What's the charge?"

"After such a lovely meal, there is no charge."

After thanking her again, I left feeling more resolved to discover who had murdered Rosa. I also felt scared.

While walking back to my shop, I decided that Bree and I needed to learn more about Rosa to solve this case.

"I'm back," I yelled.

Jasmine appeared in the doorway, holding Phoebe. "I sold three magic kits while you were gone."

"Excellent." I reached for my fur baby and headed to my office to sit. I ran a hand through my hair and looked down at Phoebe, whose warm body lay curled on my lap. "I think I need to give Ron one more chance to see if I can get more information. What do you think, Phoebe?" *There's still something Ron's not telling me. I feel it in my gut.*

Phoebe looked up, blinked, and yawned.

"I'll take that as a yes." *Lordy, I'm getting as bad as Bree.*

I was mid-text to Ron when the store phone rang.

"Mystery Shop. How can I help you?" I answered with a positive uplift at the end.

"This is Felicity Ortega."

I sucked in a breath and frowned. "Sugar, your father called me and shouted an earful of accusations. The only thing he didn't accuse me of was running a brothel."

A breathy sigh came through the phone. "Sorry about that. Mom was distraught when she found out. He's so protective. Does the shop owner still have the furniture?"

With a haughtier tone than intended, I said, "The last I heard, Mr. Craft doesn't like to sell haunted furniture."

"Oh?"

I chuckled, imagining her facial expression. "Mr. Craft once sold a possessed vase that caused many problems, so he tries to be careful."

Silence.

In a squeaky voice, Felicity asked, "Oh, my. Did he know it was possessed?"

"Nope. Are you still interested in seeing the writing secretary?"

"Yes, but we need to wait until Dad leaves for a conference."

I grinned. *Felicity and her mother are sneaking around. He must've given them an earful, too.*

"Can we call you back, with a time?" Felicity asked, using a wheedling tone.

"Sure."

"Perfect. Um, I mentioned that Mom is into researching our ancestry." Felicity raised her tone an octave at the end like she asked a question.

I examined my nail polish while waiting for her to finish.

Felicity blurted, "She wants to ask the ghost some questions about our lineage."

I frowned again, only this time at the phone. I knew the phone couldn't care less and she couldn't see me. "I'm sure that'll be fine as long as she has her questions ready and it doesn't take too long. We're doing this after hours and will want to go home and eat. No longer than twenty minutes for her questions."

Sounding relieved, Felicity said, "Perfect. I'll tell her."

Perfect this and perfect that. I rolled my eyes. *What's with twenty-somethings and that word? Is it the new awesome?* "Please, let us know when you want to come as soon as possible."

"Will do. Thanks again, and sorry about Dad."

When I finished the call, I phoned Mr. Craft. "Good news."

"It's been a slow day. I could use some," he said, sounding a bit down.

"Felicity Ortega phoned. She and her mom plan to sneak up here when her dad goes out of town. They'll call to confirm the date."

"Excellent! Sounds like he's a piece of work. Could Phoebe come to visit for an hour this afternoon? She is such good company."

I smiled. "I'll bring Phoebe over after her afternoon walk."

He said, "Wonderful," before hanging up.

At least he didn't say "perfect."

Feeling more upbeat, I decided not to text but instead phone Ron.

"Mystery, is everything okay?" He sounded alarmed.

"Why wouldn't it be?" I asked. My good feelings slid to the floor.

"No reason. Just asking," he said with an evasive tone.

"I'd like to meet at Big Spring Park a little after six and discuss what's going on," I said.

Silence.

I'd call it a pregnant pause, but no one was in a motherly way. While I waited, I thought about my plan to ask Bree to be there, out of sight, so she could intervene if the not-so-friendly haint showed up. If she tried to use work as an excuse to not come, I'd remind her that Jasmine and Kaya were closing our businesses tonight.

Sounding defeated, Ron said, "I'm not sure it would do any good."

"Maybe not, but I need more facts to help you. I'll meet you on the red Japanese bridge," I said and disconnected before he could decline.

Then I phoned Bree. "I need your help."

CHAPTER 23: BRIANNA

After taking Prissy home, I drove to Big Spring Park to meet Mystery. I found a parking spot only two cars away from her Prius.

I opened the trunk and pulled out the disguise Mystery had given me this afternoon.

I stuffed my hair under a long blonde wig before placing a wide-brimmed hat on my head. I smiled at my reflection in the car window and donned my sunglasses to complete the disguise.

Wow. I don't recognize myself.

I hurried toward the bridge while scanning the area for Ron. Other than Mystery, I spotted a homeless man lying on a bench to the left of the path and a young couple holding hands near the Museum of Art.

Good, I made it in time.

Ducks paddled in the lake, and geese fed on the grass near the path. I gave them a wide berth before sitting on a bench next to the bridge.

Mystery leaned on the railing of the red Japanese bridge and looked down at the koi. The multicolored fish of all sizes crowded together and rose to the surface to greet her.

"What took you so long," she whispered.

"Traffic." Then, pretending not to know Mystery, I pulled a book from my purse to read. Minutes later, I saw Ron approaching in my peripheral vision.

"The koi know this is a favorite spot for people to feed them," Ron said, smiling.

Mystery whirled to face him, her hand over her heart. "You scared me. You shouldn't sneak up on people that way." Her tone was far from kind.

He focused on his shoes. "Sorry about that." After a shrug, he looked up. "Can we walk? I've been chained to a desk all day."

"Good idea. I could use the exercise."

She didn't mention that the stress related to the case had further reduced her Girl Scout Thin Mint Cookie supply.

They took the path leading toward the hotel that sat on the park's edge.

While Ron and Mystery strolled in companionable silence, I struggled to be unobtrusive while staying in earshot. As I followed, I observed the long shadows moving across the grass and extra-wide concrete paths used by walkers and cyclists. There was a golden hue to the light as the sun crept closer to the horizon.

I jumped to the right to avoid being mowed down by a family of cyclists.

Ron turned to look at Mystery. Dark circles and the gray stubble on his typically clean-shaven face made him look older and tired.

"Has work been busy?" Mystery asked, sounding concerned.

I moved a tad closer to better hear.

He nodded. "More so than usual."

Mystery cocked her head. "Did you sign up the new account you mentioned?"

He nodded again.

Isn't he the chatty one today? She'll have to push harder for more information.

"Ron, do you still want us to help investigate your case?"

He looked up sharply. "Yes! The way Detective Ricci is hounding me with questions, I fear he'll show up at my business, cuff me, and haul me to jail in front of my employees."

That would be humiliating. I imagined my feelings if something like that happened in front of Kaya.

"Then you need to tell me everything. I can tell you're withholding information," Mystery said, her tone insistent.

Ron's shoulders drooped.

"Let's stop at the hotel, sit on the porch, and have a glass of iced tea. You can tell me what you're holding back while we cool off," Mystery said.

The path approaching the hotel split around a circular pool with a fountain shooting water high into the air. The white noise of falling water made it harder to hear anything.

A light breeze blew the spray onto me, offering some relief from the late afternoon heat that reflected off the concrete. I inhaled the clean smell of water and smiled.

A canal with five feet of flowing water ran between the paths when they rejoined before entering a large concrete tunnel.

Mystery called out, "Hello" once she was in the tunnel. The word bounced off the walls several times. She looked at Ron and smiled. "Sorry, I can't resist an echo."

When the path emptied out the other side, the shadows had deepened, and lights in the hotel twinkled through the panes of glass.

Two squealing little girls shot out of the hotel and raced toward us.

Ron and Mystery shifted to the right to avoid a collision.

I did the same.

Harried-looking parents chased them, murmuring, "Sorry," as they rushed past.

The encounter forced Ron and Mystery into close contact. He reached out and pulled her closer.

Mystery looked into his eyes and offered a reassuring smile. "Sugar, is there something you're not telling me? Because the more I know—"

A small rock hit Ron's ear. His eyes popped wide with apparent shock. When he touched the wound, his hand came away bloody. Backing away, he raised his hands like Mystery had pointed a gun at him.

What's wrong with him? I turned to see where the rock came from. I saw no one. A slight blur of haze crossed in front of a nearby bush. *Ghost?*

Another rock grazed Ron's temple, causing him to bleed. He staggered back and swayed.

Mystery rushed forward and tried to help. She was reaching to steady him when that blur of haze pushed her hard.

Mystery lost her balance and pinwheeled both arms to no avail before toppling into the canal. Falling flat on her back, she went under and came up gasping. She looked fighting mad.

A pair of alarmed ducks squawked and took flight.

I looked for the culprit but saw nothing.

Soaked to the skin, Mystery tried to stand but kept slipping on the algae that covered the concrete bottom.

Ron was nowhere in sight.

Where did he go?

Several people who were having drinks on the hotel's balcony stood and peered over the rail. Two of the men raced down the stairs.

Stepping forward, I said, "She can't get out without help. Can y'all pull her out if she can work her way to the edge?"

"We can try," the younger man said.

I was on the wrong side of the canal to the men, so I raced the short distance to the connecting bridge and dashed across to join them.

Mystery mumbled under her breath while wading toward the side of the canal. She grabbed the edge in time to prevent another slip.

"You're going to owe the Bad Habit Jar big time after that stream of cursing," I said.

She glared up at me.

I backed away, hands held in front of me. "I'm just saying."

The men each took an arm. After several unsuccessful tries, they heaved a soaking wet Mystery out of the water.

Water streamed from her, flooding the concrete at her feet. The two men backed away to avoid getting wet.

Mystery stood like a drowned poodle, dripping and shaking.

"Are you all right?" I asked.

Rubbing her arms, she nodded. "Thank you so much for your help. I'm not sure if I could've gotten out by myself."

The older of the two men asked, "Did that guy who ran away push you? Should we phone the police?"

A blonde, middle-aged woman in a classic black dress with pearls handed Mystery a towel. "I saw the whole thing. He backed away from her with his hands up. The moment this lady reached to touch him, she went flying into the drench. It was like someone gave her a vicious shove, but he didn't touch her." She gave her

MURDER IN THE CEMETERY

head an incredulous shake. "Were there bees or hornets buzzing y'all?"

"Not that I saw. Why?" I asked, still feeling dazed.

"He ran away waving both hands around his head like he was running from bees or something," the helpful woman said.

I never saw any of that because I was focused on Mystery.

"Ran away?" Mystery dried off while searching the area for Ron. "He's gone?" She looked for him again while toweling her hair. "He left me like this?"

As if reading my thoughts, the lady in black said, "If I were you, I'd forget this guy. He deserted you. What if you'd been injured?"

Blushing with embarrassment, Mystery nodded and returned the towel. "Thanks. That's good advice. I'm going home to take a hot shower."

The woman accepted it. "At least it's warm tonight. Otherwise, you'd freeze to death."

We thanked everyone again before I led Mystery back toward our vehicles.

I wondered if she felt as confused as I did.

People who passed us stared at Mystery and whispered after they walked past.

"You stink of canal water," I said, creating more distance between us.

"I shudder to think about all the fish poop in that water," she said.

"Don't forget the ducks," I added.

She shot me a searing glance. "Is that supposed to make me feel better?"

"Sorry."

The sun retired as the moon showed up for her shift. Dark blanketed everything except the splotches of illumination provided by lights along the paths. Insects whirled close to the bulbs.

When I reached Hot Stuff, I opened the front trunk and pulled out a beach towel that I kept there, along with charging cables and a heavy-duty extension cord. I closed it and offered the towel to Mystery. "You can spread this over your car seat."

"Thanks." She took it and dried her phone and Apple Watch.

She was hair-pulling mad if her clenched jaw and narrowed

eyes were any indications.

"I'm calling Ron right now. He owes me an explanation!"

"And an apology," I added.

She harrumphed. "He's not answering."

"Try texting him," I said.

Mystery nodded. She showed me the text before she sent it. *What happened? How could you leave me that way?*

No reply.

She opened her car door, placed the towel over the seat, and tossed her phone onto the passenger seat.

"Bree, I'm going home to take a long hot shower. We can discuss this tomorrow."

I stepped forward to hug her.

Mystery raised her hand in a stop gesture. "I appreciate it, but there's no reason for you to get sopping wet."

"Drive safe. Have sweet dreams," I said.

"I'll be happy if I don't have nightmares tonight."

CHAPTER 24: MYSTERY

I woke to Bree's customized ringtone. Cocking open one eye, I mumbled under my breath and grabbed my phone. "Bree, it's six in the morning, and I didn't sleep worth a darn last night. So, this better be good."

"Sorry, I wondered if you would have nightmares. Did Ron call or answer your text?"

"Let me check." I squinted at my phone. "No. Can you believe it?"

"I'll admit the Ron I thought I knew, wouldn't have abandoned you last night or failed to return your calls and texts."

"Why are you calling so early?" I asked.

"I'm meeting Chris for breakfast."

"You'll get up this early for Chris, yet you whine about meeting me to walk?" I said, sounding as cranky as I felt.

She chuckled. "Oh, I complained about the time to him, too. Anyway, I really called because he told me Rosa's body was released from the state lab."

"That's nice. So why are you waking me after last night's ordeal?"

"Rosa's funeral is this morning at Berryhill Funeral Home," she said.

I grunted and stretched.

"If you can arrange it, this might be our opportunity to talk to folks who knew her." Bree yawned. "I think we should meet there."

I yawned, too. *Dang things are contagious.* "I can handle this on my own if you need to be at your shop today."

"I *need* to go with you. Ghosts often attend their funerals. Remember Victoria?" Bree asked.

"How can I forget! Lordy, I hope Rosa doesn't send people running in terror from the funeral home the way Victoria did in that church."

"My thoughts exactly. After the ghost's performance last night, there's no telling what she'll do. There may be a large crowd. It may work better if two of us are there asking questions," Bree said.

"I'll meet you there. Go have fun and eat some bacon for me." I dragged myself out of bed while Phoebe stretched, yawned, and shook herself awake. While I trudged to the kitchen, Phoebe raced toward the rear of the house. I heard the flapping of the dog door leading to the fenced backyard.

Bree's right. The funeral is the best way to collect information about Rosa from her friends and family.

After a cup of coffee, I checked online. *Drat! The service is scheduled at the same time that I open my shop. I'll need more caffeine for this.*

I popped a fresh pod in my coffee maker and called Jasmine. The heady scent helped clear the fog from my brain.

Phoebe pushed through the dog door and stood, tongue out and wagging her tail.

"Jasmine, can you open this morning?" I explained the circumstances while feeding and watering Phoebe, who scampered around my feet.

"No problem. Hope y'all find out something interesting," Jasmine said, sounding way too perky for my mood.

I looked down at Phoebe's upturned face. "You're staying home today."

Phoebe lay down and put her chin on her crossed paws.

I swear she understands what I'm saying the way Prissy understands Bree. "I have too much to do today. So, I'll put down extra food, and you can have a good run in the yard while I'm gone. I'll leave the doggie door open." I turned to get ready and stopped. "Don't even consider escaping from the fence."

CHAPTER 25: BRIANNA

I turned off Memorial Parkway into the crowded parking lot of Berryhill Funeral Home.

Mystery exited her car and waved as she walked toward me.

I dragged myself from Hot Stuff and gave her a quick hug. Her energy felt much calmer than last night.

Mystery gestured at the rows of cars. "Either Rosa was a well-known person, or there's more than one event."

I stood a moment, trying to determine the best place to enter.

"Bree, which way do we go? I've never been inside this facility because my family and friends consider it to be a *white* funeral home."

"There's no official segregation in the South regarding the funeral industry," I said. "However, my observation has been that folks tend to self-segregate when it comes to funeral homes and hair salons."

Mystery nodded. "True. I could use this funeral home, but I'd be concerned that the staff wouldn't know how to properly handle my hair and makeup needs. I plan to use Serenity Funeral Home on University Drive because I have confidence that my cousin Derrick has all the right products to make me look good. When folks come to say their final goodbyes to me, I want to look my best."

I studied my friend's short dark curls. I wouldn't know how to style her hair. I barely know what to do with my own.

Berryhill had a Georgian architectural style with a central main entrance and matching wings on each side. The red brick, combined with the beige and white accents, oozed Southern charm. The sidewalk led to a covered porch with beautiful decorative double glass doors. People were entering through these doors and the ones on the right wing.

We chose the main entrance and walked into an elegantly decorated room that extended the entire length of the center section. Two viewing rooms opened off it. A visitation was in progress in the room to the left.

"Good morning!" A well-groomed, dark-suited man greeted us with folded hands. Are you here for the Hanson viewing or the Lopez service?" Before I could answer, he waved a hand toward a desk to my left, where a matronly woman sat. "If you want to make arrangements for a future event, our receptionist can assist you."

Goodness, the way he said "future event" it sounded like plans for a birthday or wedding reception.

"The Lopez service," Mystery said.

He gestured to our right. "They are in the chapel." He then turned to direct the next group of people entering the door like a funeral traffic cop.

We entered the chapel and stopped to take it in. The room was large with wooden pews with cranberry-colored padded seats on each side of a wide center aisle. A combination of four large Venetian bronze chandeliers and canned lights created the perfect lighting effect.

When my gaze traveled to the front, where the casket sat between two ornate floor lamps, I saw Rosa's ghost. She floated near a weeping Latina woman in her mid to late forties.

"It's Rosa," I whispered before hurrying down the aisle.

I want a word with that ghost. What am I going to say? Why did you push my friend into the water? Who murdered you? Better yet, how am I going to manage this in front of her grieving mother and a chapel full of witnesses without ending up in Huntsville Hospital's psychiatric unit?

I was four feet away with Mystery in my jet stream when Rosa's ghost looked up and locked gazes with me.

She scowled and dissipated.

Dang! If she'd stay put and tell me who killed her, this would be easier.

Before I realized it, we were hemmed in by a line of people moving toward Rosa's mother.

"What happened?" Mystery whispered.

"She pulled a Houdini on me," I whispered back.

"Well, heck!"

When I reached Rosa's mother, I said, "I'm sorry for your loss. I can't imagine what it would be like to lose a child."

Only a few inches over five feet, and what Lucille would call "pleasingly plump," she looked up at me with red-rimmed eyes. "Were you friends with my Rosa?"

As I live and breathe, what do I say to that? I stuttered out, "We only recently met."

I stopped by the coffin and marveled at how they'd covered the gash on Rosa's forehead. Her body looked more serene than her jealous and vindictive spirit.

I whispered to Mystery, "Go mingle and do some eavesdropping. Signal if you hear anything interesting. I'll do the same."

Several older women sitting in a front pew discussed concerns about Rosa's mother. I drifted on.

Three men standing to one side were discussing sports, so I kept walking.

Several children raced up and down the center aisle until a pregnant woman in her twenties glared and said, "Siéntense!"

With downcast eyes, the kids scooted into a pew and sat. They were quiet—at least for the moment.

Across the room, Mystery gestured for me to join her.

A group of three women were huddled together talking. I could tell they weren't related, so I mentally named them the Three Amigos after the movie.

I sauntered closer and halted when I heard, "She hated Rosa. It wouldn't surprise me one little bit if she killed her."

I walked closer. "Excuse me."

Mystery joined me.

Three pairs of eyes focused on us, one set looking curious, the second wide with surprise, and the last narrowed with suspicion. I explained our mission to solve Rosa's murder, since we had found her body. I avoided the topic of ghosts.

The tall, dark-skinned woman still eyed me like I might kidnap the corpse at any moment. With a melodious Jamaican lilt, she said, "Quid pro quo. First, you tell us about the murder scene." She shrugged one shoulder. "Then maybe we will tell you what we know." She pointed at me. "You go first."

Mystery cocked a hip and crossed her arms. "Quid pro quo doesn't mean maybe."

"True," the Jamaican woman agreed.

After brief introductions among us, I relayed the facts.

The three women leaned closer, listening with wide-eyed fascination.

When I finished, Maria, a well-padded Latina woman with long glossy black hair, screwed up her face and said, "I think it was Linda. She hated Rosa."

"That's true," agreed Candy, a wide-eyed, skinny blonde with a quarter-inch of dark roots.

Before Mystery or I could say another word, a priest asked everyone to be seated.

Unwilling to let my sources of information out of sight, I followed the three women into a pew. Mystery joined me. Before sitting, I glanced around the chapel and locked gazes with Detective Ricci.

"Guess who's here?" I whispered. I looked toward the rear of the chapel.

Mystery looked over her shoulder. "I should've guessed Detective Ricci would show up."

He stood with his arms crossed at the back of the room. His tight expression radiated disapproval as he glared at us.

I gave a little wave.

He arched a dark brow.

"He doesn't look one bit happy," Mystery said.

Feeling like a child plotting to steal a cookie under the watchful eye of her father, I sat next to Candy, who was chewing gum like a masticating cow.

I tried to pay attention to the priest, hoping to learn more about Rosa's life, but he droned on and on in a boring monotone.

Mystery whispered in my ear, "Lordy, if he recorded this, he could market it as a sure-fire way to cure insomnia. Where was he when I couldn't sleep last night?"

I suppressed a chuckle, before falling prey to the mind-numbing words of the priest.

I jerked awake when Candy nudged me and said, "It's over."

Feeling groggy from my brief nap, I blinked a few times and stood. "Where's the burial going to be?"

"Valhalla Cemetery on Winchester Road," Candy said, smacking her gum.

"Are y'all going?" I asked.

"No," Amoy said with her melodious Jamaican accent. "I'm starving."

After a brief discussion, we agreed to meet at Cracker Barrel on Drake Avenue to discuss Rosa.

As we were heading toward the nearest exit, Detective Ricci stepped in our path. "You ladies aren't snooping into *my* case, are you?"

Mystery crossed her fingers behind her back. "No, Sir. We're on our way to lunch."

He cocked a disbelieving brow before letting us pass.

I followed Candy's white Toyota to ensure I wasn't being dumped. Mystery followed me.

Mystery and I parked and met the Three Amigos inside. The gift shop area was a prime example of sensory overload. Colorful displays of merchandise were everywhere, each vying for my attention. The smell of fresh-baked biscuits and brewed coffee made my mouth water. A Taylor Swift song blasted from the speakers.

We wound our way between displays and shoppers to a podium where a young woman asked how many of us there were. She marked something down before grabbing menus and wrapped silverware. We followed her like ducklings past bustling waitstaff wearing brown aprons toward a round table for five.

When I passed the vast fireplace stacked high with fresh logs, the scent of ashes caused my nose to twitch with irritation. I was taking in the plethora of old stuff covering the walls when a motion caught my eye. I paused momentarily when a framed photo of a woman from another era moved. The ghostly image of her face scanned the crowd. *Jeez just like Hogwarts.* I looked to see if anyone else had seen her, but no one noticed. Heeding advice given to me by Mom when I was a child, I didn't acknowledge the ghost.

Maria, Candy, and Amoy sat opposite Mystery and me. We moved the advertisement and game on the table to the center to have more room. A child and an older gentleman were seated at the checkers table across from the fireplace. *Like a checkers player, I need a strategy.*

Amoy picked up her menu and said, "I'm glad they finished the service early. Ten minutes from now, this place will be packed."

"Amoy is a unique name. Does it have a special meaning?" Mystery asked.

"It means beautiful goddess."

Mystery perused the breakfast menu. "I only had a protein bar with my coffee this morning. I have a hankering for a fried egg and crispy bacon with a warm blueberry muffin."

All I could think about was chicken and dumplings with some cooked vegetables.

A gray-haired waitress with three gold stars and Kate embroidered on her apron took our beverage orders.

After she left, I raised my voice to be heard above the din of conversation and country music. "How did you know Rosa?"

Candy discreetly deposited her gum into a tissue that she placed in her purse before saying, "We all worked together for the same nursing agency."

I nodded. "Tell me why Linda hated Rosa."

The three women exchanged wary glances.

"Come on. We've come this far," Mystery said, sounding exasperated.

Amoy looked at Maria, "You brought it up, you tell her."

Maria sighed, rubbing her right thumb inside the palm of her left hand. "A couple of months ago, Linda and Rosa shared the care of a cancer patient during weekdays. Linda was on days. Rosa had the night shift."

Kate returned, distributing tea and coffee along with creamers. "Do you need anything else?"

We all shook our heads.

I tasted my sweet tea while waiting for the story to continue.

Maria also sipped her iced tea before saying, "Rosa told me she suspected Linda was taking some of the patient's pain meds because the supply was going down too fast. So, she started counting the pills every night and documented everything."

"Does this happen often?" I asked.

Amoy replied, "On occasion. It's usually a family member sneaking some pain pills. This time Rosa swore the husband wasn't the one, and she was right."

"What did Rosa do with all her information? Did she confront Linda?" Mystery asked, stirring her coffee.

Maria shook her head.

"She ratted Linda out to our supervisor," Candy said, blushing pink. "Sorry to interrupt. Go ahead, Maria."

Silence fell.

I twirled my index finger in a circle. "And..."

Maria shifted in her seat before blurting, "Linda was stealing a couple of pain pills every night. She was addicted. The whole thing came to a head when she overdosed on the job. She took some Oxy combined with fentanyl that she'd bought on the street. The patient's husband was home and called 911 when he found Linda unconscious on the floor. The paramedics saved her using Narcan."

I sat back in my seat. "Whoa, that's serious." *Ron never mentioned anything about this incident.*

"Darn right, that is serious," Amoy said. "She nearly died. If that was not bad enough, the company lost the contract, and Linda lost her job and nursing license. Until she goes through treatment and proves she can remain clean and sober, she cannot work as a nurse."

"How did Linda handle all that? Did she go into treatment?" Mystery asked.

Maria shook her head, looking sad. "She blamed the whole thing on Rosa. Claimed Rosa ruined her life because she reported the missing pills."

Sounds like denial to me. "Has anyone seen or heard from Linda lately?" I asked.

Amoy's mouth tightened. "No. She is out there doing her thing. Based on the fit of rage Linda had when she was fired, I would say she is capable of killing Rosa."

"She was throwing furniture around. Our supervisor called the police," Candy said.

Mystery pulled out a small notepad and pen. "What's Linda's last name?"

"Weber," Amoy said, leaning back in her chair.

Candy fidgeted with her napkin. "You won't tell Linda we told you about this, will you?"

"No," I said.

Kate arrived with a tray full of food bringing the conversation to a halt.

Mystery leaned closer and whispered, "I'll put Jasmine to work locating Linda Weber as soon as I return to the shop."

CHAPTER 26: BRIANNA

It was Kaya's night to close, so I left at six to meet Mystery at the Cajun Steamer. To my surprise, there was a parking spot open in front of the place. I exited the car, opened the door to the restaurant, and took a step back. *Wow, it's loud in here.*

Mystery stood next to the hostess station, hands over her ears, looking distressed.

She yelled, "Can we eat outside?"

The young woman crewing the station nodded.

The overall interior décor was cliché trailer-trash Cajun. The photos displayed on the walls and laminated on the tables would leave the impression that everyone in Louisiana was poor, resided in shacks, and did nothing but shuck oysters. This is far from the truth.

The right side of the establishment contained wooden booths that seated four. The middle was full of tables shoved together for larger parties. The left was dominated by a large U-shaped bar decorated with Mardi Gras decorations. Cajun restaurants seem to find it desirable to decorate for Mardi Gras year-round. *Laissez les bon temps rouler!*

The hostess grabbed two menus and led us past the bar and out a side door to a narrow open patio, wide enough for two rows of small tables. A black wrought-iron fence surrounded the area. The moment the door to the entrance to the restaurant closed, the noise level dropped.

Sighing with relief, I pulled out a chair at our table located across from the door. "Y'all should get hazard pay, so you can afford hearing aids."

Mystery giggled, but the hostess placed the menus on the table without comment and left. A blast of Cajun music escaped when she opened the door to go back inside.

Heck, she's probably so deaf she didn't hear me.

Mystery peeked over the top of her menu. "Bree, have you ever been to Louisiana?"

My eyes perused the food options. "Yeah. You?"

"Tyree and I went to the low country Mardi Gras in Lafayette the year before he died. It was lots of fun, the food was fabulous, and the Zydeco music was eardrum-piercing loud. If you ever go dancing, take earplugs."

"I'll keep that in mind. I'm ordering the Crawfish Enchiladas," I said, laying down my menu.

"Sounds good. I'm going to try the Cajun Seafood Medley. Looks like some kinda seafood casserole."

When our waitress appeared in tiny shorts and a low-cut Cajun Steamer shirt, I wondered if the sexy dress was required. We gave her our orders along with requests for margaritas and ice water.

I rested my elbows on the table and steepled my fingers. Due to the funeral today and work, Mystery and I hadn't taken the time to talk about the ghost attack at the park. The mere thought triggered a visceral response of heart palpitations for me.

I cleared my throat. "I'm still recovering from the last few days. It's not often that I see my friend get thrown into a canal with ducks and large carp."

I noticed that Mystery was concentrating on slowing her breathing. I wondered if she was also reliving the experience.

"You want to talk about it?" I asked.

"That assault was not only mortifying but frightening," she said, hand over her heart.

A noisy car raced down the street, swerved around a slower vehicle, and shot through a red light. It barreled down the road, belching exhaust.

I glared after the vehicle. "Where's the police when you need them?"

"They can't be everywhere. That guy is in a hurry to find a wreck," Mystery said.

The waitress appeared and placed our margaritas and ice water on the table along with napkins. "Your food should be ready soon." She flounced away. The guy at the table across from us couldn't take his eyes off her.

I picked up my drink and sipped at the salty rim.

Mystery took a gulp of hers. "I could've used your wine and dark chocolate therapy last night, but I was teetotally exhausted by the time I drove home and washed off the muck." She drank another large slurp. "I went straight to bed but didn't sleep well. Had nightmares off and on all night."

Using a soothing tone, I said, "I can see why."

Her eyes welled with tears. She seemed surprised by her intense reaction and dabbed under her lashes with a napkin. "The bottom was slippery with algae and other disgusting things I'd rather not think about, like duck and fish poop. I kept falling every time I tried to stand."

"I know. To be truthful, I wasn't sure how we'd get you out of there. Thank goodness those two guys came to the rescue."

She shook her head and looked down. "All the people sitting on the patio saw the entire fiasco." She looked up. "I was humiliated."

I nodded. "It was awful." I visualized the situation. Mystery flying through the air after she was shoved. Arms pinwheeling. The screech when she landed in the water. Her sputtering to the surface. Suddenly, it seemed humorous.

Brianna Olivia Kelly, that was NOT funny. I covered my mouth with a napkin while attempting to hold in my subdued chuckles.

Mystery stopped wiping her eyes and glared at me from across the table.

I wouldn't blame her if she threw her water at me. Why can't I stop laughing?

"Sorry." Bursting into gut-wrenching guffaws, I continued to repeat the apology between bouts of chuckles.

Mystery crossed her arms and shot another sharp glare first at me, then at the guy staring at us like we'd crossed the centerline and fallen into the ditch of insanity.

The guy dropped his gaze to his phone.

Her laser-stare had no effect on me, except to increase the

intensity of my laughter binge. It would have to run its course. Tears coursed down my cheeks while I held my contracting stomach.

As her anger drained, she, too, saw the humor and started giggling.

Ten minutes later, we wiped away our laugh tears and tried to gulp deep breaths. I felt like I'd had an emotional steam cleaning. My abdomen was contracting like I'd completed a round of crunches.

After drinking some water, I cleared my throat. "Let's get back on track." I sipped more of my frosty concoction and licked the salt from my lips. Before I could say more, the waitress arrived and placed our fragrant food entrees in front of us. I closed my eyes, sniffed, and made an olfactory journey to the land of bayous, spicy food, alligators, and Cajun waltzes.

The waitress asked in a disinterested tone, "Does everything look okay?"

All I could manage was a nod.

Mystery pulled her plate closer and picked up her fork. "I wonder why that woman said Ron acted like he was being pursued by bees?"

"I don't care if he was chased by a poltergeist, I can't believe he left you that way! He didn't even wait to find out if you had been injured. I'm going to ask around. I know a couple of women who went to dinner with him. I want to know what he's hiding."

Mystery's eyes widened. She leaned forward and lowered her voice. "Bree, do you think he killed his wife? Gave her too much pain medication to hasten her death and then led his friends to blame Rosa?"

"Who knows?" I said, jabbing at my food. "I'm glad we went to the visitation because the Three Amigos gave us a clue."

"Do you mean like the movie?"

I nodded. "What did Jasmine find out about Linda Weber?" I asked before stuffing my mouth with my crayfish enchilada.

"Nothing yet. I was out the entire morning, so Jasmine had a backlog of work today. It's the first thing on her agenda tomorrow." She raised her drink and toasted, "Here's to happy hunting."

CHAPTER 27: MYSTERY

The next morning, I peeked into Jasmine's office. "Sugar, I thought about Mama's advice to you."

Jasmine whirled around in her chair to face me. "Ms. Lucille has given me so much advice. The woman should write a blog."

Chuckling, I said, "Specifically, the one about doing background checks on those so-called boyfriends of yours."

"Yeah? You think I should do it on everyone I consider dating?" Jasmine entwined her fingers across her stomach.

"Maybe. In fact, I also want you to check out Ron after you check out Linda Weber. I'm beginning to think you can never be too safe."

"Will do. You want me to do this on company time?"

"Do Ron's and Linda's on company time. You're welcome to use the search engines to run only basic criminal checks on your guys off the clock," I said. "Nothing too invasive." I set the rules about confidentiality and the other issues regarding the information she might glean.

Jasmine nodded. "Sounds fair. When do you want yours?"

"I want Linda's information ASAP, then Ron's."

"Oakey dokey." Jasmine turned toward her monitor.

My mouth dropped open. "Did you just say oakey dokey?" *Good grief, what twenty-one-year-old says that?*

Jasmine glanced over her shoulder, looking confused. "I guess I did. I've been hanging with Ms. Lucille. All her little sayings are contagious."

I left shaking my head. Jasmine always wanted a mother like mine. Too bad she had to wait until she was an adult to be emotionally adopted.

Jasmine could mine a wealth of information on Ron, but I knew I'd have to gain information from the Camellia Express to find the grittiest of dirt.

I might as well start the ball rolling. *Good grief, now I sound like Mama.* I walked to the front and leaned against a counter before calling Bree's store.

With an uplifting lilt, Bree said, "Chocolates and Delights. Ten percent off on all chocolates until Friday."

I lowered my voice an octave and tried for a Scottish brogue. I knew it was a bad idea, but I couldn't help myself. Besides, she deserved it after laughing like a hyena at the restaurant the night before.

"I'll be wanting something sexy for me woman. You got any of those crotchless panties?"

Sounding more reserved, Bree said, "Yes, the store carries a selection of those."

"Well, now, will you be modeling them for me, lass."

Silence. "We don't model any of our items."

I covered my mouth and swallowed a giggle. I felt sure Bree's face was pink by now.

"That's too bad, lass. How's a man to know what stirs his loins if he canna see the item on a real woman?" I intended to push a bit more, but I started laughing.

"Mystery Lucille Jones! Don't you have anything better to do than taunt me?"

From her spiky tone, I could tell Bree was spitting mad. Resuming my fake persona, I said. "Now, now, lass. Dinna be poppin' your cork."

The connection died.

I looked at the receiver. Bree had hung up on me again.

The bell on the door rang like it would shoot into orbit. Bree, red-faced and hair flying like flames, tromped to the counter.

I knew I should look apologetic, but I couldn't help myself. I burst into a belly-wrenching laugh.

Bree's complexion deepened from red to puce. "I'm glad you think this is funny."

All I could do was hold my stomach and try to breathe between bouts of laughter.

Bree crossed her arms and launched her deadliest stink-eyed glare.

"Sorry." I giggled. "Really, I am. I couldn't resist." I wiped my eyes. "Now that you're here, I need your help."

Her shoulders hovered under her ears, stiff and unyielding. "You have a weird way of asking. You've got to stop baiting me this way. I always think it's another one of those sex fiends calling."

I lifted my chin. "You've baited me with prank calls before."

Bree shrugged one shoulder. "True, but you always figure out it's me right away. It's not fair."

"Is it my fault you're not good with voices?"

Bree rolled her eyes. Her shoulders settled back down to their normal position. "Good thing you're my best friend. What do you want?"

"You mentioned asking your customers about Ron. Could you do that for me? There's something more going on here, and I can't let it go."

"I'll call a few of my regulars to tell them about the chocolate sale and then ask about Ron." Bree paused and tapped her chin with her forefinger. "Who you really need to ask for help is Tiffany. Since she lives in the Twickenham district, she knows most of the gossip and the residents. She's at the heart of the Camellia Express."

"That's true. Let's ask her to join us for dinner tonight. The poor soul is still trying to adjust to being alone."

"Sounds good. That way, we won't contact the same people."

"My treat. It's the least I can do for y'all's efforts," I said.

Bree finger-combed her hair into place. "And for nearly giving me a stroke. I'm in the mood for Mexican. Let's meet at Little Rosie's."

An hour later, Jasmine handed me a page with Linda Weber printed at the top. "This is all I could find."

"Thanks." I perused the page. "My, my, Linda has been a naughty lady."

Since losing her job, Linda had been arrested twice. Once for trying to use a forged prescription and once for alleged possession of a controlled substance.

Addiction is a life-changing event, and not in a good way.

The first charge sent her to mandated substance abuse treatment. *If I'm lucky, she may be clean and sober by now. She hasn't gone to trial for the possession charge yet, so she's not in jail.*

Her current address and her probation officer were listed. I called Bree.

When she answered, I asked, "Is Kaya working today?"

"Yep. She's unloading a new shipment of lingerie. Why?"

I explained my plan to visit Linda's home.

"I'm game. Besides, I don't want you going alone."

After alerting Jasmine that I'd be gone for about an hour, I left out the back door and found Bree waiting in Hot Stuff.

Within fifteen minutes, we parked outside an apartment complex.

"This is the same complex where Rosa's ex-husband resided. No wonder that address sounded familiar," Bree said.

Linda's apartment was located in Building A to the left on the second floor.

Bree led the way to the stairway with all the stealth she possessed.

She whispered, "I don't want to alert the nosy manager in the next building that I'm back trying to question one of her residents, at least not yet." She put her finger to her lips and started up the stairs.

I followed.

When we reached the door, Bree nodded at me, indicating I should take charge.

I tapped on the door.

No answer.

Bree mumbled, "Please don't make me talk to that meddlesome manager again."

I knocked louder.

A hoarse-sounding voice said, "I'm coming. Don't get your panties in a wad."

The door opened the width of a chain lock. "Who are you, and what do you want?"

A pale face framed by stringy, dark blonde hair peered out at me. I could barely tell the one eye peering out at me was blue because the pupil was so large.

Either she had her eyes dilated for an exam or she was high on something. *Marijuana?*

I introduced myself and Bree. "Can we come in to talk?"

"Talk about what?"

"We wanted to ask you some questions about Rosa Lopez," I said, noticing the dark smudges under her eyes.

Linda let loose a string of words that would have cost my employees five dollars to place in the Bad Habit Jar.

"Why do you want to ask me about her?" Linda asked, turning red in the face.

"We're trying to figure out who murdered her," Bree said.

Linda's eye widened. She slammed the door shut.

Bree and I exchanged surprised looks. I knocked again. "If you can tell us where you were, it may remove you as a suspect."

Silence.

Bree stepped closer and banged on the door with the heel of her curled fist. "Would you prefer to tell us, or the cops?"

The door opened a slit. "What happened to Rosa?"

Does she not know, or is she playing games? I explained what I knew, including the date of the murder.

"I didn't do it. I was still in detox at Huntsville Hospital. Have you checked out her crazy husband, who lives in the next building? He'd get drunk and beat her."

"He was one of the first people I questioned. Can you think of anyone else?" Bree said.

"Could be one of the guys she was sleeping with. She kept trying to hook up with a rich guy, so she could divorce her lousy husband. Claimed she needed financial security."

"There was more than one?" I asked.

"There were three that she talked about. Could be more for all I know."

"Did she give you names?" Bree asked.

"Nope. She was secretive about who they were, like I might steal one of them. She gave them nicknames."

I nodded to encourage her to continue. When she didn't, I

asked, "What did she call them?"

"She called one 'Numbers,' and the second was 'Salsa.' I got the impression he must be Mexican, too. She once told me that he put salsa on almost everything."

"What did she call the third one?" I asked.

"I can't remember right now. My brain's a bit foggy."

More like drugged out.

Bree flipped her hair over her shoulder and asked, "Can you prove you were in detox when Rosa was murdered?"

"Just a minute." Linda walked away and returned with a cell phone. She tapped in a number and pressed the speaker icon. The phone rang.

A female voice said, "Huntsville Hospital psychiatric unit."

"This is Linda Weber. Can I speak with Julie?"

"I'll see if she's available."

Recorded music played until a pert voice said, "Hi, this is Julie."

Linda lied and said that she needed a verbal confirmation of the dates she was in detox for her probation officer.

After asking a few questions to make sure she spoke to Linda, Julie confirmed the dates that Linda was in the hospital, which included when Rosa was murdered.

I handed Linda my card. "Give me a call if you remember the third guy's nickname," I said.

She took the card and glanced at it before closing the door.

We left without alerting the nosy manager.

Bree drove out of the parking lot with a look of relief on her face.

"I guess we're back to square one," I said.

"Not exactly," Bree said. "I need to check with the Three Amigos to see if anyone knows who Numbers, Salsa, and our mystery man could be."

"Seems obvious to me that Numbers is Ron since he's an accountant," I said.

"That, or she was seeing a bookie," Bree said.

*

When I walked in the door of Little Rosie's that night, the blast of noise made me want to retreat. Between the salsa music and the reverberating acoustics of the place, it's always thought-breaking loud when crowded. I tried to take in all the colorful decorations while searching for my friends.

The line to order snaked down a nearby aisle. Bree and Tiffany waved for me to join them toward the rear of the queue.

I salsa-stepped to the music while passing the waiting patrons. "I'd forgotten how loud it is here," I yelled.

Bree leaned closer and handed me a napkin with writing on it. "This is what we want. Tiffany will get a table on the enclosed porch where it's quieter, and I'll get a selection of salsas."

"Sounds like a plan," I said.

Fifteen minutes later, I carried a tray with three margaritas, chips, white queso, and the order buzzer to the table for four where Bree and Tiffany were waiting.

"This is much better. I couldn't hear myself think in there." I unloaded the tray and the square black buzzer. "Do we need anything else? Napkins? Utensils? Straws?"

"Got it all," Bree said.

We dug into the chips and the selection of salsas. Ten minutes later, the device vibrated on the metal table.

"Hold the table, Tiffany. I'll help Mystery carry the trays."

When we returned, the heady scent of spices enveloped me, causing me to salivate. We ate first, enjoying the food while it was hot.

When we were waistband-stretching sated, Tiffany said, "Bree told me that you need my help."

I exchanged glances with Bree. "Before I start, what I'm telling you is not for public consumption. In fact, it can only be discussed with our staff."

"I remember the confidentiality clause in my contract." Tiffany mimed zipping her lips.

I told her about the strange happenings involving Ron.

Tiffany sat back in her chair, hand over her heart. "I'd think you were pulling a prank if I hadn't experienced those things in my house last April." She leaned forward. "Good Lord! The drink flying off the table and bowling ball incidents are disturbing enough, but this spirit hitting Ron with rocks and pushing you into the water, that's personal."

"And violent," Bree added.

"Bree and I think it has something to do with Rosa Lopez," I said before taking a sip of my drink. "We can't be sure because she won't manifest during the incidents, so Bree doesn't have a visual ID when it's happening."

"I did see her briefly at the funeral home," Bree added.

"Are we looking into this because you like Ron, or is it only curiosity?"

I sat back and considered the question. "It's business now. Ron's hired me to get rid of his ghost." I caught her up on a small part of his story.

"That didn't answer the part about liking Ron," Tiffany said.

"True. Ron's the first guy I've been interested in since Tyree's death." I leaned forward and slapped the table. "This whole thing became personal for me when I was attacked. If this haint assaulted me, who else will it try to harm?" I sat back and glanced toward Bree, who gave me a look that seemed to say, *and...* "We're also trying to help Rosa's ghost cross over."

Bree scraped the last cheese dip from the bowl with a chip. "It has become a serious situation. Whoever Ron's ghost is, there seem to be no limitations to what it will do." She pointed the cheese-laden chip at me. "That's why you need to steer clear of Ron until we figure this out."

"I agree with Bree. I'll set the Camellia Express in motion," Tiffany said.

While they worked out their call list, I sipped my margarita and pondered my next move.

I'm beginning to wonder if I should steer clear of him forever.

CHAPTER 28: MYSTERY

While suppressing a yawn, I knocked on the back door of Mr. Craft's shop. I could feel an afternoon slump sneaking up on me, ready to entice me to take a nap. Phoebe pranced beside me, anxious for her visit. I suspected she wheedled multiple doggy treats out of him.

When he opened it, his wide, frightened eyes alerted me that something was amiss.

"What's wrong, Mr. Craft?"

"Thank goodness you're here. I was about to call you because Felicity has been acting up something terrible. I hate to trouble you, but could you get Brianna to talk with her? She has a way of controlling ghosts."

I handed him the dog's leash. "I'll see if she can come right away."

I was happy to leave the angry haint to Bree, since she has methods of controlling them that I lack. My dead phone was charging, so I rushed back to my store, sprinted past Jasmine, and out the front door. I assumed Bree would be at the register or putzing around with the merchandise. If so, she may not hear me pounding at the rear door.

Kaya Mendez stared at me slack-jawed when I ran into Chocolates and Delights.

I huffed, trying to catch my breath, "Where's Bree?"

Kaya hooked a thumb over her shoulder. "In the back. Is everything okay?"

I hurried past her to the storage room without explanation.

Bree turned when I entered. "What in the name of the living? Is there a bomb threat or something?"

I held the stitch in my side and tried to catch my breath. "Mr. Craft looks terrified. Felicity is acting up."

"Acting up how?" Bree put down a box and crossed her arms.

I placed my hand on my chest. The rapid beat of my heart pounded against my palm. "I don't know. Mr. Craft asked me to hurry and get you."

Bree poked her head into the retail area and told Kaya, "I'll be back in a few minutes." She grabbed me by the arm. "Come on. We're going the back way. It's faster."

We rushed out the rear door and dashed past the dumpster that no longer smelled of rotten bananas but now smelled like cat urine. When we arrived at the rear door of Craft's Antiques, we could hear Phoebe barking.

Bree pounded on the door.

Mr. Craft opened it, clutching the leash in a trembling hand.

We squeezed past.

"Thank you for coming, my dear. Felicity is upset about something, but I don't know what to do," he said.

Broken glass littered the floor.

Bree looked toward the furniture. "Wonder what set off this ghostly fit of temper?"

She closed her eyes and took several deep breaths to lower her shields. When she opened them, she said, "Mr. C, her arms are crossed, and her eyes are blazing with anger. I'd say she's pissed."

I nudged her forward and whispered, "Do something."

"Felicity, why are you so upset?" Bree cocked her head and listened. "She's pacing back and forth and ranting about her relatives not coming to claim the brooch."

Mr. Craft dropped into a nearby chair. His chest heaved as if he'd been jogging. Phoebe stood guard in front of him, ears forward, tail up.

Bree threw her hands up in frustration. "You need to understand; we've done everything we can. Unfortunately, Felicity Ortega's father is interfering. They plan to come when he leaves town."

Bree crossed her arms and listened to Felicity's response before shaking her head. "No, Felicity. It's your fault this is taking so long. We could've delivered it by now if you'd told us where to look for the brooch."

A glass full of water flew across the room and smashed against the wall.

Out of the corner of my eye, I saw Mr. Craft cringe.

That's it! She's going to cause him to have a heart attack.

Before Bree could open her mouth to intervene, I stepped forward and slammed a hand on a nearby work table. "Stop it right now!"

Everyone flinched.

"You're behaving like a spoiled child." I gestured toward Mr. Craft. "This gentleman is paying to help you achieve your goal. It's not his fault that your great, great, great whatever won't stand up to a controlling father." I exhaled an explosive breath and crossed my arms. "I've driven hundreds of miles to meet with your relative, but you don't seem to appreciate that either." I pointed toward the secretary desk, hoping I was pointing at Felicity. "Furthermore, your namesake's father called and accused me of fraud. I don't have to put up with that kind of abuse." I swept my right hand to indicate the mess. "This good man tries to help you, and you destroy his property. You should be ashamed of yourself." I wasn't yelling, but my words held the cutting tone of a thousand razor blades.

Bree took a step forward and touched my shoulder. "Felicity's sorry, Mr. Craft, and promises to be more patient. She won't break anything else."

Mr. Craft pushed himself to his feet, steadying himself with the help of his cane. Phoebe still stood guard in front of him, hackles raised.

"I can't begin to understand how hard this has been for you to wait all these centuries. You're forgiven, my dear."

"She said, 'Thank you.'" Bree closed her eyes and took several deep breaths.

I knew from past experience that she'd restored her shields. *Wish I knew how to do that trick.*

Mr. Craft looked at us. "Can your two furry kids stay with me?

They calm my nerves and make me feel safe."

Bree nodded. "Sure, Mr. C. I'll bring Prissy over after the glass is cleaned up. We want to make sure the dogs don't injure their paws. That way, you'll have double protection."

I squeezed his shoulder. "That would be great for me, too. I need to unload some boxes. Phoebe thinks it's her job to supervise *everything*."

He chuckled and reached down to rub Phoebe's ears.

Mr. Craft looked exhausted, so we suggested he take Phoebe into the retail area until we cleaned up the glass.

"Thank you, my dears."

Once everything was clean and safe and we were back in the alley out of earshot, I asked, "Bree, why are all these ghosts throwing temper tantrums?"

"Most people can't see or hear them, so they throw a fit sometimes to communicate. I'd try to hurry Felicity's relatives along if I were you. Our Gray Lady is getting antsy."

CHAPTER 29: BRIANNA

That night in my living room, Tiffany raised her glass of Merlot. "To the Camellia Express, may it continue to circulate gossip for centuries to come."

"Hear, hear!" I said, clinking glasses with her and Mystery.

They sat on my long sofa that faces my fireplace. The large oil painting by Pierre hangs above the mantle.

The painting is important because the woman looks remarkably like me. Her flowing red hair trails behind her as she rides a green dragon past a castle with flapping banners.

Pierre was already a ghost when I first met him in Paris. When he took me to the gallery to see some of his work, I knew I would purchase this painting. I've always had a thing about dragons.

What I didn't know at the time, was that Pierre attached himself to the painting to follow me home.

Prissy and Phoebe lay cuddled between Tiffany and Mystery. Phoebe's gentle snores provided a rhythmical background like the ticking of my grandfather clock.

My Asian-styled rectangular cherry coffee table had a large blown-glass dragon stretched across the middle. Mom purchased it for me on one of her vacations to Milan, Italy. It's amazing that she was able to transport it home without breaking it. A selection of chocolates and red wine shared the area, providing a unique mingling of aromas.

I was seated in my comfy, yet sleek, recliner that faces the large screen TV on the opposite wall.

"This is my idea of stress relief—chocolate and wine. Yum!" Tiffany said, licking her chocolate-smeared fingers before wiping them on a napkin.

"What did y'all find out?" Mystery asked. She took off her shoes and wiggled her toes.

I raised the footrest of my recliner. "Before we begin, I'd like to say your need to know about Ron's past has been profitable for me. Using the guise of calling certain customers about my chocolate sale was a huge success."

Mystery rolled her eyes. "Glad it worked out for you, but what did you discover about Ron?"

I set my glass on the end table. "Nancy Abbott told me that Ron asked her to dinner six months after his wife had died. They had a lovely time, so she thought they'd clicked. He asked her to a movie on the second date but kept looking over his shoulder and acted paranoid. When they came out after the show, his car had been keyed. She said he looked more scared than angry. As Lucille would say, he dropped her like a hot potato. Poor woman still hasn't figured out what happened."

"Sounds familiar," Mystery said.

"I spoke to two other women who reported similar incidents," I said before popping a square of chocolate into my mouth. I chewed and continued, "Irene Barnett reported she was Ron's date and cohost for an employee cookout at his home. A Latina woman with long curly hair showed up and Ron asked her to leave. He threatened to call the police. Irene went to her car afterward to get something she forgot and saw the woman lurking around. When she was ready to leave for the night, the air had been released from all four of her tires. Ron wouldn't let her call the police."

Mystery frowned. "Did anyone else see anything?"

"No, but Irene's still upset about it."

"Wow!" Tiffany said, wide-eyed. "The man is cursed or something."

"Katherine Dobbs told a similar tale," I said. "In her case, Ron was eating at her home. He came out and found one tire punctured." I sipped my wine and placed it next to me. "After each incident, Ron stopped all contact. Every one of those women is still confused about what happened. It's clear that Rosa did her best to warn away women from Ron when she was alive."

Tiffany wiped her hands on a napkin. "There seems to be a pattern here. I spoke with Jessica Hartley. She was one of Carol's good friends. She visited Carol while she was sick. According to her, something weird was happening while Carol was bedridden the last month."

I gave an involuntary shiver. "What do you mean by weird?"

"It took three glasses of wine to get it out of her. She suspects that Ron had an affair with the full-time night nurse."

"Interesting!" I picked up my glass and raised it in a salute to Tiffany. "Tell us more."

"She admitted to never seeing the woman and Ron in a compromising position, so it was more like a vibe," Tiffany said.

Mystery looked impatient, if her bopping foot was any indication. "Can you be more specific?"

"It was hard to get her to explain. Jessica said the nurse gave her dirty looks if she hugged Ron and that he appeared uncomfortable every time the nurse was in the room with them."

"Do we know the nurse's name?" I asked, wondering if more than one nurse was involved with Ron.

"Rosa. Jessica only knew her first name," Tiffany said.

We were silent for a bit while sipping wine and munching on chocolate.

Tiffany's brow furrowed as if she was in deep thought. "Do we know what nursing service Ron used? Maybe one of the other nurses knows more."

Mystery set down her empty wine glass and sat forward. "There's more you need to know." She filled in some of the missing information, including what we learned from the Three Amigos about Linda Weber and the firings.

Tiffany cocked her head. "Since they are women, don't you mean the Three Amigas?"

"That's not how they say it in the movie," Mystery said, jutting her jaw.

Tiffany looked ready to argue that there were three men in the movie, which is true. She looked at Mystery and then me.

Mystery also looked at me for confirmation.

I shrugged. *It's not worth the effort.*

Tiffany pressed her lips together and rolled her eyes.

CHAPTER 30: BRIANNA

At seven on Friday night, Mr. Craft stood looking out the window of his shop, waiting for Felicity Ortega and her mom. Mystery, Jasmine, Tiffany, and I stood behind him, discussing how to best handle the guests.

"I was surprised when Felicity called to say her Uncle Henry was having open-heart surgery. Her dad left this morning for Denver," Mystery said.

"Nothing like last-minute plans." Tiffany flipped her hair over a shoulder. "Not that I have a busy social calendar since Jason died. I never realized how many events and dinners I attended related to Jason's work."

"I hope her uncle survives his surgery," I said.

Jasmine walked around, examining some of the items in the store. "I hope our ghost doesn't start throwing things again."

Mystery's brow puckered with a concerned look. "Don't we all."

"Her temper tantrum cost me over three hundred dollars," Mr. Craft said, rubbing his forehead.

A black Mercedes slowed and pulled in to park, its lights slashing across the windows as it turned into the space.

Two women left the vehicle and approached the front door.

I nudged Mystery. "I think this family is in the cloning business. Those two women could be sisters of our Gray Lady."

Mr. Craft unlocked the door. "Please come inside, ladies. I hope your journey was pleasant."

The younger woman said, "It was an easy drive."

While Mr. Craft relocked the door, Mystery made the introductions.

Jennifer Flanker's eyes glittered with anticipation. She wore a light blue suit that screamed Chanel. "I can't wait to meet my long-lost great-great-grandmother. First, I want to apologize for my husband's nasty phone call. He can be a bit much at times. When he announced he was taking off to Denver, I couldn't wait a minute longer to make plans to come."

I resisted an eye roll. *A bit much? He was downright hateful and demeaning, according to Mystery.*

We had discussed the situation before the two arrived and didn't want to spend hours while Jennifer researched her entire family tree. I patted Mr. Craft's bony shoulder. "This gentleman is footing the bill to help your relative pass on with her journey. We all have had a long day of work, so we ask that you keep your questions to a reasonable number."

Jennifer lifted her chin. "Of course."

We followed Mr. Craft to his storage area. He caned his way to a corner and pointed at the antique secretary. "Brianna is psychic. She will handle all the communication with the ghost."

I readied myself by closing my eyes and taking a deep breath to center myself before lowering my shields. I nodded to our Gray Lady and smiled. "Felicity Abbot, these are your kin, Jennifer Flanker, and her daughter, Felicity Ortega."

The two stepped forward, their gazes roaming around the piece of furniture.

"Oh!" Felicity jumped back and shivered.

I grinned, always amused by people's first ghost encounters. "She touched your face."

Felicity rubbed her cheek. "It was like a cold electric shock." Her eyes were as round as a wheel.

Jennifer rubbed her arms. "It's cold in this corner. Oh, my!" Her hand flew to her face. "She touched me, too."

Mother and daughter looked at each other, delighted smiles crinkling their eyes.

"I normally communicate with my mind, but I'll speak my

questions to Felicity aloud so you can hear them, and repeat her answers to you."

Jennifer pulled a small journal from her Brahmin purse. "I'm ready. I only have a few items to clarify. It shouldn't take more than five minutes."

Mr. Craft said, "We'll give you some privacy."

The rest of our crew followed him to his office.

Jennifer asked a multitude of questions about the family, including information about the causes of death for numerous ancestors.

When we finished and knocked on the office door, Prissy greeted us, her tail fanning the floor. Phoebe did her cute, happy-to-see-you prance.

Felicity's smile widened. "Well, hello. Aren't you two the cutest?" She squatted and crooned to the two dogs while petting their squirming bodies.

Jennifer watched, grinning. "She's always been an animal person."

Mr. Craft eased out of his chair. "Don't get old, ladies. Your joints get creaky."

We gathered in a semicircle around the secretary. Jasmine shifted from foot to foot. Tiffany's eyes glittered with anticipation. Felicity and Jennifer stared at the antique while huddled close together.

Jennifer turned and placed her hand on Mr. Craft's arm. "After we're finished, I'd like to discuss buying this family heirloom. I promised my ghostly granny that I would keep it in the family."

He gave a slight bow. "I'm sure we can come to an agreeable solution."

Wonder if he'll add on the cost of Felicity's hissy fit.

I rubbed my hands together. "Okay, it's time to find the brooch and pass it to its new owner." I turned to face the spirit. "Who leads the search?" I paused. "She says her namesake."

Felicity stepped forward, wringing her hands. "I hope I don't break anything."

I repeated the ghost's instructions. "Pull out the top right drawer."

She touched the handle like it might be hot and pulled it open.

I nodded to the ghost. "You need to trigger a latch hidden in the back. It's small, but it's supposed to pop up a false bottom."

Jennifer clapped her hands. "How wonderful! A false bottom. I'll have a place to hide things from your father."

Felicity's brow furrowed as she reached inside the drawer. Her mouth tightened as she fumbled around inside.

"Got it!" She pulled out the false bottom and found some papers that she handed to her mother. Then she reached back in and retrieved the brooch. Its elegant gold setting held a substantial oblong ruby the size of a quarter. We all crowded around for a closer look.

Jasmine said, "Wow. It's beautiful."

Jennifer's eyes filled with tears. "According to the birth records I've found, her birthstone was a ruby."

Felicity's hand flew to her mouth. "We have the same birthstone?"

Jennifer nodded. "I promise we will cherish this and pass it down to future generations."

I found I was misty-eyed. "Felicity's smiling and crying at the same time. She wants to touch each of you once more. She's ready to cross over."

First Jennifer, then Felicity touched their cheeks with startled smiles.

Jennifer said, "I wish I had the gift to see her."

I shook my head. "Be careful what you wish for, Jennifer. It's a blessing and a curse." I turned and asked the specter, "Are you ready?" I paused and listened. "She wants you to know she's waited a long time. Mr. Craft, she thanks you for reuniting her with her family and apologizes for breaking your things when she was in a state."

He bowed. "Forgiven, my dear."

I smiled, touched by what I'd heard. "Felicity wants Jennifer and her namesake to know she loves you both."

Everyone took several steps back except for me.

I felt a strange power fill me with an overpowering bliss and opened my arms wide. "The love of God embraces you and waits for your arrival. Go to the light." I saw a bright light fill the room. Smiling and crying, I lowered my arms. "She has safely made the journey."

Jennifer and Felicity hugged each other, both in tears.

I closed my eyes and took a deep breath to shield myself from the strong flow of emotion in the room. Then, feeling centered, I walked over and put my arm across Mystery's shoulders. "This is what makes it all worthwhile."

Jasmine joined us, tears glistening in her eyes. "That was so, so...."

"Cool," I said, grinning.

"Beyond cool. It was amazing," Jasmine said.

Jennifer came over to Mr. Craft. "Why was my spirit relative apologizing?"

I stepped forward and described Felicity's outburst of frustration due to her husband's accusations and delay tactics.

"I want to pay for the damage. You can add it to the bill for the furniture." She pulled out a credit card and handed it to Mr. Craft.

"Thank you, but it's not necessary," he said, flushing.

"Yes, it is, because you paid for the investigation and helped Felicity move on." She looked at me. "What do you call it?"

"Cross over," I said

Mr. Craft led Jennifer into his office.

While he finalized the purchase and set up the secretary desk's delivery, everyone else was interested in the papers found in the drawer.

Felicity carefully unfolded them. "It's a house deed!"

Mystery chuckled. "I bet someone was looking everywhere for that piece of paper."

Jennifer walked out of the office waving a bill of sale. "It'll be delivered tomorrow. I know just the place to put it."

"That's great, Mom. What will you tell Dad?"

"I paid for it out of my account, so, your daddy doesn't need to know where it came from. Besides, he'd never believe what we experienced today."

"What about the brooch?" Felicity asked.

"It was found, and we received it. That's all he needs to know."

Jennifer and Felicity hugged each of us and left to drive back to Vestavia.

Jasmine waved. "I hope they make it home safe."

Tiffany nodded. "It will be past ten o'clock before they get there."

Mystery heaved a sigh. "Well, team, one case solved and two to go."

Jasmine looked confused. "I thought it was only who killed Rosa Lopez?"

"There's also the true identity of the ghost haunting Ron. It could be Rosa or his wife, Carol," I said.

CHAPTER 31: MYSTERY

The Saturday morning staff meeting started with coffee and doughnuts. We oohed and aahed over the selections and the sugary scent filling the air.

Feeling upbeat, I picked out a glazed chocolate doughnut. "I'm happy to say one of our mysteries is resolved. As Mama would say, Mr. Craft is pleased as punch. He not only got rid of a high-tempered ghost but also sold the secretary desk for a nice profit. He paid me early this morning, so now I can pay Tiffany and Bree their commissions."

I handed out commissions and paychecks to my staff before discussing current business.

After the meeting ended, I made shooing motions. "Go forth and be profitable."

Jasmine said, "Off to wash my clothes. I'll see you this afternoon."

Bree asked, "Is it okay for Prissy to stay and visit Phoebe a little longer? They're all curled up asleep, and I hate to wake them."

"Fine by me."

An hour later, two dark-complected men wearing hoodies entered the shop and furtively glanced around. The one with a mustache nodded to his cohort. A warning bell dinged in my mind. *Shoplifters? Robbers?*

They separated. Mr. Mustache veered in my direction, and the other guy went a different way.

With my heart pounding in my ears, I texted Bree. *SOS!* I knew from past experience that shoplifters were usually thwarted if a second person showed up.

"Welcome to the Mystery Shop. Can I help you find something?"

Mr. Mustache said, "I want a magic kit for my nephew's birthday."

I lost track of the second guy. I turned and found him looking into a case at the back of the store. *How did he get back there so fast?*

"Are some of the kits more advanced than others?" Mustache Man asked, moving closer to me.

I took a step back to protect my space and to escape the strong smell of sweat and cigarettes that assaulted my senses. "Yes, does your nephew need a beginner's kit or the advanced one?"

"The beginner."

I tried to locate the second man as I headed toward the beginner's kits. *Where did he go?*

I handed Mr. Mustache a beginner's kit.

He was reading the back of the box when the bell jingled.

Bree rushed in.

We both turned to face her.

She held up her phone and took the hooded man's photo. "Should I call 911?"

Before I could answer, Phoebe and Prissy began barking. I heard cursing come from the back of the store.

With a gruff tone, Mustache Man bellowed something in Spanish.

I ran toward the noise.

The second man hobbled from the back dragging a growling Prissy, who'd sunk her teeth into his right ankle. A bug-eyed Phoebe held on to the cuff of his other pants leg.

He stopped, kicked his foot into the air, and sent Prissy flying like a football over a display case. Bree scrambled to catch her but dropped her phone in the process. It clattered to the floor.

Phoebe had lost her grip on the man's pants by the time I charged him with the fury of a crazed mama moose. His eyes widened when he saw me running at him with my hands shaped

179

like claws, ready to rip his eyes out.

The two men barreled toward the front door with both dogs nipping at their heels.

Bree backed away and let them pass.

"Stay!" I yelled while leaping forward to grab the snarling dogs before they could slip outside.

Bree rushed forward and locked the door.

I slid to the floor with relief.

The dogs ran to me, perhaps thinking I was injured. I hugged them close. "Good dogs. Are y'all okay?" I checked them for injuries.

Bree picked up her phone, checked it for damage, and said, "What's going on? Do I need to call the police?"

"I'm not sure." I recounted the sequence of events. "I want to check to see if anything is missing before alerting the cops." I stood and righted my clothes.

Bree hugged me. "So glad you're okay."

"Thanks for coming so quickly. I sensed something was wrong when they came through the door."

"You didn't recognize them?"

I shook my head. "We have the entire store under camera surveillance. I'll have Jasmine pull up the footage when she comes in this afternoon."

Bree frowned. "I think I need to have y'all put cameras in my shop. I get an occasional shady character." She pointed. "I see blood on the floor." She leaned over to examine Prissy's teeth before rubbing her head. Then with a singsong tone, she said, "You bit that mean man, didn't you? Good girl!"

Prissy's tail beat against her leg with each wag while she licked Bree's hand.

"You were brave, too," Bree crooned to Phoebe, who pranced around them. "I need to get back to my store. Let me know what you find. Remember, we're meeting Tiffany for lunch." Bree leashed Prissy and left by the front door, sending the bell into a merry jingle.

After fifteen minutes of searching, I discovered nothing was missing, but some papers on my desk had been moved. *Strange. Maybe the shoplifter didn't have enough time to steal anything.*

CHAPTER 32: BRIANNA

Mystery and I met Tiffany at Garuda at noon. After we placed our orders, the waiter brought us iced Thai tea and salads with ginger dressing. Mystery reported what she discovered after the incident with the strange men in her shop. "Jasmine should have the camera footage handy by the time I get back."

"That sounds scary." Tiffany forked a bite of lettuce. "I phoned Ron and asked what nursing service he used with Carol. I told him I was helping you find more information about Rosa."

Mystery poked at her salad. "Good, I don't want to talk to him after the incident in the park." She looked up. "I've lost contact with The Three Amigos."

Tiffany paused before taking a bite of her salad, but said nothing to correct Amigos to Amigas, the feminine version.

Mystery sighed, "I'm ashamed to say I forgot to ask where they work. Glad you found out about the agency." She gave an embarrassed-looking smile. "I guess I'm not much of a detective." She sighed again and mixed the ginger dressing with her salad.

I squeezed her shoulder. "I don't blame you for being upset. I'm still pretty ticked at Ron myself." I looked at Tiffany. "What did Ron say?"

Tiffany leaned forward and lowered her voice. "He sounded uncomfortable during the call. The agency he used is Elite Home Nursing Care. He admitted with great reluctance that Rosa had been fired after Carol died."

I looked up from eating. "That's interesting. Did Ron say why?"

Tiffany's brow furrowed. "He started mumbling a bunch of nonsense before finally telling me Rosa called him in a rage and blamed him for her termination."

Mystery's brow furrowed. "She probably thought he reported her romantic overtures."

I thought while chewing. "Maybe, but I can't imagine Ron doing that under the circumstances. Did he know where she went to work after being fired?"

Tiffany shook her head. "According to the Camellia Express, several of Carol's friends called the agency complaining Rosa was too friendly with Ron. That is probably why she was fired."

I stopped chewing and swallowed. "That makes more sense to me."

"It's a big mystery. I think Ron knows more than he's telling, but he wouldn't say and rushed to get off the phone." Tiffany dabbed the corner of her mouth with the napkin.

I took a deep breath. "I wiggled some information from Chris when I talked to him today."

Tiffany shot me a sly grin. "I bet you had more fun getting your information than I did with grumpy ole Ron."

My face flushed with heat.

Mystery and Tiffany put down their forks and gave me their full attention, which intensified my reaction.

"They got the autopsy information yesterday." I stabbed some lettuce. "I can't believe how long it takes to get an autopsy report back."

"And..." Mystery said, twirling her finger in a hurry-up motion.

I frowned, since I usually do that gesture to her. "The cause of death was due to an aneurysm caused by the head wound."

"And the manner of death?" Mystery asked, sounding impatient.

"Murder," I said.

Tiffany frowned, looking confused. "I know the police were treating the case as a suspected murder, but how do they know she didn't just trip and hit her head on the tombstone?"

I flipped my hair over one shoulder and leaned in. "Because Rosa had a broken jaw where someone had hit her."

The revelation landed like a four-thousand-pound hippopotamus on the table.

I reached for my tea and tried to wash down the sudden lump in my throat. I exchanged glances with Mystery. "It feels somehow more ominous now that it's official."

The waiter interrupted the conversation by delivering steaming dishes of fragrant Thai food to us.

We were silent while sampling our lunch.

"I love this dish," Mystery said, smiling.

I smirked. "You must. Have you ever tried any other dish on the menu?"

"I think about it from time to time, but never do."

Tiffany picked up her chopsticks. "Let's get back to business. I wonder how much of a punch it takes to break someone's jaw?"

I chewed and swallowed. "Chris said the punch was powerful enough to unhinge it."

Mystery's mouth sagged open. "Now I'm freaking out again. The more I learn, the worse I feel."

I eyed Mystery with concern. "You might want to call Dr. Stone and see her again. She helped you after Tyree died. All this has been stressful."

CHAPTER 33: MYSTERY

I felt like I'd been hit with a cast iron skillet and had the headache to prove it. I slouched in my office chair and rubbed my temples while trying to puzzle out the information Bree had relayed about the autopsy.

I never noticed that Rosa had been hit on the jaw. But then again, I'd only seen one side of her face. I shivered. "Lordy, dead bodies give me the heebie-jeebies. Bree's right, I need help to process this mess."

I dialed Dr. Charlene Stone, Ph.D. While I waited for the answering service to pick up, I thought, *If Doc could help me wade through my grief after Tyree's death two years ago, she can help me make some sense of this fiasco.*

To my surprise and delight, Dr. Stone had a cancellation at four o'clock, so I booked the appointment. After disconnecting the call, I walked into Jasmine's office. "I know you're working on background checks, but I need you to watch the front while I see Dr. Stone this afternoon."

Jasmine swiveled to face me. "Is it about Ron?"

I took a step back. "Yeah, why?"

"I finished my check into his background." She swiveled her chair from side to side. "I've been looking for the right time to talk to you."

My hand covered my forehead while I sank into a nearby chair.

Heaven and earth, what now?

"As Ms. Lucille would say, he's clean as a whistle. No tax problems. No major debt. No arrests. *However,* Ron was investigated regarding the death of his wife." She paused, her right leg bouncing. "She had a ton of money and a humongous insurance policy."

I lowered my head into my hands. "Good Lord. What else did you find out?"

"Ron came under suspicion after a home-health nurse was fired by her agency because of reports of an alleged affair with him. Someone alerted the police that the nurse or Ron might have overdosed his wife, so he could inherit sooner."

Wonder if that was Sarah? The memory of her accusation at the fireworks loomed in my mind.

Jasmine continued, "After Rosa was fired, she attempted suicide for some reason. I don't have any details beyond that. Do you want me to continue looking?"

I shook my head and told her what I'd learned during lunch.

Jasmine did her neck thing. "And you give me a hard time about the guys I date! Does Ms. Lucille know? She likes him."

"No, and don't tell her. I keep thinking there's more to this story. Are you still seeing Doc?"

"Once a week. I've got a lifetime of dealing with my mom and her men to process. Doc said I'm codependent and have been an enabler to Mom. Once she explained, I looked it up online." She did her neck thing again. "I have to admit, she's right."

I patted her shoulder. "Keep going."

She nodded. "I'll cover the store but remember, I have a six o'clock date, so I need to leave at five-thirty."

"I'll be back in plenty of time," I said.

I crossed and recrossed my legs while sitting in Dr. Stone's waiting room. If Mama were here, she'd tell me to quit being so antsy. Typically, the lobby's aquarium helped to calm me, but not today. I felt like my intestines were being fed into a wood chipper.

When Dr. Stone opened the door, she smiled a greeting. Then, after observing me for mere seconds, she asked, "Do you need a ginger ale for your stomach?"

I nodded. "You know me so well." I stood and began rubbing

circles on my stomach as I entered the therapy room. I sat on my favorite perch on the golden-beige, conversational sofa.

I glanced around to see what had changed. The wall with all of Doc's diplomas, licenses, and certificates looked like she'd added two new training certificates. The same stained-glass lamps cast subtle colors on the walls around them.

Doc entered the room and handed me a frosty can of Vernor's Ginger ale and a napkin. "Did you eat too many Girl Scout Thin Mint cookies again? Is that why your stomach is queasy?"

I accepted the cold, sweating can. "Not yet. If things don't improve soon, I may succumb to a cookie binge."

We each slid back into our seats across from each other. Doc picked up a pen and chart off the table next to her and offered an encouraging smile. "How can I help you?"

After taking several sips of the ginger ale and crossing my legs, I gave her a general report about my Ron situation.

Doc's eyes widened at times. Toward the end of the story, her brow furrowed. "It sounds like encounters with ghosts are almost a daily occurrence with you."

I shrugged. "Not daily, but as you know, my best friend is a psychic, and my business does paranormal investigations."

"I remember. How do you want me to help in this situation?" Doc asked.

"I guess I'm in shock and denial," I admitted reluctantly.

"I can see why. How long have you been dating Ron?" Doc asked.

"We've had five dates, but he and my late husband had been acquaintances for years." I placed my drink on the table and clutched a throw pillow like a teddy bear. "Everyone I know thinks he's a great guy, including me." *At least until lately.* "Surely the police would've arrested him if he had murdered his wife, right?"

Doc's stern expression made it clear she was unconvinced. "I'm a criminal profiler as well as a psychologist. There are cases where the police know who committed a crime, but they can't find enough evidence to prosecute the guilty party. District attorneys don't like to take cases they can't win because of minimal or circumstantial evidence. As a result, our prisons are full of dumb convicts, while the smart criminals know how to cover their tracks."

My heart sank to the pit of my already unsettled stomach. Tears blurred my vision. "Ron's smart."

"Are you in love with this guy?" Doc asked, nudging the tissues closer to me.

Stunned by the question, I sucked in a breath and held it. *Am I?* I exhaled and said, "I've a strong sexual attraction to him, and I admit, he's often in my thoughts." I paused to wipe my tears. "This may sound crazy, but I'm worried for his safety. I don't know who this jealous ghost is, but she's dangerous."

"How do you know this ghost is female and jealous?"

I gave a more detailed account of the incidents involving the women Ron had dated since his wife's death, including me. As I continued, I noticed Doc covered her mouth with her hand. "Bree thinks it's either Rosa Lopez or Carol, Ron's deceased wife. My bet is on Rosa."

Doc shook her head and dropped her hand before saying, "This does sound dangerous. Can't Brianna do something to help?"

"Ron hired me to discover who murdered Rosa because he's the main suspect. He hasn't asked us specifically to help his ghost cross over. Besides, the dang thing won't materialize or communicate, other than throwing a temper tantrum."

Doc sat back and thought a minute. "As crazy as this sounds, you may need to do an intervention with this spirit."

I sighed with frustration. "Great! Who's gonna do that?" I looked at Doc and asked, "Will you help us?"

"I was thinking of Brianna. She's the ghost wrangler."

CHAPTER 34: BRIANNA

Try as I might to forget Ron's situation, his vindictive ghost kept haunting my thoughts.

Pierre floated outside my open window. "Ma chérie, what has you so vexed?"

I explained Ron's case and his out-of-control poltergeist.

"Je comprends. What are your thoughts?"

"Meet me around back." I exited the rear door and paced on my covered porch.

I'd banned Pierre from my home after he entered uninvited, and tried to hug me while I was showering.

"Tell me everything, ma chérie." He floated with his chin in his hand.

"What if Ron did kill his wife? Why would he murder her if she was already terminal? I've heard that Carol had a month or so to live."

Pierre gave a Frenchman's shrug that somehow looked cooler than the American version. "Les hommes are not strong when it comes to emotions."

"So, you think he couldn't stand to watch her suffer? Maybe, it wasn't murder, but instead a mercy killing?"

He shrugged again. "Perhaps."

I paced the length of the porch, fingers tangled in my hair. Prissy poked her head out the doggie door, spotted Pierre, and ducked inside.

"I wonder if he sweet talked the nurse into doing his dirty work?" I shook my head, refusing to let my thoughts go further down that track. "Maybe Rosa misunderstood and thought Ron wanted Carol dead?" I stopped pacing.

Pierre cocked a brow. "Do you think the villain is Ron or the nurse?"

"Maybe Rosa got impatient and wanted him to herself? Heck, if things were heating up with her abusive ex-husband, she might have been desperate for a safe haven."

Pierre pursed his lips. "Her mari hurt her?"

Nodding, I rubbed my aching temples, not wanting to consider the question forming in my mind. "Did Ron lie about having a full-fledged affair with the nurse while his wife lay dying?" The thought sent a shiver over me like an icy waterfall.

I looked at Pierre. "Too many questions and no answers."

"Why is Mystery so worried about this Ron?"

"I think she's more tolerant than I am because she remembers her irrational behavior and thoughts after Tyree died. I'm sure she wouldn't want to be judged as a person based on that dark period in her life."

He nodded. "Elle l'aimait beaucoup?"

"Yes, she loved him very much. At least Tyree's death was quick. What would it be like to watch someone you love suffer, slip away, and die?" I shivered again. "Ron may have been vulnerable to any form of kindness and attention."

I looked at Pierre. "Doc would say I'm rationalizing."

"Les hommes are weak when it comes to les femmes."

My phone played Mystery's personalized ring tone.

"That's her now." I sat on the swing, answered the call, and placed it on speaker mode.

Pierre levitated near the porch.

My friend sounded winded.

"Are you okay?" I asked.

"Sorry, I was playing chase with Phoebe. That little dog is fast." She paused, still breathing hard. "Sugar, I need a big favor."

"Does it involve Ron?"

"Who else? I saw Doc this afternoon. She suggested that you need to try to do an intervention with the haint."

I pulled a page from Mystery's play book and gave a long, dramatic sigh that I hoped spoke volumes. "First, I'm not sure Ron wants his ghost-stalker to cross over. All he wants is the police off his back. Second, what are we going to do, break down the door to his house and demand he let us talk to the ghost? For chrissakes, need I remind you that he left you floundering in the canal and ran?"

Pierre cocked a brow.

"I was thinking of brownies," she said as if the statement made total sense.

"What?" I asked with an incredulous tone.

Both of Pierre's brows shot up.

"The man once told me he loved brownies with pecans. I may be a lousy cook, but I make killer brownies."

"That may be true, but why do you want me there?"

"The haint won't see you as a threat. Rosa might manifest for you."

"Maybe, but she hasn't so far. Have you forgotten her disappearing act at the funeral home? Besides, Ron knows I date a homicide detective. Why would he let me into the house? He's paranoid about the police." *Maybe for a good reason.*

"Sugar, I've got it all worked out. Trust me."

I grumbled under my breath for an instant. "Only if Pierre comes. I'd feel safer if he was there."

I looked at him with my best, *pleeese* look.

He smiled and nodded.

"Good idea," she agreed.

*

Mystery drove us over to Ron's home. The sweet, chocolatey scent of warm brownies filled the car.

"Est-ce une nouvelle manière de torturer un fantôme? To smell and not be able to eat!"

I looked toward the backseat. "If we don't get there soon, Pierre will tear into those brownies, and I'm going to climb over the seat to eat my share."

"That's why I put them there, not up front," she said.

Mature trees provided a canopy of dappled shade on the streets and lawns of the Twickenham district. A riot of hydrangeas of various colors produced showy blooms that highlighted the architecture of the majestic historic homes.

"Driving through this neighborhood lowers my blood pressure by several points," Mystery said, parking in front of Ron's home.

"Nice place." I shifted to face her. "Now, how are we doing this?"

"I'm going to ring the bell." She pointed toward the door. "You stand to the side so he can't see you right away. Then, I'll try to talk our way inside."

I slapped my forehead before giving her an incredulous look. "That's your foolproof plan?"

Mystery winked. "The brownies will make the difference. Mama says a man thinks with three parts of his body, but he does most of his thinking with his stomach."

"Madame Lucille is a wise woman," Pierre said with a nod.

"I thought men made most of their decisions further south."

"Only the really stupid ones," Mystery said.

"Il y a beaucoup d'hommes stupides," Pierre said, smirking.

I laughed.

"What did he say?" Mystery asked, scanning the backseat.

"He said there are many stupid men."

Mystery chuckled. "Amen to that."

We exited the car.

"Ready?" she asked

I nodded.

We strolled toward the door like we had all the time in the world and knew what we were doing. If only someone had told my stomach, which felt like it was performing acrobatics. I rubbed it and thought, *Why did I inherit Dad's nervous tummy when Mom could probably swallow barbells and feel fine.*

Mystery knocked before making shooing motions for me to move out of sight. She tapped her chin like she was still grappling with a plan to get inside the house.

Ron opened the door wide enough to peek out. "Mystery! What are you doing here?"

She peeled the foil off the plate and moved it closer, so he could smell the still warm chocolatey goodness of her baking.

Ron inhaled. "Brownies!" He opened the door wider and reached out.

She pulled the plate out of reach. Then with her best wheedling tone, she said, "Ron, I need a favor."

He pulled his hands back and frowned. With a wary tone, he said, "What favor?"

She yanked me into view and then crossed her fingers behind her back. "You remember Bree. She wants to install a fish pond in her back garden but isn't sure how large it should be. I told her about your beautiful pond. Can she take a peek? It won't take but a moment."

Ron shuffled his feet and looked first at me and then at the brownies. "Um, sure. That's the least I can do after recent events." He opened the door wider.

We followed him down the hall toward the rear of the house.

I looked into each room we passed, searching for the mystery spirit.

Pierre drifted behind me. I signaled for him to check the rest of the house.

He saluted and disappeared through a wall.

Ron led us onto the screened porch and out a squeaky door to an arbor-covered patio.

"You have a lovely home, but your back garden is spectacular," I said.

Pierre said, "I could haunt these pleasant surroundings for a while."

I jumped, not expecting him back so soon.

"I saw nothing," Pierre said while eyeing the pond.

Unaware of Pierre, Ron said, "Thanks. I spend a good deal of time out here." He guided us to the patio next to the fish pond.

"Wow. That's beautiful. I can see why Mystery likes it so much."

The cascade of water over the rocks created a soothing sound. Sunlight glittered like diamonds on the surface ripples and glinted off the koi's iridescent orange and red scales.

I knelt and placed my fingers into the water. The fish surfaced and nibbled them, eliciting a giggle from me.

"The fish are hungry. Would you like to feed them?" Ron asked, sounding pleased.

I stood. "Can I? That would be great."

Ron walked toward the house to get the fish pellets.

Mystery huffed and crossed her arms. "Remember why you're

here!"

"Oh, yeah." I looked around. "Carol? Are you here?"

"Hurry, he'll be back soon," she whispered.

"Carol, please give me a sign if you can hear me."

We waited for a response. Nothing.

"Try Rosa," Mystery said.

"Rosa? Are you here? Can we talk?"

"Well? Are you picking up anything?" Irritation had leaked like battery acid into Mystery's words.

I looked at Pierre.

He shook his head.

"Not so far." I cocked my head toward the house. "Here he comes. I think we will have to do something to anger the ghost. Maybe, pique her jealousy."

Mystery nodded and pasted on a smile for Ron.

When Ron reached us, he handed me a Tupperware container and said, "Only give them a handful. Sprinkle it out a little at a time. It's more fun that way."

"Don't overfeed them, or they'll get constipated," Mystery said, giving Ron a knowing wink.

When did she become a fish expert? I smiled at Ron before sprinkling a few pellets into the water. The fish attacked the pellets, some swimming over the top of their pond-mates to reach the food. I chuckled. "You'd think they were starving." When I finished, I handed the closed container to Ron and brushed my hands together to remove the dust from the food. "I really like your pond. Can I take some reference photos?"

"Sure."

Mystery also snapped a few photos on her phone. "Mama found my Granny's watercolor supplies and gave them to me. I think the waterfall and fish will make a lovely painting."

"How deep is the pond?" I asked Ron.

"Three feet along the edge and five feet in the center."

"Why so deep? I asked, before flipping my hair over my shoulder.

"It helps the fish survive during cold weather. Any more questions?" Ron asked, before glancing at his watch.

"I need to do some research before making any final decisions. Can I come back if I have more questions?" I offered a saucy smile and a wink to upset the ghost.

Pierre frowned and crossed his arms.

Ron's grin widened. "Sure, if you bring brownies."

Pierre's brows formed an angry V.

I moved closer and gave Ron a bone-crushing hug. "That's so sweet."

Before I could bat my lashes, we'd both landed in the pond. The displaced water sloshed over the rocks onto Mystery's shoes.

She jumped back and said a word that would require a dollar donation to the Bad Habit Jar at her store.

"Sacre bleu!" Pierre's rounded mouth and wide eyes showed his shock.

Ron rolled off of me and swore, as he stood in water up to his chest. He pushed wet hair out of his eyes and shot an accusatory glare at Mystery.

She held both hands, palms out in front of her. "It wasn't me. I swear. I wasn't even near you."

My attention was pulled away when I saw Pierre grappling with Rosa. I'd never seen two ghosts fight. It looked like he had the upper hand and would pin her.

When he does, I have some questions for her.

She kneed him in his ghost privates before disappearing into a mist.

He doubled over, groaning.

"I don't see anyone else here, do you?" Ron's harsh tone took on the vocal quality of a growl.

I stood, lost traction, and slipped under the water again. I gasped for air when my head breached the surface and smoothed my hair out of my face using both hands.

Mystery backed up. "Uh, oh. Bree, there's a fiery gleam in those emerald eyes of yours. Now, don't you be whipping your Irish-Italian temper into a frenzy."

I tried again to stand, pond water flowing off me like a waterfall.

"Bree, are you all right? Let me help you outta there." She bent and reached out her hand.

I reached for it.

Rosa manifested, rage contorting her face.

Before I could voice a warning, a solid push from behind

propelled Mystery into the pond. Mystery landed on Ron, pushing him back underwater. When she finally crawled off him, he surfaced and spewed pond water from his mouth.

I was sure my face was crimson when I clawed my way to the edge. Once I managed to haul myself out of the slippery pond, I stood swaying on unsteady legs, feeling like a wet Irish setter ready to explode into a hissy fit of titanic proportions.

I raised a clenched fist and bellowed, "Rosa Lopez, I order you to appear now!" I pointed at a spot in front of me.

Rosa manifested, looking both frightened and angry. She tried to float away.

Surprised that it worked, I said, "Stay!"

The spirit stopped.

I glanced at Ron, who was staring with open-mouthed shock. He couldn't see the ghost, so I said, "It's Rosa. I was concerned it might be Carol, but it's not."

He looked relieved.

I glanced back at Rosa and understood. He thought Carol might be haunting him, too.

I asked Rosa, "Who killed you?"

She glared at Ron and pointed an accusatory finger. "He knows."

I turned to look at Ron. When I focused back on Rosa, she turned to mist and dissipated to nothingness.

Ron crawled out of the water and, with my help, and we yanked Mystery to dry ground.

He looked furious. "What's going on?"

"That's what we want to know." Mystery fisted her hands on her hips and did her absolute best to look intimidating, despite looking like a dripping poodle.

"Are you telling me it was Rosa's ghost who has been haunting me all this time?" He shook his head. "I thought her stalking ended when she died."

"Apparently not," I said. I looked over at Pierre, who was now standing erect.

I repeated what Rosa said. "So, who killed her?"

Ron stepped back, his wet shoes making squelching noises. "Not me. I don't know who she's talking about."

Despite Ron's words, I could tell by his expression that he was running a mental list of possible suspects.

"I'll be back in a moment with towels." He jogged toward the house.

When he was out of earshot, I asked Pierre, "Are you okay?"

"Oui."

"I've always wondered if disembodied spirits could hurt each other."

"This was my first...how do you say... altercation. Now, we both know." He stood tall. "I will best la vicieuse the next time. She cheated."

I squeezed the water out of my hair and told Mystery about Pierre's tussle with Rosa.

"I'm sorry you got hurt," Mystery said with a concerned expression.

I pointed. "He's over there."

"Oh, sorry."

I asked Mystery, "Do you believe Ron?"

"I don't know what to believe anymore," she said, shaking water drops off her fingers.

Ron returned with three fluffy beach towels. "You need to leave."

I could tell Mystery's ire was up when she plopped both fists on her hips. Her angry vibrations shot like spears in all directions.

I raised my shields enough to stop the painful stabs.

"You have a vindictive ghost on your hands." Mystery poked Ron in the chest with her index finger. "She's not going away until her murder is solved. If you know anything that will solve the case, you need to tell us. We need to know what's happening if you don't want to be arrested for Rosa's murder."

Ron looked down and clamped his lips into a thin line, his jaw muscles flexing.

"Are you willing to go to jail over this?" I asked.

He looked up, eyes wide with panic, but his jaw remained rigid. "Find something that proves it wasn't me. That's all I'm asking." He draped his damp towel over his shoulders and reached for ours. "I need to shower. I'm meeting someone in an hour."

He walked us to the front door, eased us out, and closed it.

I looked at Mystery. "He's protecting someone."

"Yep."

CHAPTER 35: MYSTERY

I yawned wide enough to make my jaw crack, then trudged toward the office coffee machine. I hadn't slept well last night, so this three-p.m. slump was hitting me hard. I kept running possibilities through my mind about Ron and his situation. Mama has often told me, "Curiosity killed the cat," but I can't seem to help myself. I must know what happened, good or bad.

Despite a shower, I still felt grungy from my dunk in the fish pond. *Why does this haint like water so much? Whatever the reason, I'm sick and tired of it and her.*

I took my coffee and headed back toward the front of the store.

Am I putting myself and Bree in danger with this haint because I want to know the truth about Ron and his wife's death? What if he did hasten Carol's death? I kept asking myself. *Would that be murder or mercy?*

I never thought I'd be attracted to another man after Tyree died. That was part of my reluctance to think the worst about the situation.

I looked down at Phoebe. "I've known this guy for years. Yeah, I've noticed he was attractive, but I've never had the hots for him until he held me while we watched the pyrotechnics on the Fourth of July. When he kissed me, I had my own internal firework show. Is this infatuation or something more? What do you think, Phoebe?"

Jasmine walked in looking confused. "Are you talking to me?"

"Um, no, I was talking to Phoebe. I didn't hear the ping when you came in the back."

Jasmine stopped and frowned. She swung her backpack onto a counter and backtracked to the rear door.

I heard several pings.

Jasmine strolled back into the front of the shop. "I tried it several times, so it works."

I shrugged. "Guess I was too deep into my own thoughts. I'm going to open the mail."

I carried the steaming coffee to my office and eased into the chair. A stack of mail containing catalogs, advertisements, and envelopes sat in front of me. I grabbed my letter opener and dived in.

I was three-quarters through the stack when I came across an envelope with the address penned in block letters and no return address. I slit it open and pulled out a sheet of paper.

Stop the investigation, or something bad will happen.

I dropped the paper and covered my mouth with both hands. When I'd managed to lower my heart rate, I picked up the phone to call Detective Ricci. I paused when I heard a click and stared at the receiver for a moment before hanging up. When I located my mobile phone on the conference room table, I walked out back and made two phone calls.

Fifteen minutes later, Detective Ricci, Bree, and Jasmine joined me in the conference room.

"Chris would have come but he has a dental appointment to have his teeth cleaned," Ricci said.

I'd found some clean gallon Ziplock bags and had sealed the page and envelope into separate bags. We stood in a line, staring down at the evidence.

Bree reached over, held the bag with the letter in her hands, and closed her eyes. "Whoever sent this has some ugly and dangerous energy." She paused and tilted her head. "There's also a trace of fear."

Tony's expression was grim. Only his flexing jaw muscle hinted at the extent of his underlying emotion. "I'll take that to the lab." He opened a kit and took my fingerprints. "This will help us rule out yours." He pointed at Jasmine and Bree. "I'll need yours, too."

I was wiping the ink off my fingers when he pointed at me. "Leave this case alone and stay away from Ron Jeffery. He's our top suspect."

A thought rammed into my brain and burst out of my mouth. "I think my office phone has been tapped."

Tony's jaw dropped.

Jasmine popped out of her seat like bread out of a toaster. "What?"

"Are you sure?" Bree asked as she rubbed her forehead.

I explained about the phone clicking. "My former boss had her phone tapped once by a competitor. The clicking was how we knew."

Jasmine rushed from the room, causing the rest of us to look at each other with where-is-she-going expressions.

She returned carrying a box and sat it on the table. After carefully opening the container, she pulled out a black device about the size of a man's hand with two short antennas, one with a blue stripe, the other with a red one. "One good thing about working in a shop that sells spy equipment is what you need is handy. This is a listening device finder. Give me a moment to read the directions."

"Who would bug *your* phone?" Tony asked.

I shrugged. "I have no idea how anyone got access to my office."

Jasmine popped a battery into the device. "This is a Protect 1207i, a Multi-Frequency RF bug detector that covers six different frequency bands and is often used by law enforcement. It's our top-of-the-line product."

Tony leaned closer. "How much does something like that cost?"

"It retails for about a thousand dollars," I said.

Bree's eyes popped wide. "Wow. No wonder Jasmine was so careful opening the box."

We followed Jasmine to my office and waited in the hall while she swept the area.

Prissy and Phoebe stuck their noses inside the room and sniffed. "Found one."

"Where?" I asked, squeezing into the room.

"The phone."

Tony eased past Bree and said, "Let me in there, Mystery. I want to take it out and bag it. There may be fingerprints."

Both Jasmine and I backed out and let Tony inside.

After the device was extracted, Jasmine checked her office, but found no listening devices. The storeroom was also clean. She worked her way back to the restroom.

"No bugs," Jasmine said.

Who would want to listen to someone while on the toilet? The thought sent a shiver over me.

When Jasmine entered the conference room, the device indicated another bug. Methodically, she checked the coffee area, the fridge, and the shelf near the window that held a proliferation of house plants. Nothing.

When she approached the conference table, it showed a frequency. She crawled under the table. "Found it!"

"Don't touch it," Tony said. Grunting, he got under the table and bagged the device. He crawled out, red in the face, and struggled to his feet. Once there, he rubbed his right knee. "Keep going. Let's make sure there aren't any more."

Jasmine swept every corner of the retail area with the device and found nothing else.

Tony gestured toward the conference room, where we all took seats.

I felt stunned. I couldn't understand why anyone would find me important enough to put listening devices in my shop.

With a grim look, Tony said, "I think we need to check your home and car."

I turned to Bree with my most beseeching expression. "Can Kaya come over here until we finish?"

"Sure. Kaya's only putting away a new shipment of Spanx. Send her back when you're finished." She looked down at Phoebe, whose tail wagged with anticipation. "Why not have Phoebe come to my shop and visit Prissy while you're looking for more bugs?"

"That's a good idea. Phoebe thinks she should supervise *everything*." I leashed them both and handed Bree the leads.

"Come on, girls. Doggie treats at my place." Bree opened the door, allowing a stiff wind laden with the smell of rain to sweep into the store. Her red mane flew wildly around her face as she led the dogs next door.

When Kaya arrived, I gave her a list of simple things to do while I was gone. She'd filled in for Jasmine in the past, so she knew the basic procedures.

Jasmine, carrying the bug detector, followed me to my Prius. She turned on the bug detector and started scanning my car. The frequency meter flared near my right rear bumper. She slid under the car. "Get a bag, Detective. Looks like a tracking device to me."

Tony donned gloves and grabbed an evidence bag from his kit. He shrugged off his suit jacket, handed it to me, placed a large plastic bag on the ground and lay on his back under my car.

When he came out, I dusted off the back of his starched white shirt. "Good as new."

We slipped inside, and I started the car.

"I can't get over how quiet this car is, but Brianna's Tesla is even quieter," Jasmine said.

I harrumphed. When I pulled onto the street, Tony followed me. I parked in the garage and waited until he joined us before closing the door to keep out the blustery wind.

Jasmine scanned every room and closet in my home and then did the same outdoors.

When she entered the back door, Tony tilted his head toward my Keurig coffee machine. "Mystery, can we sit and discuss this with a cup of coffee?"

"Good idea."

Once we were seated around my breakfast nook table, Tony took a sip from his mug and said, "I have several questions. Who planted the devices? When and how did they gain access to your store?"

"Don't forget the third question—why?" I said.

Jasmine piped up. "I don't know who, but I have a guess about how the devices were planted."

Tony turned toward Jasmine, who sat to his right, and gave an encouraging nod.

"Mystery, remember when Prissy and Phoebe ran those two suspected shoplifters out of the store?"

Tony's eyes widened.

I raised my chin. "Bree told you that Prissy is a good watchdog. So now, Phoebe is doing her part."

"But they're so small," Ricci said incredulously.

"Tell that to the guy who hobbled out bleeding," I said, crossing my arms, before relaying the entire story.

Tony took notes. When he finished, he looked up and asked, "Did you call the police?"

"No. I never found anything missing."

His shoulders drooped.

"I kept the video footage. I had a hunch it might come in handy," Jasmine said with a smug grin.

Tony perked up. "Can you send it to me?" He handed Jasmine a card.

"Sure thing."

He paused and rubbed the back of his neck. "To be on the safe side, I think you should use that fancy contraption and check Brianna's shop and car."

Jasmine's eyes widened. "Good idea."

Tony turned his lie detector eyes in my direction. "Now, tell me everything again."

CHAPTER 36: BRIANNA

To my surprise, one of my favorite detectives was parked behind my shop when I pulled into the small back lot. I got out and waited for Ricci to join Prissy and me at the rear door.

He exited his car and bent to greet Prissy. "I saw a video where you were a brave dog and ran off a possible shoplifter. Good girl!"

Prissy closed her eyes and leaned into the hand rubbing her ear.

"What brings you here on a Tuesday morning?" I eyed his tie, which sported an image of Elsa from *Frozen*.

Noticing my interest, he ran his hand down the tie and blushed. "I wanted to fingerprint some areas in Mystery's shop that the suspects touched in the video, but her place isn't open yet."

"She'll be here in about fifteen minutes. Come in and have a cup of coffee."

He smiled. "A cop never turns down a good cup of Joe. I see why Chris likes you so much."

I opened the door and gestured Tony inside. A single barred window dimly lit my almost empty storage room. I turned on the lights as I made my way down the hall to the conference room. Once there, I brewed coffee, saying, "I was beginning to wonder if Chris had lost interest?"

Tony stopped jiggling the change in his pockets. "What makes you say that?"

I shrugged. "I haven't seen much of him lately."

He walked over and patted my shoulder. "My poor wife has the same complaint about me. Huntsville's murder rate is up. We have one detective on medical leave, and his partner is vacationing. It's shortened our case rotation, so we're both working our off days." He dropped his hand. "Believe me, you're on his mind."

I smiled with relief. "Good to know."

The comforting smell of coffee filled the room. I poured the dark brew into two mugs.

"I take mine black." He reached for a mug.

"I remember. Is that a cop rule or something?"

Ricci shrugged and took a sip. "Good."

I doctored mine.

"Were you surprised when Jasmine also found a tracker on your car?" he asked, blowing on his coffee.

I shrugged. "Yes and no. I'm like Mystery. Who would go to the trouble?"

"Is this murder in the cemetery the only case you two are sticking your noses into?"

I felt my face grow hot. "Yes."

He pointed his finger at me. "You need to stop snooping before you get hurt."

I heard a car door close in the back.

"That's probably Mystery."

Ricci followed me to the storeroom and out the back door.

Prissy burst out the door behind us and greeted Phoebe, who sat beside Mystery.

"What's going on?" Mystery looked from Ricci to me.

He explained his mission.

"Where do you want to start?" Mystery asked.

"The conference room," he replied.

Once we were all inside, Mystery turned on the lights and prepared to open while Ricci dusted certain areas of the conference table.

I helped by turning on her open sign.

Mystery was unlocking the door when Ricci came into the shop area.

"Have you moved those magic kits since those guys were here?"

She shook her head.

He dusted a magic kit.

"Why did you dust that particular one?" I asked, curious.

"In the surveillance video, Mystery handed him this kit and later replaced it. I'm sure you clean the glass counters often, but I'm hoping you don't wipe these plastic-wrapped boxes."

"Good assumption. The merchandise gets Swiffer dusted every so often but not wiped," she said.

When he finished, he said, "You need to clean where I dusted so you don't get this mess on your clothes."

Mystery nodded. "Thanks for the warning. I'll do it now."

"One more thing. Since each of you has a garage door to your storage areas, I suggest you both park your cars inside so people have less access to put on another tracker."

Mystery and I looked at each other.

"I'm calling a garage door company to put a remote on mine. I don't know why I didn't think of it before," I said.

Mystery waved her hand in a dismissive gesture. "Don't bother. I'll call Zach. He can pick up the kits and install both of them."

"Great," I said.

Tony drained his coffee and handed me the still-warm mug.

"It wouldn't hurt to check both cars for bugs daily until we figure this out," he said.

Mystery grabbed her keys. "I'll move my car now, if you'll stay and watch the front."

He nodded.

I grabbed my phone, which also serves as the key to my Tesla. "I'll do the same."

CHAPTER 37: BRIANNA

By dinner time, I was shaky-kneed starving. It was Kaya's day off. I had spent most of the day unpacking and displaying orders of Swiss chocolates and Parisian lingerie between waiting on customers. Needless to say, my day had been more physical than usual.

Mystery and I had ordered a large Special from DJ's Pizza. The restaurant isn't high on atmosphere, so we always opt to eat it at one of our homes. We were seated at my breakfast nook table.

"I thought it would be quieter to discuss the case here while we eat," I said.

"True," Mystery said, her gaze glued to the pizza box. She opened it.

The fragrant steam filled my senses, triggering my mouth to water and my stomach to growl.

Prissy and Phoebe looked up at us and whined.

Mystery and I both shot them our no-begging looks.

They tucked their tails and headed toward their brimming food bowls.

Mystery smacked her lips. "This is my favorite pizza. Their crust is thin and crispy."

"Mine, too." I grabbed a slice, stretching the cheese until it broke. "Have you heard any news from Tiffany and her sources?"

Mystery shook her head while chewing. Then, after swallowing, she said, "Just the same old stuff."

"Darn, I was hoping for some new insights."

After eating several large slices, I felt sated and sat back, patting my happy stomach.

Mystery finished the last piece and pushed her plate away. "I can't eat another bite."

I cleared the plates to the sink to soak and returned.

"Have you seen Chris lately?" Mystery asked, her brow wrinkling with concern.

I shook my head and pulled my glass closer. "He's called and texted. His department is slammed. I'm a bit worried about him."

"Why?" Mystery asked, her stare intensifying.

"He sounds tense and tired."

Mystery nodded. "Y'all's schedules haven't lined up lately, that's for sure. This may be something to consider. Dating a detective can pose problems."

I eyed her. *Is she trying to discourage me from continuing to date Chris? She was the one doing the matchmaking that night at Bonefish Grill.* I struggled to keep my tone neutral. "Like what?"

"Well, you know...."

I gave her my spit-it-out look.

She shifted in her chair and waved a hand in the air. "The crazy schedule, for one thing."

"My schedule is irregular, too." I cocked my head to the side. "Anything else bothering you?"

Mystery's gaze softened. "Bree, it's a dangerous job." She sighed. "I hate to say it, but he could get killed. I would hate for you to suffer like I did when Tyree died."

There it was, laid out on the table next to the empty pizza box. My biggest fear about the relationship.

I gulped the last of my wine. "I don't want to deal with this right now."

She was on a roll and not ready to stop. "Then there's the high rate of alcoholism and suicide with cops."

I slammed my hand on the table. "Are you accusing Chris of being a suicidal alcoholic?"

Mystery winced. "Well, no. But—"

She opened her mouth to speak, but my glare closed it.

Silence filled the room for several long moments.

After hitting my internal reset, I took a deep breath and decided to change the subject. "Tony told me we have to stop snooping about Rosa's murder." I hitched a shoulder. "You must admit the whole bugging situation is a bit creepy."

Mystery studied me while she wiped the sauce off her hands with a paper napkin. I could tell by her compressed lips and the energy radiating from her that she was trying to decide if she wanted to let go of the issue about Chris or bulldoze ahead.

Her shoulders rose and fell with her sigh. "Knowing my shop was bugged gave me nightmares last night." She shivered. "I hate to quit, because I think we're making progress."

To break the tension, I stood and retrieved the wine bottle. I refilled our glasses and thought a moment. "Let's take our wine into the living room and get comfortable while we take a second look at our suspects and witnesses."

She rose and followed me, careful not to slosh any wine from her glass. "What witnesses? I'm not aware there were any."

I placed my glass on the table next to my recliner and raised the foot rest to ease my aching feet. "I assure you there were multiple witnesses."

Prissy leaped to my lap, circled twice, and collapsed with an exhale of doggy breath.

Mystery chose the couch. "My feet have had it today." She arranged the blue decorative pillows to her liking and slipped off her shoes, so she could stretch out.

Phoebe jumped up and joined her for a cuddle.

"I've two theories about the witnesses," I said, dragging it out to torture Mystery a bit.

She sighed. "Will you just tell me already?"

"When we arrived, six ghosts were looking at the body."

An expression of realization spread across her face, followed by a small hopeful-looking smile. Then her shoulders slumped. "Haints can't testify."

"True. However, ghosts can describe the killer. It would give us some leads."

She gave a grudging nod. "What's your other idea?"

I put my hands behind my head and gave a knowing smile. "I'm beginning to believe Ron either saw the killer or suspects who it might be, but doesn't want to admit it."

She stiffened. "Like Ron is in denial or something?"

I sat forward and placed my hands on the arms of the recliner. "Maybe. Or..."

Mystery slammed her hand on the sofa, causing Phoebe to jump and look around. "What? You're killing me here!"

I shot her a smug smile. "Think about this the next time you call me impersonating someone."

She glared and pointed her index finger at me. "You're a grudge holder."

"Maybe so, but at least I'm not an impersonator." My smile widened.

She held up her hands. "I surrender. What's your theory?"

"I'm beginning to believe Ron is protecting someone."

She sat up, once again startling Phoebe. "Like who?"

"Sarah. She might have come to the cemetery that morning to pay her respects to her good friend."

Mystery's eyes widened with excitement. "She hated Rosa. It makes sense. They could have gotten into a tussle."

I nodded.

"So where do we start?" she asked before taking a sip of wine.

"At the cemetery."

Mystery's eyes widened. "No way! I'm not going to interview haints in the dark."

I chuckled. "No, silly. In the morning."

CHAPTER 38: BRIANNA

I whipped my car through the gates of Maple Hill Cemetery.

Mystery's tires squealed when she pulled in behind me.

I braked to a stop at the square concrete marker 34, got out, and leashed Prissy.

Mystery soon joined me with Phoebe. "What's the rush, Ms. Lead Foot?"

"I'm feeling antsy, I guess. I just want this interrogation to be over."

She squinted her eyes. "What's the problem?"

"The last time we were here, I had to clear these ghosts for Ricci. Remember?"

The light breeze helped to relieve the rising early morning heat.

Mystery placed her hand over her mouth. "Oh, I see." She dropped her hand. "They may not be too happy to see us."

The golden morning light gleamed across the polished granite headstones. Chirping birds flitted from tree to tree playing feathered tag.

After spotting three of the ghosts not far from Carol's grave, I approached at a run, fearful they would leave.

Prissy kept pace beside me.

When I stopped short of the disembodied spirits, Prissy pressed against my leg, her tiny body trembling.

I waved hello and smiled. "Hi, I'm Brianna. I need to ask you some questions about the woman murdered near here a few days ago."

Mystery stopped behind my left shoulder, huffing as if she'd just run a sprint.

Phoebe sat next to Prissy, her ears cocked forward.

A perfectly coiffed spirit who looked as if she'd died in her early forties crossed her arms across the front of her Chanel suit. She raised her chin and said, "Young lady, you were rude to us the other day. I'll have you know, I was only trying to sniff the cologne of that gorgeous hunk of a police officer."

It's true that scents are one of the few things that spirits can enjoy. I resisted an eye roll and swallowed my comeback about snooping. "I apologize for my rude behavior. I was trying to protect the police officer. My friend and I are trying to solve the murder of Rosa Lopez and need your assistance."

The three ghosts looked Mystery up and down, glanced at the dogs, and then returned their gazes to me.

A lady ghost who looked to have died in her eighties produced a gentle smile. "Now, Roberta. She's apologized. Let's help her."

Roberta turned her head away from me. "You're too soft for your own good, Josi."

No help there, I thought, my frustration building.

Mystery nudged me and whispered, "What's happening?"

I ignored her because the third ghost, a woman with a teased hairstyle, said, "We didn't see it happen. We belong in section 37." She pointed to her left. "We were coming this way to talk with some friends that day."

I sighed my disappointment. "Do you think the other three spirits with you saw what happened?"

Mystery tugged at my arm. "What did they say?"

I patted her hand. "Give me a minute."

Josi said, "That would be Margaret, Theresa, and Bernice. They were already here when we arrived."

"Could I talk with them?" I asked, trying to keep any hint of impatience out of my tone.

Josi waved a hand in the air and smiled. "Child, Bernice isn't here anymore."

"Where is she? Did someone move her?" I asked.

I knew if a body was moved to a new location, its spirit often followed.

Josi laughed. "Lord, no. Bernice crossed over on Sunday." She leaned forward like she was telling a big secret. "You see, Bernice died of a heart attack a mere hour before her great-grandbaby was born. Her strong desire to see that child kept her earthbound. On Sunday, her family visited and brought the little tyke with them. Bernice was so happy to finally see him that she joined her husband in the light."

I felt my mood lift. "That's wonderful. What about Margaret and Theresa?"

Roberta said, "They saw you drive up and wisely returned to their graves."

Mystery stomped her foot. "What's going on!"

I raised a finger. "Excuse me, ladies." I proceeded to give a Cliff Notes explanation.

Mystery pursed her lips. "Find out where these two haints are buried? Then we can do a house call."

More like a graveside call, I thought.

Roberta raised her chin again. "None of your business. Go away!"

I was losing patience and could feel my face growing hot from anger. "Who is being rude, now?"

Josi shot her friend a disapproving look, then turned her gaze on me. "If you find this Rosa's killer, will it help her cross over?"

"That's what I'm hoping to achieve. Rosa deserves justice," I said.

Josi nodded. "Follow me."

I explained the plan to Mystery.

"Sounds good. Give me Prissy. I'll stand back with the dogs."

As it turned out, Margaret and Theresa were neighbors with side-by-side headstones.

Josi leaned down and said, "Quit hiding down there and come talk to this young lady. She's trying to help that poor woman murdered in section 34."

The two ghosts popped up. Margaret had a large physique with several chins. Theresa had the skin-and-bones build of someone who'd died a lingering death.

After introductions, I asked, "Did you see what happened?"

They both shook their heads.

Margaret looked over her shoulder towards Carol's gravestone. "I was hanging out down here minding my own business."

Theresa rolled her eyes. "That would be the first time."

Margaret crossed her arms. "Do you want to tell this?"

Theresa flipped a hand. "No. Go ahead."

"I usually don't surface until dark unless something interesting happens."

Theresa sniffed. "She's the nosiest ghost in this cemetery."

Margaret glared at Theresa before turning her back to her neighbor. "I heard a bunch of yelling and screaming, so I poked my head out to see what was happening, but the gravestones blocked my view. By the time I'd floated up, a white car was speeding out the nearest gate like a grave robber."

"Did you get the tag number?" I asked, hoping for a break.

Theresa laughed. "We're ghosts. Why would we even think about getting a tag number? Nobody can see or hear us, except you."

Feeling frustrated, I asked, "Do you know what kinda car it was?"

"Maybe," Theresa said with a sly smile.

In the world of the living, this would be where I'd slip my informant a twenty. However, this was ghostdom, and the desires and needs are different.

I crossed my arms and huffed. "What do you want?"

"They're asking for a bribe?" Mystery asked, her eyes all squinty with disapproval.

I gave a helpless shrug.

Theresa held up two fingers. "First, I want you to tell my daughter where I hid my wedding rings. I want them passed down to my granddaughter. After that, I'll be ready to cross over."

"And your second favor?" I asked.

"They want two bribes?" Mystery asked, her tone heavy with disapproval.

"I'll explain later," I said.

Theresa pointed at Josi. "She wants to cross over really, really bad. Will you help her?"

I looked into Josi's hope-filled eyes.

"I'll do my best," I said, hoping the task was achievable.

Theresa looked over at Josi.

Josi nodded. "That's good enough for me."

Feeling generous, I looked at Margaret. "Anything I can do to help you?"

Margaret shook her head. "I'm waiting for my husband, Joe, to pass. He comes to visit every Sunday."

I took out my phone and made notes while the two ghosts told me the details of their requests and where to find Josi's grave when the time came.

That completed, I asked, "What kinda car drove away after the murder?"

Theresa smiled. "It was like my son's four-door Honda Accord, only white."

CHAPTER 39: BRIANNA

Mystery and I sat at my conference table, ready to eat sandwiches we'd brought from home.

After eyeing my peanut butter and banana sandwich with a longing expression, Mystery closed her eyes, smiled, and inhaled. "That banana smells delicious."

I ignored her while I cut the sandwich in half.

"No siree, there's nothing quite as comforting as a peanut butter and banana sandwich." Her gaze lasered in on it. I was surprised the peanut butter didn't melt.

"What kind is yours?" I asked.

"Ham and cheese."

I noticed hers was already sliced in half. "Let's trade a half sandwich."

A smile lit her face. "Great idea."

I ate a bite of her sandwich, chewed, and swallowed. "How do we find out what type and color car Sarah drives?"

"I could have Jasmine look it up, or you could call Chris and get him to pick something up and come eat with us," Mystery said through a mouthful of peanut butter. "It might give you a chance to see him."

I did an internal head shake. *First, she warns me to stop seeing him. Now she suggests an impromptu lunch date. What's with her?*

Then I smiled. "Good idea."

*

Fifteen minutes later, Chris arrived with a Hardee's burger and fries. He kissed me and nodded to Mystery. The scent of his Polo cologne jump-started my hormones. *Down, girl. Do not jump the nice detective with Mystery in the room.*

"Glad you called. I was already in line to order."

I smiled. Chris's energy felt warm and comforting, like a loving cuddle.

"We have news to share." Mystery said, shifting in her seat.

Chris adopted his neutral cop expression while unwrapping his burger. "About what?" I felt his walls go up, cutting off the warm fuzzy energy.

"The Rosa Lopez case, of course," Mystery said with a hint of aggravation.

"You mean the one that my partner warned you to stop snooping into?" Chris pinned Mystery with a disapproving gaze and took a large bite.

"I interviewed the ghosts present at the scene of the murder." I held up my hands. "If Tony wants to go talk to them himself, he's free to do so."

Chris choked. After gulping down part of his soda that smelled like Dr. Pepper, he wiped his mouth. "You know he's afraid of ghosts! He hasn't recovered from the last incident."

I gave a smug little nod. "That's why I did it."

"What did you learn?" he asked, looking interested.

I relayed the conversation we had with the spirits.

Wide-eyed, he said, "They wanted a payoff? It's like dealing with a bunch of deceased snitches. What did they want?"

I explained.

He nodded. "That's reasonable and right up your alley. So now you want to know if Sarah drives a white Honda Accord?"

"Yep."

"This is helpful information, but you know it's inadmissible in court." Chris shoved several fries into his mouth and chewed.

They smelled so good that I snitched one.

"I told Bree that haints can't testify, but it's still a clue," Mystery said.

"When I finish eating, I'll check for you."

I tried to be patient while watching him enjoy every bite. I knew he often had to bolt down a sandwich en route, so he probably wanted to enjoy this break in his day. Still, that twenty minutes felt like eons.

Still feeling amorous, I reached under the table and squeezed his thigh.

His eyes widened before he turned to smile at me.

When Chris finished eating, we followed him out to his unit. He opened the door and stepped aside to allow the sweltering heat to escape, along with the delicious smell of salty fries. After he started the car, he cranked up the air conditioner. Since the passenger seat was full of paperwork, we waited outside the car, in the beaming sun, while he accessed the system on his computer.

Mystery leaned down to look inside. "Where's Ricci? Doesn't he eat lunch with you?"

"Sometimes. Now that we're swamped with cases, he goes home to have lunch with Maria when he can. It helps to cool her jets."

Mystery and I exchanged glances.

Did he show up today to cool my jets?

He sat back in the seat, the air from the vents blowing his hair.

"Your sources are correct. Sarah owns a white Honda Accord, but that doesn't prove she killed Rosa."

"True, but it doesn't rule her out, either. Remember her reaction to Rosa at the fireworks display?"

He nodded, his expression thoughtful.

Mystery's face broke into an anticipatory smile. "When do we go talk to her?"

With a steely tone, Chris said, "You don't. Tony and I will handle it."

CHAPTER 40: BRIANNA

I wasn't looking forward to tonight's tasks, but a deal was a deal.

I drove down Dean Street in south Huntsville and stopped in front of the address of Theresa's daughter. I exited my car and paused to gather my resolve.

Unfortunately, the mature trees in the neighborhood blocked the street lights. Only patches of illumination shone on the well-manicured lawns. I was grateful for the tiny lights lining the walk that led to the porch.

I rang the doorbell, which sounded more like an unattractive buzz. The scent of Carolina jasmine triggered memories from my last case and caused my stomach to do the jitterbug. Shifting from foot to foot, I rehearsed once again in my mind what I planned to say.

A dark-haired woman who looked like a younger, healthier version of her ghost mother opened the door. She emanated a mixed energy field of apprehension and curiosity.

"Melody Hennessy?"

"Yes?" she said, before opening the door wider and stepping forward.

"This may sound strange, but I promised your mother, Theresa, I'd deliver a message to you."

Her mouth formed a perfect O. She took a step back. "What?

Who are you?"

Fear filled her energy field.

"Theresa's wedding rings are hidden in her escritoire. They are in an envelope taped under one of the bottom drawers. She wants the jewelry to go to your daughter, Cynthia. Please visit her grave and tell her Cynthia has the jewelry She won't cross over until it happens."

I turned and hurried down the steps to my car.

She stepped out onto the porch and yelled, "Wait! How do you know this?"

I pulled the door closed and sped away.

"One down and one to go." I only hoped Melody thought her mother told me about the rings before she died.

My next stop was to Josi's daughter, who lived in a new neighborhood near Toyota Field in Madison. I parked in front of Maggie Davis's home, careful to make sure I faced the right direction for a quick escape.

Please God, don't let her call the police.

This wouldn't be as easy as the last one because I knew what I had to tell her would rock her world. Unknown to Maggie, her mother had a secret rented storage unit on University Drive. Josi had told me the combination for the lock, and she was desperate for me to make an intervention soon. The rent would come due on the first day of September.

I faced the door. Clutching the paper in my hand, I thought about writing a note, wedging it in the door, and fleeing.

I can't. I gave my word.

I rang the bell.

The porch light came on.

A woman in her fifties answered, holding a paperback. Her short blonde bob was streaked with gray. She looked me up and down with a wary, narrow-eyed expression.

"May I help you?"

Her voice was melodious.

I hesitated; my words stuck like peanut butter in my mouth. "This may sound strange, but I'm trying to help your mother, Josi, cross over. She's stuck on this plane of existence because she failed to tell you the name of your biological father."

The book fell to the hardwood floor with a bang.

This is where she thinks I'm off in woo woo land and slams the door in my face.

"You're serious, aren't you?"

I nodded. "It's not easy for me to be here, but I made Josi a promise."

She opened the door wider and beckoned me inside. "I think I better hear this."

The home was bright and cheery, with an open floor plan that included the living room, dining area, and kitchen in one elongated space.

"This is pretty," I said.

"Thanks." She picked up the book and turned to face me. It was a battered copy of *13 Alabama Ghosts and Jeffery* by Kathryn Tucker Wyndham.

At least she believes in ghosts.

We sat on a blue leather sofa and angled toward each other.

She took a deep breath and said, "Who was he?"

I sat back, startled by her bluntness. "You don't sound a bit surprised."

"When I was fifteen, two of my meanest cousins spilled the beans that Mom was pregnant before she met my dad." She compressed her lips. A small smile tugged them loose. "In my mind, Jason Davis was my real dad, the man who loved and took care of me."

I nodded. "I don't know your biological father's name. Josi gave me the name of a storage facility, the code to get in the gate, and the lock combination. All the information and other things she wants you to have, have been stored there." I handed her the paper. "The rent is paid until September, so you might want to check it sooner rather than later."

She nodded. "I know this facility. I drive past it every day. I never realized the answers to my paternity were hidden there." She searched my face. "Why did you do this?"

"Um, Josi did me a favor, so I'm returning one. She wants to cross over."

"What do I owe you?"

I held up my hands in a stop gesture. "Nothing. Go find the unit and unearth your mother's secrets. Afterward, please visit her grave and tell her you found it, so she can have closure and go to the light."

Maggie's hand went to her throat. "We had a huge fight about this after my cousins dropped the genetic bombshell. She would never reveal who my sperm-donor, dead-beat father was, not even on her deathbed."

She rose abruptly. "Thank you for coming."

I was being dismissed.

"You're welcome." I stood, hesitated, then walked toward the door.

She opened it and said, "You never told me your name."

I pasted on my most cryptic smile. "No, I didn't."

*

Once I was back home, I called Mom.

"How is my beautiful daughter?"

"Okay, I guess. I sure can use your help here," I said, sounding a little down, even to me.

"Tell me."

I explained about my last case involving Victoria and about Rosa's antics.

There was a pause. "You have been busy. I need to work with you in person in order to train you to handle a dangerous ghost. Can you meet me in St. Augustine? My former college roommate, Betsy, needs my help. We can use it as a training opportunity."

"That's a great idea." I felt my shoulders relax. "What about Rosa? Any suggestions for handling her?"

She reminded me of the strength of my power before telling me what to try.

"So, this will work?" I asked, feeling unsure.

"Yes. Have faith in yourself and your gifts."

"I'll try."

"Trying is lying, either you do or you don't." She paused. "Why don't you ask Mystery to come with you? She'd enjoy St. Augustine. Betsy can give her some tips on ghost tours. It would be fun," she said, followed by a lilting laugh.

"I'll ask her."

After Mom answered the rest of my questions, we worked out a date to go to the oldest continually occupied city in the United States.

CHAPTER 41: BRIANNA

Mystery and I sat in Ted's Bar-B-Q eating pork sandwiches with slaw and sauce. We had decided we were too tired that night to go far for food.

"I had a good day today," Mystery said, wiping sauce off her cheek. "I wish my sales were this good every day."

"I had a busy day, too. It was about equal lingerie and chocolate sales."

"I've been thinking about expanding my ghost tours to every weekend. But first, I need to see how some other folks are running their businesses." She grinned. "I'm even thinking of getting a passenger van."

I pasted on a serious expression. "That's great! Tiffany can drive while you give the history."

"What!" She sat straight. "Have you lost your ever-lovin' mind? That woman is a five-car collision waiting to happen. I'll get sued because someone will have a heart attack, not from any haints, but from her driving."

I started laughing.

Her chin jutted forward. "You only said that to set me off on a tirade."

"Girl, you took off like a bottle rocket." I smiled. "I have a proposal."

"What? It better be good after that stunt."

"Mom and I are meeting in St. Augustine next month. You ought to come with me. The place is crawling with ghost tour companies."

She fiddled with an earring while she looked up as if searching for her thoughts on the ceiling. Finally, she looked down to meet my gaze and smiled. "That would be great! Why are y'all going? Vacation?"

"Sorta. I've always wanted to see the place. There's so much history there." I paused to sip my iced tea. "Mom and I need some time together. She wants to train me to handle malevolent ghosts by helping a friend who has a dangerous poltergeist."

Mystery rested her chin in her hand. "Good idea. We've had a few of those pop up lately."

"Exactly." I leaned closer to avoid being overheard. "Mom told me I'm more powerful than she is, but I don't believe it. She has some weird theory that my dad has some Irish fairy blood in his lineage."

"Did you say 'fairy'?" She looked both ways and lowered her voice. "Like Tinkerbell? I didn't think they were real."

I shrugged. "Who knows? I've never seen one, but Mom sure believes in them."

Mystery sat back and rolled her eyes. "Did Olivia smoke too much weed in college or something?"

I shrugged again.

She laughed. "If it's true, that would drive logical Sean over the edge."

I pictured my Irish granny telling my father about his fairy ancestors and chuckled. "He'd never believe it." I pulled my napkin from my lap and wiped my hands. "Either way, I need to be able to hold my own with dangerous ghosts."

"Amen to that!"

"Like I was saying, one of the people who owns a ghost tour business down there was Mom's old college roommate when they attended Sewanee."

"Don't they call that The University of the South?"

"Yep." I flipped my hair over my shoulders to keep it out of my plate. "It's a pretty campus. Unfortunately, her friend, Betsy, has been having problems with a spirit injuring her customers. So, the trip's a three-fer."

"Vacation, training, and haint removal?" Mystery asked.

"Something like that. Not sure how Mom will handle the naughty spook."

"You sure I won't be horning in?" she asked, wrinkling her brow.

I waved a dismissive hand. "Mom and I have already discussed it. I planned to ask you about it tonight." I took another bite of my sandwich. *I hope the tips for handling Rosa work.*

Mystery looked pleased. She leaned forward. "How did your assignment go?"

I held up a finger while I finished chewing. "Better than I thought." I explained what had happened.

She pantomimed wiping sweat off her forehead with the back of her hand. "Sugar, I wondered how you would manage all of that."

"That was easy compared to what we're doing tonight."

Mystery sat back, her eyes wide. "What do you have in mind?"

"We need to question Ron."

"Sweet baby Jesus! I was afraid you'd say that."

*

We parked and walked to Ron's front door like we'd been invited and knew what we were doing.

What is that saying, "Fake it until you make it?"

Ron answered with a smile, which morphed to round-eyed alarm. He tried to close the door, but we pushed our way in.

"Now, wait a minute!" He looked full of righteous indignation.

Mystery got in his face. "You wait. It's time to come clean. If you don't know who killed Rosa, you have a dang good idea."

"Well, I..." He clamped his mouth shut and crossed his arms.

I placed a hand on my cocked hip. "I can handle Rosa if you tell us."

He huffed. "Nobody can handle her. I'm doomed forever."

I stepped closer to Mystery and whispered, "Hug him."

I lowered my shields and centralized my energy as Mom advised last night.

Mystery threw her arms around Ron and kissed him.

His eyes widened in surprise, and he seemed frozen in place.

I heard a thump in the living room to our left.

I pulled Rosa into manifesting so I could see her, then energetically shoved her into a nearby corner. "Stay."

She struggled but couldn't get free. She glared at me with a combination of shock and malice.

It worked! "This is your chance to tell us who murdered you," I said.

Her response wasn't friendly or helpful.

"Why don't you want justice so you can cross over?" I asked.

"I'm staying with him." She pointed at Ron. "He's mine."

I passed on the information to my non-psychic friends.

Mystery looked angry.

Ron looked defeated.

"Ron, if you tell us what you know, I'll ban her from your home forever."

Rosa struggled again. "You can't do that! This is *my* home."

"She seems to think this is now her home," I said.

Ron's gaze met mine. "Can you really do that, banish her from my life?"

"Only from a location like your property, office, or car," I said.

He leaned against a doorframe. "I can't keep going like this. I'm not able to sleep or eat anymore. I'm terrified."

"You better not let her banish me," Rosa threatened, but he couldn't hear her.

He held up his hands as if surrendering and then lowered them. "I placed the flowers on Carol's grave that morning, said a prayer, and left. I had this strange sensation that I was being watched."

"Did you check it out?" Mystery asked.

He shook his head. "I needed to hurry to the office. I had a new employee starting that day. Sarah had phoned the night before to tell me she planned to drop by that morning to pay respects to Carol. I was pulling out of the cemetery when I saw a white car turn onto McClung. Sarah drives a white Honda, but I couldn't tell the make at that distance. Like I said, I was running late."

Mystery placed her hands on her hips. "Did you tell this to the police?"

He shook his head again. "All I had was suspicion. I didn't want to get Sarah in trouble." He gave me a pleading look. "Will you get Rosa out of my hair?"

I crossed my arms. "Only under two conditions. First, you tell one of the detectives working the case what you told us about Sarah and Rosa's conflict with each other and what you saw that day at the cemetery. Second, that you tell Rosa the truth about your feelings for her before I banish her."

"Okay. Where is Rosa?" he asked, looking around.

I pointed at the corner where Rosa seethed, rage contorting her face.

Ron turned to face her. "I was vulnerable when I met you because my angel, the woman I loved with all my heart, was dying. I betrayed her with you and have felt guilt and regret ever since."

Rosa reached toward him. "That's not true. We loved each other."

I relayed her message.

He sighed. "The only woman I've ever loved was Carol. I've never loved you, and you don't love me. There's a difference between obsession and love. I was only a secure means for you to leave your bad marriage."

Rosa drooped, crying translucent tears. "That's not true."

I pulled my phone from my purse. "Chris, I need you to come to Ron Jeffery's house."

"Why? Are you snooping again?"

I explained the situation.

"I'm coming." His tone sounded exasperated.

*

Twenty long minutes later, the doorbell rang. We were still in the foyer, sitting on the stairs because I wasn't sure I could keep Rosa's spirit penned if she wasn't in sight. All of this was new to me.

Ron opened the door, barely missing a swipe of Rosa's hand.

Chris walked in.

"Stay away from that corner," I warned, pointing toward Rosa.

Chris had no idea what was happening but veered away from the area. He pulled out his phone to record the conversation and began questioning Ron, who once again shared what he knew.

When the interview was finished, Chris looked my way. "Thanks. Tony and I'll talk with Sarah Shaffer tomorrow."

Rosa glared at me. "If you banish me from Ron, I'll haunt his friends."

"I wouldn't advise it," I said.

She roared a maniacal laugh.

Ron, unaware of Rosa's threat, looked at me. "Ban her. I've had it."

"Ban who?" Chris looked at Mystery, who was the only other female that he could see.

I explained the situation to Chris, who backed further away from the corner.

I gathered my energy and released it while I yelled, "I banish you from all of Ron Jeffery's property, including his home, cars, business, and the grounds."

Rosa was screaming, "Noooo," when she was sucked from sight.

"She's gone," I said.

Everyone but Chris sagged with relief. He was hyperalert, brows raised. "What just happened?"

"Mystery, it's time for us to go. I know Ron is looking forward to a good night's sleep." I jerked my head toward the door. "We can talk to Chris out by the cars."

Ron thanked me and closed the door. It sounded like he locked every lock he had.

We remained silent while going down the brick walk, which was pretty but not level.

Chris leaned against his car and crossed his arms and ankles. "What happened in there?"

I explained the banishing procedure while he tried to maintain his cop face—which slipped a few times.

I crossed my arms and cocked a hip. "What time are we going to interview Sarah and Jack Shaffer?"

He shifted to stand straight. "You're not going."

"Rosa Lopez's ghost is spitting mad about being banished from Ron's property."

Chris interrupted, "Are you sure that can be done?"

"Yes, it can. If the Shaffers did murder Rosa, she's probably haunting them now and will follow them everywhere." I paused to let that sink in. "Do you want Tony to deal with an angry ghost in the interrogation room without me?"

Chris ran a hand down his face and then shook his head. "Okay. I'll call you when we set it up."

Mystery planted both hands on her hips. "If Bree is going, so am I."

CHAPTER 42: BRIANNA

Mystery and I sat in the conference room at the police station, sipping coffee from Styrofoam cups. The whole space smelled of the brew. We decided to wait here until the Shaffers arrived.

"At least the coffee isn't burnt this time," Mystery said.

I chuckled, looking down at the concoction in my cup. The java was finally palatable after three sugars and a ton of creamer. "It's seven-thirty in the morning. There hasn't been time for it to burn yet."

Tony and Chris ambled into the room and took turns filling their mugs with the dark brew. They sat opposite us at the large oval table.

Tony chanced a sip and winced. "What's the plan to handle the ghost?"

I raised my index finger. "Plan one: Place Sarah and Jack in the interview room. If Rosa isn't there, you can proceed as normal, and I'll stand by in the observation room in case she shows up."

Chris leaned forward on his elbows, hands cupping his mug. "What's plan two?"

"If Rosa is there, I'll make a noise and hope she pokes her head through the one-way mirror."

"What happens then?" Mystery asked.

"I'll pull her into the room with me and banish her from the police station."

Looking paler by the minute, Tony asked, "What if she won't leave the room?"

"I'll go in with you under the guise of taking notes and confine her in a corner. Then, when I have her pinned, you can use some excuse to take the Shaffers out of the room. Once they're gone, give me a few minutes and I'll ban her from the station."

Tony wiped the sweat from his forehead with a white handkerchief. He placed it back into his pocket and smoothed his Casper the Friendly Ghost tie.

I grinned. *Got to give Tony credit; he has a sense of humor.*

"New tie?" I asked, arching a brow.

"Dr. Stone suggested I get it to remind me that some ghosts are only friendly, lost souls."

"That's true, but it's not the case today," Mystery said, looking around. "I almost hope she doesn't show up."

Tony nodded. "Me too. Can't you just ban her ahead of time?"

"Nope. I have to have her in sight in order to do it," I said.

Chris escorted Mystery and me into the observation room. He squeezed my hand. "Wish us luck."

Mystery moved closer to the mirror to eyeball the room on the other side. "Not much in there."

"How much stuff do you want in a room while interviewing dangerous, hardened criminals?" I asked.

She backed up. "Good point." She sat in a chair placed four feet from the one-way mirror. "Is this the same room where you saw the line-up during our first case?"

"No. That was a long narrow room with no furniture. It had a height chart on the back wall."

I heard the door opening in the next room. Bending, I whispered in Mystery's ear. "Be quiet! They can hear us if we're too loud."

Chris entered first, then the Shaffers, followed by Tony, who directed Sarah and Jack to the seats facing the mirror. Chris and Tony took the two chairs on the ends.

The preppy-looking Sarah I'd met at the fireworks wasn't the same woman who sat at the metal table facing the mirror. She looked pale; the whites surrounding her blue eyes were a roadmap of red lines. She glanced around in an almost paranoid way while rubbing her arms.

Is she cold or scared? Or both?

Jack frowned at one detective, then at the other. He was sweating despite the air-conditioned room.

Rosa ghosted through the door and hovered behind Jack, her arms crossed.

"There's Rosa," I pointed, even though I knew Mystery couldn't see the ghost.

"I don't know why we're here. We've done nothing wrong," Jack said.

Rosa's face began contorting into a mask of rage.

Jack's breath puffed out like fluffy clouds.

Ice began forming on the corners of the mirror, moving toward the center at a rapid pace. A ping alerted me to a crack in the glass surface.

"Oh, crap!" I yanked Mystery to her feet.

"What?" she blurted.

I raced toward the door, pulling her with me. Then, flinging the door open, I pushed her through and followed.

The automatic mechanism began closing the heavy metal door at a snail's pace. The one-way mirror exploded into a spray of sparkling glass shards that peppered the opposite wall just before the door closed with a bang.

Mystery backed against the wall, holding her hand over her bosom. "Did you see that!"

Fury flooded my veins like liquid fire. I stomped to the interrogation room and jerked the door open.

When I stepped inside, my breath fogged.

Papers whirled around the room.

Tony was under the table. "Do something!"

Sarah sobbed, barely visible under Jack's bulk as he did his best to shield her.

Chris was grabbing papers as they flew past his face.

"Catch me if you can." Rosa shot past me and through the wall.

I wrestled the heavy door open again and sprinted into the hall. I looked one way and then the other.

A woman's yelp, followed by male cursing, alerted me to go right.

I dashed past closed doors and skidded into the conference room where we had started the morning. A screaming woman almost mowed me down while trying to escape.

Officer Jackson, from the murder scene at the cemetery, stood, gun drawn, in a Weaver stance. He moved his Glock from side to side, searching for his invisible attacker.

I raised my hands. "Don't shoot!"

He glanced my way.

A row of coffee cups hit the floor.

He aimed toward the disturbance.

"It's a ghost. You can't kill her because she's already dead," I said.

"Aren't you the chick from the cemetery?" Jackson said.

Before I could answer, Rosa shot me a malicious smile before lofting a sugar container at him.

Jackson ducked and fired a shot.

I dropped to one knee.

Rosa flew through the wall back into the hall.

"As I live and breathe!" I followed her.

She ghosted her way through a door.

Rushing to it, I whipped it open and ran inside.

I skidded to a stop.

The older policeman had his back to me. The smell of urine filled the room. He glanced over his shoulder and mumbled some curses. The zip of his fly sent a rush of heat to my face.

"Sorry." I backed out the door, hand over my mouth.

"Bree, what were you doing in the men's room?" Mystery asked.

"Chasing Rosa."

"What was she doing in there?"

"Embarrassing me," I said while looking down the hall for the ghost.

Following my intuition, I eased back toward the interrogation room and stepped inside. I found Rosa floating with crossed arms, glaring at the Shaffers.

Jack had his arm around Sarah's shoulder while he mumbled, "It's going to be all right."

"Not for me," Rosa said, looking both sad and angry.

You're not getting away this time. I pulled in my anger-fueled energy and shouted, "Freeze!"

The results were instant. Rosa froze in place.

Sarah screamed before sliding out of her chair and under the table.

Jack whirled, his face contorted and fists clenched. He tackled me.

My head slammed against the floor. Air whooshed from my lungs.

Chris rushed over. "Get off her," he ordered, grabbing Jack by the collar.

Jackson raced in the door and helped to wrestle the brute off me.

I lay, arms and legs splayed, trying to gulp a breath, but I couldn't. My vision started to gray out and went black.

*

I opened my eyes to find a dark-haired man with brown eyes leaning over me. There was an oxygen mask over my face. I tried to take a deep breath but couldn't quite manage it. It took me a minute to remember what happened.

"Ma'am, my name is Jeff. I'm a paramedic. "Does anything hurt?" he asked. His voice reverberated inside my head like a bouncing ping pong ball.

I closed my eyes, waiting for the pain to subside. *Geez, I'm not deaf. Jack just knocked the breath out of me.* I opened my eyes but didn't have enough breath to say anything but, "Head."

Chris knelt beside me and took my hand. "She hit her head when she was tackled."

Things were a bit fuzzy, but I was managing to follow the conversation.

Jeff looked at Chris, then back down at me. "Who tackled her?"

Chris nodded somewhere to his right.

I wasn't willing to turn my head to see who or what was over there, but I could hear Tony Mirandizing someone.

After following Chris's gaze, Jeff shook his head. "This lady is lucky she's not dead. Did you see the size of that guy?"

I managed a deeper breath. "You should try...having him slam you...to the floor."

"Do you feel dizzy or have a headache?" Jeff asked.

"Head...hurts."

A blond, younger guy wearing the same uniform shirt asked Chris to move. He lifted my arm, wrapped on a blood pressure cuff, and pumped it up to a vein-popping level.

232

"Hank, when you finish that, let's put a neck restraint on her in case she has a neck or spinal injury," Jeff said, sounding worried.

Spinal injury!

Over the next several minutes, Jeff asked me questions before making me move my fingers and toes and track a moving light with my eyes.

"Is she going to be okay?" Mystery asked, her voice shaky. When she moved into my line of vision, she was hyperventilating and looked close to having a panic attack. I tried to smile to make her feel better, but my effort was feeble.

"We're taking her to the ER in case she has a concussion or more serious injuries," Jeff said.

I wanted to protest that I was fine, but I was still struggling to breathe, and my vision was becoming hazy again.

In my peripheral vision I saw Ricci lead a cuffed Jack past me and out the door.

Chris knelt and leaned close. He whispered, "Is it safe?" His eyes were wide as saucers. "Is Rosa contained or whatever the heck you do?"

I shook my head and instantly regretted it. Everything went black again.

CHAPTER 43: BRIANNA

A strong aroma of chocolate woke me. I opened my eyes and blinked until I could focus them.

I felt like a knot of tiny dwarves were mining with picks inside my head. I reached up to touch my forehead and groaned.

Mystery leaned over me, blasting me with chocolate breath. "You're awake! Don't go anywhere."

She ran into the hall. I heard her yell several times that I was awake. Her words created an echo in my mind, causing me to wince.

I looked at the IV sticking out of my hand. A contraption somewhere to my right was blipping.

Where does she think I can go?

Mystery returned, shooing a nurse in blue scrubs into the room.

The nurse replaced her look of annoyance with a kind smile when she saw I was awake. "Hi there, I'm Julie, your nurse tonight."

She asked me a ton of questions about my vision, pain level, and dizziness, among other things.

"Why am I here?" I asked. The last thing I remembered was lying on the floor at the police station.

"The doctor will be here to explain everything in a moment."

Rushing back to my bedside, Mystery patted my sheet-covered knee. "You scared the bejesus out of me. I nearly had a panic attack." She placed her hand over her heart. "After you passed out, I thought Chris would go down the hall to beat the you-know-what out of Jack."

I moved my head. The movement sent a flash of pain across my vision. "He didn't, did he?"

"No. Tony calmed him down." Her eyes were round as saucers. "It was close."

I wanted to say more, but my throat was dry. I tried to swallow, but my tongue felt like heavy grit sandpaper.

"Water."

"Right." Mystery reached over somewhere and grabbed a cup. She placed a straw between my lips.

I sipped a little of the cool liquid. "Where's Chris?"

"He'll be here in a few minutes and is staying with you tonight. He told the staff you needed police protection," she said, still looking worried.

Before I could say anything more, a rotund man wearing green scrubs breezed into the room. His gray hair circled his bald spot, and the section above his ears stood at attention, making it appear that he had an additional set of ears. He paused to pull the stethoscope from around his neck.

"I'm Dr. Holloway. I hear you were tackled by a mountain of a man."

Mystery nodded. "You should've seen it, Doc. The guy was huge. It was scary."

"We've done a CT scan, and you have a mild-to-moderate concussion. Only five to ten percent of people lose consciousness like you did, so we're keeping you overnight to make sure no brain swelling occurs. We also did x-rays. There are no spinal injuries, broken bones, or internal injuries that we've found. However, there's some bruising on your back where you hit the floor. You are one lucky lady."

"That's good," I said, although I felt lousy. The only thing that didn't seem to hurt was my nose.

Mystery crossed her arms. "If she was lucky, she wouldn't have been tackled."

The doctor proceeded to poke and prod while asking the same questions the nurse had already asked. Then, after checking my eyes with a blinding light that spiked my headache, he said, "If all goes well tonight, you'll be released tomorrow. We'll provide a list of things to avoid doing. I suggest you follow up with your physician in a day or two."

"Thanks." My stomach grumbled. "Can I have something to eat?" I asked.

"I don't see why not, since you're not nauseated and you don't need surgery. I'll tell the nurse to make it light. Let us know if your headache and blurred vision worsen."

Chris walked in the door and stopped.

Dr. Holloway didn't seem to notice. He continued, "I want you home and resting for two days. No strenuous exercise or mental gymnastics."

Mystery spoke up. "I'll call Kaya. We'll make sure your shop is covered."

"I'm sure I can go to work." I shot Dr. Holloway my best Prissy look. "I own a chocolate and lingerie shop. I won't do any heavy lifting."

"If you hadn't been unconscious when you arrived, I would say, okay." He crossed his arms. "You've been out longer than you realize, so I suggest lots of sleep so your brain can heal faster."

"No problem," Chris said with authority. "I've taken two days off. I'll be taking care of her."

The doctor whirled to face Chris, who stood behind him.

"Sorry, I didn't mean to alarm you," Chris said, offering a hand to shake.

Dr. Holloway shook it and looked back at me, and smiled. "Glad to know your husband will be seeing to your well-being."

Mystery burst into guffaws, one hand covering her mouth as if to hold the outburst inside, the other clutching her stomach.

The doctor looked confused.

Chris said with an impish grin, "We're not married...yet."

My jaw dropped. *Yet!*

"Well, um, good." The doctor ran a hand over his bald pate. "I'll check on you later." He left without a backward glance.

Mystery was now holding her stomach with both hands, still unable to control her laughter.

I glared at her, though it cost me. "It wasn't that funny."

She managed to straighten and wiped laugh tears from her eyes. Chris placed a white paper bag on the rolling tray table and leaned in to kiss me. "I brought you some vegetable soup from Panera."

That perked me up. I smiled up at him. "You're my hero twice in one day."

He blushed. "I don't feel like a hero."

Occasional giggles still bubbled out of Mystery.

Wincing, I pushed myself up in the bed and fumbled with the remote to elevate the head.

Chris rolled the table up to me, took the soup container out of the bag, and pulled the top off.

The smell of the hot concoction caused my empty stomach to rumble.

I was probably unconscious when lunch was served.

The crinkle of the clear plastic covering for the flatware and napkin seemed extraordinarily loud. All my senses seemed heightened.

Mystery came over and patted my shoulder. "I'll leave you in Chris's hands." A giggle escaped. "Y'all behave, now."

"Thanks," I said, my voice sounding weak.

She left, but I heard her giggling in the hallway.

Strange. Is her behavior due to stress or her relief that I didn't die? My stomach grumbled again, reminding me to eat. I spooned the soup into my mouth and let the melody of flavors play across my tongue. "Yum! Thanks, it's just what I needed."

Chris smiled. "I'm going to answer some work emails and texts while you eat, if that's okay?"

"Works for me."

The silence was both comfortable and restorative to my overloaded senses. While eating, I tried to assemble my fractured thoughts about the events that led to my being squashed flatter than a fritter by Jack. I couldn't recall doing anything but yelling, "Freeze." *I didn't move toward them or anything. What triggered Jack to react that way?*

Before I realized it, I'd finished the last drop of the soup. I wiped my mouth and hands. "That was wonderful. I already feel better."

Chris lowered his phone and smiled. "I'm glad." A furrow formed between his brows. "I feel so guilty. I should've been there to protect you from Jack."

"I was so busy chasing Rosa, I'm not sure you could've kept up."

"When Jackson discharged his weapon, Tony and I thought someone had been shot, so we ran to the conference room."

I rolled my eyes and regretted it when a sizzle of fire shot across my forehead. "Is Jackson in trouble?"

"What do you think?" Chris shook his head. "He fired his weapon in the police station at an unseen assailant, for chrissake."

"So, when Jack tackled me, you were in the conference room?" I asked, feeling confused. My thoughts were slowly lining up.

"I heard you yell, "Freeze," so I ran back to the conference room. When I arrived, Jack was on top of you. Sarah was screaming and crying under the table. What the heck happened?"

I started with escaping the exploding glass and then explained the entire chase from the conference room to the men's room, then back to the interrogation room.

Chris chuckled. "We heard about you disturbing Andy's flow at the urinal. The guy may not be able to pee straight again."

Heat flooded my face while I relived the moment. "If Rosa wasn't already dead, I could've strangled her at that moment."

"What happened in the conference room?"

I explained the situation in more detail. "Jackson was under attack, but I'd warned him that it was a ghost and that his weapon was useless."

"Bullets can pierce walls and travel a long distance. Jackson's round missed an officer sitting at his desk by inches."

"That was a close call," I said.

"We'll need an official statement when you feel up to it," Chris said.

I clenched my bottom lip between my teeth while trying to decide. "Can we just discuss it now and make it official tomorrow? I need to decompress but I'm still kinda dizzy and feeling tired."

He pulled the chair close to the bed and took my hand. "Sure."

In more detail, I described what had happened in the conference room and my confusion about Jack's reaction. By the time I finished, my eyelids were closing.

Chris lowered the head of the bed and pulled my covers up. "Take a nap. I'm right here to protect you."

His warm hand took mine before I drifted to sleep.

I woke feeling cold and pulled the thin blanket higher. I looked to my right.

Chris still held my hand. He slouched low in the chair, lightly snoring.

I settled back into my pillow before glancing around the room for the air-conditioning vent that blasted the cold air.

Rosa levitated in the left corner.

I sucked in a breath.

"Don't worry. I'm not pissed off at you anymore."

"Is that what you call it?" I asked. "You need to enter an anger management group for ghosts."

"All I wanted was a good man to love and to take care of me." She cocked her head. "And a couple of kids, so Mom would stop hassling me." Her shoulders drooped. "I failed on all counts."

I was tempted to remind her that trying to steal another woman's husband while on her deathbed isn't the correct way to go about it. I knew I wasn't up to another tantrum, so I kept my mouth shut.

Rosa shook her head. "I kept picking the wrong guy."

"You aren't alone. It's a problem for many women," I said, while rubbing my temple.

"You ever pick a loser?"

I laughed, sending a jolt of pain across my forehead. "I've had my fair share."

She pointed at Chris. "You're lucky. I think he's a keeper."

I looked at him and smiled. "The jury is still out, but I think you may be right."

"I didn't mean for you to get hurt," Rosa said. "Now you know how I felt when Jack plowed into me."

I stiffened. "What happened?"

"They pulled to the curb, and Sarah shot out of the car and hurtled toward me. While Jack was still in the car, Sarah and I started fighting over the flowers. We were doing our best to yank each other bald. The minute I shoved Sarah to the ground, he came out of nowhere and slugged me like a sledgehammer. It was an automatic reaction. He didn't hesitate a minute."

That caught my attention. I powered the head of the bed up a bit. "When I yelled, 'Freeze" at you, Sarah screamed and slid under the table. Jack tackled me immediately. It seems like any threat to her triggers Jack to protect her."

Rosa nodded. "He's a loaded gun of fury. She strikes me as emotionally fragile. When I worked as a nurse for the Jeffery's, Carol comforted Sarah more than Sarah supported Carol."

"Tell me every detail of what happened in the cemetery again," I said.

She did.

"If you'll let me, I can help the police convict Jack," I said.

"How? Dios mío, I'm a ghost! I can't testify in court."

I explained my plan.

She listened intently and nodded. "That just might work. What do I do?"

"First, I want you to haunt the Shaffers, especially Sarah. She's the weak link. Jack's already proven he'll do anything to protect her."

She rubbed her jaw. "De veras. He hits hard."

"Second, stay out of the police station."

Rosa laughed. "You should've seen your face when you walked in on that cop pissing."

I crossed my arms and glared at her. "Do you want my help or not?"

She covered her mouth to stop a giggle. "You have to admit it was funny."

"Fine, I don't have to help you." I raised my chin and turned away from her. The motion set off a rock drummer inside my head.

"Sorry." She floated closer. "Yeah, I want your help."

"Then, stay away from the police station!"

"I will." She raised her right hand like she was being sworn in to testify.

"Good. Don't you have some folks to haunt?"

She gave a jaunty salute. "Sí, señorita. Good luck." She then ghosted through the wall.

CHAPTER 44: BRIANNA

I'd been released into Chris's care and given permission for a short stop at the police station to make a statement. To my surprise, I still felt hypersensitive to light, noise, and scents, so I shoved my sunglasses onto my nose for the trip there.

Chris helped me out of the car. "You sure you're okay to do this?"

In truth, I felt like a professional wrestler had body-slammed me about ten times.

"No, but I want it finished."

I was moving like an arthritic old woman and wondered if I'd ever feel normal again.

"Did the doctor give you any pain medication?" Chris asked.

"Only Tylenol. He doesn't want me to have anything else for several more days. I think he's worried I might spring a leak in my brain or something."

Once inside, Chris led me to an interrogation room I'd never seen before. The room smelled of Lysol.

"We'll take your statement here. The other one is undergoing repairs."

"I'm not surprised. That one-way mirror is history." I eased into a chair and breathed through the pain.

He patted my shoulder. "I'll be back in a minute with Tony. Do you want coffee?"

"No. Thanks." The thought of burnt, late-morning coffee didn't appeal to me.

Chris left the room and closed the door, sealing in the silence.

I looked at the one-way mirror and began to shake. I relived the shards of glass hitting the wall yesterday like I was back in the event.

*

Sarah slid down the chair under the table. Jack rose from his chair and turned toward me with a look of pure violence. The full-body hit slammed me to the floor. His massive bulk crushed my chest so my breath couldn't get past my throat.

*

When the door opened, the sounds of the station rushed in, sucking me back to the present moment.

Chris knelt by my side. "Are you okay? You're white as rice."

I gulped a few breaths, realizing I'd stopped breathing. "Flashback."

Tony took the chair opposite me. "I've had a few of those. Scary stuff."

Chris stood and handed me a bottle of cold water. "I remembered the nurse said to keep you hydrated."

"Thanks." I unscrewed the cap and sipped some, letting the sensation of swallowing ground me.

Chris sat next to Tony. They turned on the equipment, did the initial interrogation ritual, and we began. We were finished within fifteen minutes.

After turning everything off, I asked, "What happened to Jack?" I still felt shaky.

"We booked him for assault in the first degree, which is a Class B felony," Tony rubbed his forehead. "He's already lawyered up and is out on bail." Anger flashed across his features before he resumed a neutral cop expression. "He didn't even spend the night in jail."

"Will he get away with it?" I asked, feeling vulnerable.

Chris shook his head. "We have the whole thing on tape."

"Can I see it? I need to reconcile this in my mind."

The two detectives looked at each other.

"Are you sure you want to do this, Brianna?" Tony asked.

"Yes. I need to see it."

242

Mom always said the only way to survive my psychic gifts was to face my fears head-on. I needed to do the same with this attack.

We moved down the hall to a room with a computer. Chris left and ten minutes later returned with a thumb drive. He leaned over me, keyed in a code, and plugged in the drive. The smell of his Polo cologne was comforting.

Seeing the events from the camera's view near the ceiling was strange. First, Sarah screamed and slid below the table. Then, just as I remembered, Jack rose, lowered his shoulder like an offensive tackle, and creamed me. No hesitation at all.

"This makes sense to me now," I said, stretching to ease my muscles.

"What makes sense?" Chris asked, placing his warm hand on my shoulder.

"I'm ready to give my unofficial statement."

Tony's eyes widened. "What do you mean?"

"Rosa visited my room last night."

Chris stiffened. "What? When?" He huffed. "I was there and didn't see or hear anything."

I patted his hand. "While you were sleeping. I woke up cold, and there Rosa was, floating in the corner. She felt bad that I'd been hurt."

Tony eyed me with curiosity. "What else did she say?"

"Rosa told me about the murder. I know this isn't admissible in court, but I think if you use what she told me, Sarah will cave."

The two men looked at each other again.

Since they didn't say no, I started.

"Rosa followed Ron to the cemetery that day. She hid behind a large headstone and watched him put the flowers on Carol's grave. She said he leaned against the stone and talked for a while, and cried."

A sharp twinge of pain stole my breath for a moment.

"His graveside visit made Rosa furious. In her obsessed mind, Ron loved and belonged to her. So, it infuriated her to overhear his words of love and his apology for the affair. When he drove away, she walked to the grave and saw it was the exact arrangement of flowers that Ron had brought Carol every week while she was ill. The whole scene was too much for her."

Chris rubbed his chin. "Sounds like Rosa was consumed by this fantasy relationship with Ron."

"Still is, because Rosa felt Ron was her ticket to everything she ever wanted. She still wants him in death, but she may have to contend with Carol if she reaches the other side."

Tony nodded. "My wife would be that way."

"Rosa picked up the flowers and planned to throw them away when she heard a car pull up."

Chris leaned forward. "Who was it?

"The Shaffers. Rosa said Sarah bolted from the Honda before Jack had even stopped it."

Looking impatient, Tony tapped his finger on the table.

"The two women were scratching each other and pulling hair like feral cats over the flowers Ron put on Carol's grave. Rosa gained the upper hand and shoved Sarah, who tumbled to the ground."

I paused to catch my breath. My bruised ribs protested any efforts toward a deep breath.

Brow furrowed with concern, Chris leaned closer and touched my hand. "Do you need some Tylenol?"

I gently shook my head, pleased that my brain didn't feel like gelatin sloshing around anymore.

"Rosa said that she looked up in time to see Jack hurtle toward her like a stampeding bison. He hit her with his right fist. She flew off her feet and hit the corner of Carol's gravestone."

"His immediate protective attack sounds similar to the one on you," Chris said.

I nodded. "Do you remember Jack's reaction to Rosa at the fireworks and Ron saying, 'Sarah's high-strung, and Jack will do anything to protect her'?"

"Now that you mention it, yeah," Chris said, looking pensive.

"So, this sounds like a case of voluntary manslaughter, not murder," Tony said, smoothing his Daffy Duck tie.

"Seems that way. Rosa agreed to stop haunting everyone and cross over if Jack is arrested and charged for her death," I said, holding the ribs on my left side.

"That's comforting," Chris said with a smirk. "Now, all we need is a confession or tangible evidence."

"I have a plan," I said.

"Mio Dio!" Tony sat back in his chair. "I'm not sure I want to hear this. Does it involve a spook-chase, discharged weapons, and a charging former college football right tackle?"

"As I live and breathe, I certainly hope not." My hand rubbed my ribs. "The weak link is Sarah. If y'all tell them you have an eyewitness to the event, it will get their attention."

Tony nodded. "I'm listening."

"Then, tell them the step-by-step progression of what happened. Sarah will believe you. Jack will know y'all have them dead to rights."

Chris smiled. "It's the truth. We don't have to reveal the witness is a ghost."

"You've got the idea," I said. "The Shaffers will assume it's a living witness. Make sure you start with Sarah and list all the charges she will face. I'm counting on Jack to do almost anything to protect her."

"What about Rosa?" Tony asked with a wary tone.

"What about her?" I countered with a teasing one.

He frowned. "Will Rosa be present or not? We don't need another...incident."

"I negotiated that, too. Rosa offered sincere apologies for her bad behavior and agreed to stay away from the police station."

Tony's hitched-up shoulders lowered. "Good. I had an emergency appointment with Dr. Stone yesterday after work. By the way, she wishes you a speedy recovery."

I smiled. "I'm glad my referral to Doc is helping." I rubbed my hands together. "So, when do you plan to interview Sarah?"

Tony sighed. "Let me guess, you want to observe the interrogation."

I grinned. "Of course. I have to make a report to Rosa. If you would prefer for Rosa to be present..."

Tony raised both hands. "That won't be necessary."

CHAPTER 45: BRIANNA

After lunch and a nap, I sat behind the one-way mirror next to Mystery. When she discovered from Jasmine, who heard it from Kaya, that I could observe Sarah's interrogation, she phoned Tony and raised Cain until he agreed she could come, too. She used the old "Brianna may-need-emotional-support" ploy.

Sarah faced the observation mirror, sitting next to her attorney, Harris Parker. I didn't think Sarah could look worse than the last time I'd seen her, but she did. Her unwashed blonde hair looked drab and hung in strings. She wasn't wearing makeup, and the dark circles under her eyes looked like bruised grapes.

"Man, she looks awful, like they drug her straight out of bed after a bout of the flu," Mystery said.

"Rosa's been haunting the couple, so Sarah's probably sleep deprived, bless her heart. Being cuffed and brought in for questioning couldn't have been pleasant either," I said, thinking about my sleepless nights as a child, trying to pretend the specters didn't exist.

Sarah's attorney was her opposite in appearance. Parker was dark-haired, well-groomed, and impeccably dressed in a charcoal suit with a burgundy tie. Everything about him screamed exorbitant legal fees.

The door to the observation room opened.

We turned and a woman walked inside. I recognized her from

the news.

I nudged Mystery and whispered, "That's assistant district attorney Marge Johnson."

She looked professional in a dark blue suit, crisp white blouse, and heels. She paused before pulling an empty chair next to me. After she had settled into her seat and introductions were whispered, she asked, "Which one of you is the psychic?"

Mystery pointed at me.

She eyed me up and down. "The stories about your ghost chase are hot news around the courthouse."

I slid an inch down the chair. *I'll never live this down.*

Ms. Johnson crossed her long legs, placed a legal pad in her lap and ran a hand through her jaunty, short brown hair.

I wondered, *Why is she in here with us?*

We watched through the one-way mirror as Tony and Chris entered and took chairs on either end of the table.

Parker eyed Tony's Daffy Duck tie with open disdain.

Tony had told me earlier the tie was a gift from his youngest granddaughter. She slept over last night while her parents were on business travel and insisted that he wear it today.

Parker glanced at the screen of his laptop and cleared his throat. "I demand to know why you've insisted on bringing my client in for questioning. She had nothing to do with the incident involving her husband's recent arrest for the assault on," he looked at his notes, "Ms. Brianna Kelly."

His voice was a deep baritone that I'm sure would demand respect during a trial.

Tony didn't address his remarks to Parker. Instead, he homed in on Sarah. "We're here to question you about the wrongful death of Rosa Lopez."

I've often heard attorneys don't like to be ambushed. Parker's expression of wide-eyed confusion said it all.

Sarah looked down, refusing to meet Tony's gaze.

Chris took over. "During a previous questioning, Mrs. Shaffer, you denied going to the cemetery on the morning of Rosa Lopez's murder. We have a witness who saw your white Honda Accord there."

I thought, *He didn't mention the witness was a ghost.*

Sarah appeared to be shrinking under the weight of the

accusation.

"What witness was this?" Parker demanded with a prickly tone.

Chris didn't answer.

Tony spoke up, forcing Sarah and her attorney to shift their attention. "A second person witnessed an altercation at the graveside of Carol Jeffery between you and Ms. Lopez. Y'all were fighting over some flowers left earlier by Ron Jeffery. Isn't that true?"

Sarah's pale face flushed as she sat straight. With clenched fists she blurted, "She was stealing Carol's flowers!"

Parker closed his laptop. "That's it. My client isn't answering any more questions. Come on, Sarah. We're leaving."

Tony leaned back to better focus on his opponent. "I'm afraid not. Your client lied during a previous interrogation with the police."

Chris Mirandized Sarah, before asking her to stand.

Parker's jaw dropped. "See here! My client has committed no crimes."

Chris cuffed Sarah's wrists behind her back.

"Your client is being charged with third-degree assault." Chris looked at Sarah. "This misdemeanor is punishable by up to a year in jail and a $6,000 fine."

Sarah drooped and begin to sob.

Chris adjusted his stance to keep her from hitting the floor, and then eased her back into her chair.

Parker stood, face reddening under his tan. "This is preposterous." He turned toward Sarah. "I'll get it reduced to community service."

Tony held up his hand. "Our witness also observed Jack Shaffer hit Rosa Lopez after she pushed his wife to the ground. The extreme force of his blow broke the victim's jaw and slammed her head against the gravestone. By report, neither Sarah nor Jack checked the victim to see if she needed medical attention."

Sarah moaned, "I'm sorry. We should have called an ambulance. Jack was only protecting me. He thought I was in danger."

Parker sliced his arm in the air. "Don't say another word until we've had time to discuss this privately."

Tony continued. "Mrs. Shaffer is being charged with aiding and abetting her husband's voluntary manslaughter of Rosa Lopez. This carries more dire consequences than the first charge." Tony shot Parker a viper smile. "I don't believe you can get this one reduced to community service."

Parker eased down into his chair. Sweat glistened on his brow.

Ms. Johnson stood, startling us, and walked to the observation room door. "Nice to meet y'all. I may be phoning y'all about a disturbance occurring in my home at night." She left as quietly as she arrived.

Mystery looked at me and whispered, "Where's she going?"

I shrugged.

A few moments later, the interrogation room door opened and Ms. Johnson strode up to the table, some papers in her hand.

Parker shot to his feet. His eyes focused on the papers.

Ms. Johnson handed part of the papers to Parker. "Officers are currently arresting Mr. Shaffer on several new charges, including the manslaughter of Rosa Lopez." She paused and offered a gotcha-smile. "We also have affidavits from Mr. Sánchez and Mr. Pérez, who were arrested yesterday for criminal surveillance. Their fingerprints were found on listening devices planted in the Mystery Shop and tracking devices on Mystery Jones's and Brianna Kelly's cars. They reported that Mr. Shaffer hired them to plant the devices, so he could monitor Ms. Jones's and Ms. Kelly's activities related to the murder of Rosa Lopez."

Parker sank once again into a nearby chair. His golf-course tan paled.

"We also have subpoenas to obtain DNA samples from both Sarah and Jack Shaffer. We will be matching it to blood and hair samples found on the victim's body." She handed additional papers to Parker who looked like he'd been side-swiped by an eighteen-wheeler.

He took them with reluctance.

She slid her card over the table to him. "This is where you can reach me."

CHAPTER 46: BRIANNA

The morning was beautiful, and the slight breeze smelled of sunshine. A smattering of ghosts drifted here and there, looking curious. To the dead, any visitors to the cemetery qualified as entertainment.

The distinctive chirp of a male cardinal seemed to be sounding an alarm. I cringed, praying that the hyperacuity of my senses would gradually fade back to normal.

Mystery, Chris, and I strolled to Rosa's gravesite in Valhalla Memory Gardens, where she had agreed to meet me.

The grass hadn't yet covered the dirt. The small flat stone of gray granite boasted a bronze plaque with her name and the dates of her birth and death. Someone had filled the bronze vase to the left of the plaque with artificial red roses.

Rosa floated over it.

"Nothing fancy like Carol's angel." She ran a hand over the flowers, causing them to move. "I was hoping for Maple Hill, but I guess this is good enough."

"I think it's nice," I said.

"She's here?" Mystery asked, eyes fixed on the roses. She looked anxious.

I didn't blame her. Rosa had only expected me.

I pointed toward the ghost, who'd shifted to her left. "Over there."

Mystery gave an uncertain wave.

Rosa stared at her with a confused expression.

"I brought Mystery and Chris with me. Chris wanted to tell you the current status of your case."

"That's good." Rosa raised her chin and looked down her translucent nose at Mystery. "What's she doing here?"

"I think the two of you have some issues to resolve."

"We'll see. But first, what's happened with Jack and Sarah Shaffer?"

I nudged Chris and nodded.

He looked where I'd pointed and described Sarah's interrogation.

Rosa laughed. "I wish I'd been there. At least I was at the house when Jack was arrested." She gloated. "Sounds like they had a horrible weekend."

I relayed what she said.

Chris ignored her sarcasm. "When Jack discovered that we knew everything and that Sarah was going down with him, he made a deal with Marge Johnson, the assistant district attorney."

"What deal?" Rosa asked, floating closer.

"Explain the deal," I said, fearing she wouldn't like it. I certainly didn't.

"Jack agreed to confess to voluntary manslaughter if Sarah's charges were dropped," Chris said.

"Dropped!" Rosa flung her hands in the air and ghost-paced above her headstone. "She left me lying there. Did you know I didn't die right away? If she'd called an ambulance, I could have lived." She pointed a finger at Chris. "Jack Shaffer didn't even check on me. All he did was console her while I lay there bleeding!" Angry tears filled her eyes. "He'll protect Sarah no matter what. I was such a fool to believe him."

I stiffened. Leveling a severe look her way, I said, "There are still unanswered questions."

Rosa crossed her arms. "I'm not saying I'll answer them."

"Several people have overheard your phone conversations with two different men. One was nicknamed Salsa."

She gave a dismissive flip of her hand. "That's José. He works with Ricky. We flirted back and forth, that's all. I would've been no better off with Jose, than I was with Ricky."

"What about the third guy?"

"What third guy?" A wary look cloaked her face.

"Come on, Rosa. You're a schemer. You would've had a plan B."

She recrossed her arms and presented her profile. A ghostly tear slid down her cheek.

She's hurt over something. The words, *"He'll protect Sarah no matter what. I was such a fool to believe him,"* circled my brain.

Realization hit me like a rogue wave. "You were having an affair with Jack."

Chris and Mystery simultaneously said, "What?"

Rosa slumped. "He told me he loved me and that he'd take care of me." She shook her head. "I was such a fool."

I told Chris and Mystery what she said.

Chris ran his hand through his hair. "This puts a different spin on things. Jack wasn't just protecting Sarah, he was hiding the affair." He cleared his throat and widened his stance. "Regarding your belief that you could've been saved, I have some information for you." He held up a piece of paper. "According to the autopsy, the initial head wound caused a ruptured blood vessel that would've made you a vegetable if you'd lived."

Rosa's eyes widened. She floated back, hands over her mouth. After a few moments she said, "Thank goodness that didn't happen. I'd hate lying in a hospital bed being a burden on Mama. She deserves better."

She ran a hand through her spectral curls. "I guess I can live with that outcome, even if it's not fair." Then, she realized what she'd said and gave a resigned laugh. "Guess I can't 'live with it' since I'm dead."

An uncomfortable silence fell, disturbed only by the faint sound of cars passing on Winchester Road.

After a moment, I broke the silence. "I think you two ladies need to resolve your differences about Ron. I'll tell Mystery everything you say."

Chris excused himself to let the two women, one living, the other dead, duke it out.

Mystery placed her hands on her hips. "I don't appreciate you throwing things around and pushing me into the canal."

Rosa chuckled. "You were funny slipping and sliding on all

those algae on the bottom."

I glared at her.

Rosa looked contrite. "Sorry. I couldn't think straight when it came to that man. Dios mío, I've never thought straight when it came to any man. I was so sure I could make him love me." She wiped away a tear. "Will you and Ron marry someday?"

I relayed the message, curious to hear what my friend would say.

Mystery paused. "I don't plan to date that wuss of a man ever again, let alone marry him. How he handled this whole situation showed a lot about his character."

Rosa seemed to be contemplating those words. "I wonder if he could ever forgive me? I've done some spiteful things to him. Will you call him? See if he'll come? I need to make amends."

I shrugged. "I'll try."

The only way that I managed to talk Ron into coming was to assure him Rosa would cross over and never bother him again if he did.

While we waited for Ron's arrival, Mystery and Rosa continued to discuss their differences. Chris sat on a nearby wall and watched the antics of two squirrels scampering around the base of a nearby tree.

Twenty minutes later, Mystery placed her hand over her heart. "I forgive you, Rosa. Unfortunately, it won't be the first or last time a woman goes batty over a man."

"Thank you."

We all turned when we heard a car approach. Ron parked and got out of the Porsche.

"I always loved that car," Rosa said with a wistful tone.

Ron stopped short of our group, looking uncertain of his welcome. "She's not going to attack me again, is she?"

Rosa laughed.

I shot her a squinty-eyed glare. "No, she won't." I gestured for her to begin and relayed her words.

"Ron, I apologize. I went off the deep end and thought we could have a life together. I see now that it would never have worked. You'll always be in love with Carol."

When I relayed the message, Ron nodded with a contemplative look on his face.

From Mystery's expression, I suspected she agreed with Rosa.

Ron stepped forward and scrubbed a hand over his face. "I have one question that keeps me awake at night. Did you kill Carol? Even if it was to shorten her suffering? I need to know. I'm not sure I can live with the guilt if our...our, you know, led you to do that."

Rosa jerked back as if slapped. Her lips thinned with anger before she flew into a round of Spanish cursing. "I was a nurse! I saved lives and helped the suffering. I'd never kill a patient. Not even for you."

Ron looked first relieved and then ashamed for asking.

Rosa's brown eyes widened with a look of wonder. She pointed. "It's the light!" She raised her hands like a child to a parent. "I feared that God wouldn't accept me. Ya vengo! Gloria a Dios!"

I turned and shaded my eyes. "It's here for you. Are you ready?"

"Yes!"

I've watched many disembodied spirits walk into the light, but Rosa was the first to leap into it with open arms.

My heart filled with joy and wonder. *I'll never tire of seeing this wonderful passage.*

I turned to Ron. "She's crossed over."

Ron rubbed the side of his face. "Do you think she told the truth...about Carol's death?"

"Ron, I understand your doubt since ghosts can lie. In this case, I know Rosa told the truth."

"How?" he asked.

"When a person murders another person, their soul is marked and claimed at death to be transported to hell."

I didn't share the gruesome details that Mystery, Chris, and I have witnessed in the past. I looked at Mystery and Chris.

Mystery shivered and rubbed her arms.

Chris paled.

"This didn't happen to Rosa. She leaped into the light."

Ron nodded. "Okay. Mystery, I'll come by to pay my bill tomorrow." He turned and walked back to his car.

I walked over and hugged my friend. "Are you okay?"

"I will be. Right now, I'm going home to indulge in some Girl Scout Thin Mint cookie therapy."

"Um, we need to talk about your granny sometime," I said.

She gave me a funny look. "Is that the ghost I felt at Mama's on the Fourth of July?"

"Yep."

She ran her hands through her curls. "I may need some chocolate ice cream to go with those cookies." That said, she left.

Chris and I held hands while walking back to our vehicles.

He squeezed mine and said, "This whole case has me thinking about love and us."

"Yeah?"

"I think what we have is special. I was terrified when you passed out at the station. I can't bear the thought of losing you."

I smiled and bumped him with my shoulder. "I don't want to lose you either. But I must admit, the dangers involved in your job do cloud my thoughts. I worry that you might be killed."

He nodded. "After this case, I'm having similar concerns about your paranormal activities."

I let that sink in for a moment.

Chris placed his arm across my shoulders. "I think we need to make our relationship more of a priority. Things are difficult with the demands of our careers, but I'm willing to try."

"Me, too." I winked. "We can sneak in lunches or *other activities* between dates."

Chris grinned briefly before assuming a serious look. "I promise to be more careful. It's different now that I have someone that I love."

My heart pounded. *Chris loves me.* It was then I realized that I also love him.

We stopped and looked deep into each other's eyes as if seeking confirmation.

He wrapped me in his arms and kissed me.

The End

Until

MURDER IN THE LIGHTHOUSE

ABOUT THE AUTHOR

Shirley B. Garrett, Psy.D. is a three-time Silver Falchion finalist. She uses her former career as a psychologist to create realistic characters and plots. Dr. Garrett is also an artist in the mediums of watercolor, oil, and acrylic. She enjoys ballroom dancing, traveling, and hiking with her husband, Bob.

Dr. Garrett is available to speak at book clubs, conferences, and conventions.

https://www.shirleybgarrett.com
Facebook.com/ShirleyBGarrett
Twitter.com/ShirleyBGarrett
Instagram.com/ShirleyBGarrett

Look for the third book in the Brianna Kelly Paranormal Series,

MURDER IN THE LIGHTHOUSE

Made in the USA
Columbia, SC
30 March 2023

14235507R00146